BROKEN GENIUS

BROKEN GENIUS

<A Will Parker Thriller>

DREW MURRAY

OCEANVIEW PUBLISHING
SARASOTA, FLORIDA

ISBN 978-1-60809-388-5

Published in the United States of America by Oceanview Publishing

Sarasota, Florida

www.oceanviewpub.com

10 9 8 7 6 5 4 3 2 1

PRINTED IN THE UNITED STATES OF AMERICA

For Christine

ACKNOWLEDGEMENTS

There are a number of people that have been part of bringing this novel to life, and I'd like to thank them here.

To my family for their unwavering support. Especially Christine for being the first reader, most dedicated fan, and the finest partner in life that anyone could ever ask for. We are the best team.

To Melissa Edwards for seeing the potential in the book and appreciating Will Parker for all that I imagined him to be. Your support and advice has been indispensable. To Pat and Bob Gussin and everyone at Oceanview. What a privilege to get to work with such a talented team of professionals! To Benee Knauer. Your sage editorial advice taught me a great deal I will never forget.

To Kelley Armstrong for being a guide, a coach, and sometimes even a counselor. You were always encouraging without ever letting me take any shortcuts. You said I'd thank you for it later, and here I am. Thank you!

To John, Bev, Pat, and Clarissa from my writing group for their crisp and constructive feedback on early drafts.

To my fellow thriller authors who provided hard-earned wisdom from experience. It was invaluable, and I appreciate every bit of it. Simon Gervais, Kim Howe, Kathleen and Michael Gear, Sandra

Brannan, Heather Graham and her husband, Dennis, thank you very much.

To Betsy Glick, Public Affairs Specialist at the Federal Bureau of Investigation in Washington, D.C., and the agents at the New York Field Office for taking the time to share information with me and other writers about the incredible work done by their agency. Any errors in procedural details are for artistic purposes and entirely my own.

Finally, to all my friends who have been a part of the journey to getting this book finished in all the many different ways you showed it, you were there when I needed you. You know who you are, and I can't thank you enough.

BROKEN GENIUS

CHAPTER ONE

<March 10, 2011>

The night I was supposed to fly to Japan, I didn't know how little time I had left before my personal apocalypse. Had I, there's one thing I would have changed. The one thing that wakes me in the night, my teeth clenched so tightly I think they're going to crack. The one thing that puts blood on my hands and a death in my ledger. The one thing that won't let me go.

I wouldn't have made a mistake.

Yeah, I know, everyone makes them, and all that. But not me. I started my first company before I could drive. The company I really became known for, the one that became a household name, came later. Valued at over $1 billion pre-IPO, CastorNet is what the Valley calls a *unicorn*. They're not as rare as they once were, but people still sit up and pay attention when they're run by a guy in his twenties.

That wasn't enough for me. I wanted a place in the history books. When I got to Japan, I'd close a deal that would put my name alongside Jobs, Gates, and Zuckerberg.

While I was supposed to be popping the cork on a bottle of Cristal on our private jet, I was instead sipping a stale, green smoothie, huddled around a computer screen in the dark with a hairy, bearded guy, trying to get the FBI off my back without blowing everything up.

"The payload's been delivered. Coming online now," said the hairy guy. The glow of the monitor reflected off his wild beard, giving him a spooky profile in the dim room. "What are you going to tell the guys at Fukushima Semiconductor when you don't show up to complete the takeover?"

Jack Walton. My right hand, and oldest friend. The Woz to my Jobs. Brilliant programmer, but like the legendary Wozniak he didn't have a head for business. Building CastorNet was all me. He was the only person I could trust with what we'd agreed to do for the FBI. If word got out, it would be a disaster.

"I'll make it in time to close the deal. I'll take the jet when we're finished here. I just won't have time to check in at the hotel, which means I'll have to shower at the airport."

"Noble sacrifice, considering this deal's going to make you a billionaire," said Jack, noting the distaste in my voice. "But first, wherever this guy is, we have to find him."

"We will. Then that FBI dude, what was his name? Salazar something..."

"Burke," said Jack, rolling his eyes. "Special Agent in Charge Salazar Burke."

"Whatever. Details," I answered, waving my hand back and forth. "Then we can get on with Fukushima while Burke takes credit for our genius."

The Agent had shown up on our doorstep from the LA Field Office with a problem. This sick fucker, Bruce Sterling, had kidnapped a girl named Kate Mason, right out of her college dorm. The FBI said he'd taken some other girls before, all of whom turned up dead, and in each case, he'd used our software to livestream his exploits with them. While the media hadn't gotten a hold of the story, they could.

The negative press from that revelation would be bad, but I was sure Ace Prior, our Operations guy, would be able to contain it. He's good and calm in front of the camera. Then Burke showed me and Jack pictures of Sterling's previous victims. It's easy to stand on your high moral ground when it's just an ideal. Words on a page. Or in a mission statement. But when you see the things Burke had to show, it changes you. It hits you on a level deeper than intellect, right at the part of your brain that evolved from a furry little mammal whose drive was survival from predators.

Burke told us he had to find Sterling before he did those things to this Kate girl. It didn't matter who Kate was or where she came from. You see someone facing that kind of horror, you help. But that doesn't mean you have to throw away everything you've spent years building. CastorNet's most valuable product was secure, private messaging and live video streaming. Which meant if anyone found out what Jack and I were doing for the FBI, we'd be finished.

"Will, the marketing push on privacy starts tomorrow," said Jack, tugging on his beard. "Are you sure it won't get out that we have a back door . . ."

"Don't call it a *back door.*"

"What should I call it?"

"A trap door."

"Will, that's not a real thing! You can't just make it a thing because you want to."

"I bet I can after the Fukushima deal closes. It's totally going to be a thing."

"Maybe then," acknowledged Jack with a sigh.

"It's just you and me in this room, and the minute this is over we get rid of the trap door," I said, checking the time on my iPhone. "Get the patch in a critical release and send it tomorrow."

"Send me the patch, and I'll get it in the queue."

"You have it. It's in the same directory as the change to the payload."

This is the reason I needed to be there: to make sure stuff gets done. Developers, even brilliant ones like Jack, need to be managed.

"I don't have it," Jack said. "You made the changes to the payload."

I felt a knot twist in my stomach.

In the final push to version 1.0, we had a hackathon to complete the first Beta version. Back then, a lot of people chose to work from home. Jack thought that made it easier for people to work for twenty-four hours straight. I thought it made it easier for people to get distracted.

So, I embedded a routine in our software to monitor the developers. It took a picture using their own webcam, with the message "Don't get distracted. Get back to work!" along with their physical location.

I thought it was hilarious. Jack called it "demotivating." Whatever. It worked.

Now we were using that app to get a location on Sterling and give it to the FBI. One quick change to the code to suppress the message pop-up on Sterling's screen, and we were ready to go. Without that change, Sterling would know immediately that someone had found him. What would he do to Kate then? And who would he tell about our trap door?

"I didn't do it," I said, swallowing hard. Jack was about to tell me he misunderstood me and everything's fine. "I was busy with the Fukushima deal all day. You made the changes to the payload."

"I know what I did, Will, and I didn't make the changes. This is your Trojan, not mine. I told you that. After the daily stand-up."

"But you tested it."

"There was no test!" said Jack, typing frantically to bring up the code. "Why would we need to test your code? You're a genius. You hate it when I test your code."

Good point. Totally true.

"So, change it now," I said, leaning over his shoulder, "quick!"

"I'm working on it," he said pounding the keyboard hard enough to rattle the empty can of Red Bull on the desk. The screen changed as a swarm of text and numbers appeared in the editor. "Okay, here's the code—where do I go?"

I grabbed Jack's chair, rolling him aside. "I'll do it. Get on the phone to Burke. Tell him we need more time."

Any second Sterling could trigger the trap door, and seconds later that message would appear on his screen. The pictures of Sterling's victims flashed through my mind in a staccato slide show as I scanned the code. I just needed a minute to block out the pop-up message and then force the update onto Sterling's machine. Messy, but it would work.

I remember every app I ever wrote, and this was no exception. My fingers a blur on the keyboard, I found the message module and started commenting it out. Before I could finish, I heard a distinctive, warbling ringtone. A special ringtone I'd set up on my phone so I'd know I had another funny webcam shot of an intern. Only now it wasn't going to be an intern and it would be anything but funny. For a second my fingers froze, my mind forming this idea that maybe I hadn't heard it.

"Did it just happen?" Jack asked from the other side of the desk, phone in hand, shattering my illusion.

I pushed back from the workstation, the knot in my stomach tightening into a wave of nausea. I took out my iPhone. There was a message.

The picture showed what looked like the unfinished basement of an old house. A chair sat empty in front of a concrete wall, floor beams just visible at the top of the frame. In the corner was the get-back-to-work message, along with the IP address and physical location on a map. The app had worked.

But without the changes I'd been frantically working on, the same message I was looking at was also on Sterling's screen.

"What do we do?" Jack was pale underneath his hairy face, the blueish glow of the monitor making him look like a corpse.

"Is that on mute?" I whispered, pointing at the phone.

"Yes," said Jack.

"Are you sure?"

"Yes!"

"Then we do nothing."

"What?" Jack threw his arms up in the air.

"What can we do? The second Sterling touches the computer, the message disappears and no one else will ever know."

"Are you serious, Will? What about the girl?"

"Get Burke there!" I said, handing over my iPhone with the location.

"What if they can't get there?"

"Tell them to hurry!"

Burke must have come on the line because Jack started talking very rapidly. I pulled up the livestream console and punched in Sterling's ID. Online but inactive. Maybe he'd booted up his computer and walked away. A red button turned green, crushing my hopes. He was launching a live feed. My finger hovered over the mouse. I wanted to stand up and walk away, but I couldn't. I had to get control of this somehow. Time, that's all I needed.

"Burke says local PD SWAT are on the way," said Jack. "But it's going to be a few minutes."

I clicked the button. The video stream came up. The chair was still empty.

"Is that live?" he said, looking over my shoulder. "Can we hear anything?"

I reached out and turned up the volume on the expensive self-powered external reference speakers I'd bought for every workstation in the office. Not even Facebook had them. All we heard was the sound of a fan running. Perfectly reproduced, but still just background noise.

"See? He's not even there," I said, clapping my hands. "If he had the stream on auto-launch, maybe the message was already gone."

I tried to calm my breathing. I'd been here before, on the edge of disaster, but it always worked out and there was no reason to think this time would be any different. Jack and I stared in silence at the screen. One minute. Two. Ten. We watched the minutes tick off on the clock in the corner of the screen. Where was the damn SWAT team?

Then came a new sound. The low grinding of something being dragged, combined with the shriek of metal on concrete, perfectly clear through the expensive speakers.

A person backed into the frame. A big guy, wearing a golf shirt with sweat stains under the pits. He looked unkempt. Messy. Unclean. My upper lip lifted in disgust. Gross.

The man spun around, stepping back to reveal another chair. Metal. But this one wasn't empty. I recognized Kate Mason from her pictures. She was bound and gagged, her eyes as wide as golf balls, threatening to burst out of her head. Her chest rose and fell rapidly, taking panicked, shallow breaths. She strained against the rope holding her in place. I recognized the rope as the round, multi-layered type from the climbing gym.

"Tell Burke to hurry up!" I shouted, my voice cracking.

The door opened behind us and a tall, thin man popped his head in. Ace Prior.

"Will, I think you need to look at the news. It's Japan." There was a warning tone in his voice, but I didn't have time for it.

"Not now!" Jack and I thundered in unison. Ace held up his hand and backed out of the door.

Jack went back to the phone, begging Burke to hurry. On-screen, Sterling pulled the empty chair into the frame and sat down in it.

He threw his arm around Kate's shoulders like a brother. No. Too intimate for that. Like a boyfriend. A shiver went down my spine making me shift in my seat.

"SWAT's one minute out," said Jack from the desk. "They're getting into position."

Bruce Sterling's dirty face broke into a smile, revealing a mouthful of surprisingly white and perfect teeth. I clenched my jaw, recoiling from the screen. Something about his smile made me want to hurl up that stale green smoothie.

Please hurry, I silently repeated over and over in my head. There was still time. There had to be. SWAT was outside for fuck's sake. What was taking so long?

Sterling leaned forward into the camera, looking right into the lens. His gaze penetrated my soul from a thousand miles away. He licked his lips and cleared his throat like a predator preparing to feast.

"I'm not distracted," he said with a wink. "Let's get back to work."

Get back to work. The message. He'd seen it! Time was up.

"Tell them to go," I shouted at Jack. "They've got to go *now*!"

Sterling leaned back into his intimate embrace of Kate.

"So, what do you think, Kate? Are you my opus? My final masterpiece? Why don't we go out with a crescendo?" he said, his eyes sparkling with excitement.

When he raised his hand again, it held a long, cruel-looking chef's knife. He leaned in, nuzzling Kate's pale, unblemished neck, pressing the knife flat to her chest as it rose and fell. I covered my face with my hands but I couldn't stop myself from peering through my fingers.

"They're going now," said Jack. "They're going in!"

From those stupid, expensive speakers, I heard a distant crash followed by the flat crack of explosions. But with a final flash of the knife it was too late.

"Oh God!" groaned Jack behind me.

I screamed. I know I did, but to this day I can't remember what it was I screamed. Maybe it was nothing. Maybe it was just a guttural, feral howl that carried more emotion than words. But I know it was loud. I'd made a stupid, rookie, intern-level mistake not double-checking the code and now I watched a young woman let out her final breath in a silent scream. There was blood, so much blood.

The door to Jack's office opened one more time.

"Will. Jack. You need to see this." Ace again. He looked upset. Despite his calm demeanor, Ace had a stubborn streak. He was known to sometimes refuse to take no for an answer. By the cross of his arms, this looked to be one of those times.

"Not now," I gasped. Jack was too busy silently sobbing into his palm to say anything at all.

"Yes, now!" said Ace. "You said Fukushima Semi is right next to the nuclear power plant, right?"

"What?" I couldn't shift gears to connect to what he was saying.

"There's been an earthquake in Japan," he continued, undeterred.

"So what? They happen there all the time." More explosions and muffled shouting bellowed from the reference speakers as the SWAT team crashed into the room. I reached over and turned the volume down.

"Are you playing video games?" he asked, throwing his hands up in the air.

"No," I said through clenched teeth.

"Yeah, well this earthquake triggered a tsunami," Ace continued. "A big one. And it just hit the Fukushima-Daiichi nuclear power plant. The reactor's in meltdown."

I grabbed the recycle bin from under Jack's desk just in time to catch the green vomit smoothie. Ace backed out of the room, his job done, message delivered.

As I gasped for breath between heaves, I knew two things with certainty: first, I would never be able to unsee what Sterling did; second, I could feel my place next to Jobs, Gates, and Zuckerberg slipping through my fingers.

CHAPTER TWO

<Present Day>

A chime rings out from a speaker on the dresser, reverberating off tall glass walls. The sound from the mindfulness app reminds me of a temple in Okinawa. Once again chasing away the demons in my mind.

I keep my breathing slow and even. In. Out. Just as I'd been taught. I remember the smell of cypress and incense. The feel of bamboo under my feet. The taste of salt air from the ocean. With each breath, I push them away, one by one, until all that's left is my breathing.

Stillness creeps into every corner of my mind and body. My shoulders relax. The steady thump of my heartbeat slows and fades away. Thoughts of Bruce Sterling and Fukushima will come back, they always do, but for now, there's peace.

My phone vibrates in my lap, the familiar pattern for work, shattering the calm.

I open my eyes to a dark room, the moon reflecting off the ocean. Dim light pours through floor-to-ceiling glass around my bedroom. The time on the phone says it's too late to be today and too early to be tomorrow.

The number is for FBI Headquarters in Washington. I swipe to answer.

Seven and a half minutes later, I'm showered and dressed, with this sweet travel bag I got from Kickstarter strapped to my back. As I step out into the night, the Southern California breeze coming off the Pacific is warm. Big oak doors close behind me with a satisfying thunk of the magnetic locking system. A Bureau car waits in my driveway.

"Nice place," says the driver, gazing up at the ultra-modern collection of concrete and glass boxes. Young guy. White shirt, black tie. Bureau employee. Civilian. "Whose is it?"

"Mine," I answer, tossing my bag in the back seat before climbing in the front.

"Wait, they told me you're an Agent."

"Special Agent."

"Damn, the pay band sure is different for *Special* Agents," he says, steering the car down the long driveway.

It's not the first time I've heard comments like that. Won't be the last, either. I may have walked away from Silicon Valley, but not the comforts. After the Sterling incident, I needed a change. I'd been *taking* for a long time and needed to *give* instead. Give away my money? Not a chance. I still own a large part of CastorNet, but someone else runs it.

A winding road led me to where I am now, giving something more valuable than money to the FBI: my time and talents. Theoretically, I work in the Cyber division, but reality is, I get called for any major case with a tech angle.

I've logged a lot of time on the road. But even for me, a wake-up call in the middle of the night from Assistant Director Burke, followed by a ride in a Bureau jet, is highly unusual. I love highly unusual.

"Big case?" the driver asks.

"Homicide," I answer, without elaborating.

There's a high-profile sense about the case, but Burke wouldn't say what exactly, just that it's top priority and sensitive. He told me to get on the plane, and I'd be met by another agent at the other end. A handler, if I know Burke.

He doesn't like to let me work alone. I get it. The Bureau is a place that elevates structure and procedure to an art form. Burke is a product of that environment. So, it's natural we don't see eye to eye on my approach, which I call efficient, but he says is undisciplined, or something. What really chaps his ass though, is that I'm successful. I close cases.

Traffic's light this time of night, even in LA. But somewhere out there in the darkness, someone's dead. Who? Burke didn't say. Why me? Whatever it is, it's more than murder. Middle of the night and skipping about ten different protocols for the AD to put me on a Bureau plane? Sounds political.

Whatever it is, I'll find out soon enough. Until then, I rest.

Hours later, the plane lands at a midsize airport as the sun breaks over the horizon. The Gulfstream was all right. The one I had was nicer, but you know, government modesty and all. Lavish interior or not, I know what each hour of flight costs. Someone thinks it's really important that I be here right now.

The plane taxis to a hangar far from the commercial terminal. I look out at the fence line. Anonymous warehouses. Sleazy strip clubs. No trees. Thick green weeds poking up through cracks in the asphalt. When the door opens, I take a deep breath of humid but not sweltering air. My world is New York, and California. This isn't either. It's somewhere in between.

There's another car waiting for me. Dodge Charger. Gray. Indiana plate with a dent in the bottom-right corner. No covert LEDs in the grill or the headliner, so it's not Bureau. A rental.

Standing next to it is a tall, well-built, African American man, his back ramrod-straight as usual, tie flapping in the breeze. Thomas Decker.

"Will Parker, as I live and breathe," he says with a smile. The one that car salesmen use to say: *you can trust me.*

"Decker. How'd they get you out of New York?"

"Love of country," he says, taking my hand in a grip so firm that I stretch my fingers out when he lets go. "How's LA?"

"Hasn't fallen into the ocean yet."

"Well, there's still time," he says, popping the Charger's trunk. "Let me get your bag."

As he tosses in my Kickstarter bag, I recall what I know about Decker: born in Chicago, raised in NYC. Football fan. Still loves the Bears, otherwise a real New Yorker. Military out of high school. Then college on a GI bill. Followed by the FBI. Last I heard, a Special Agent, Counter Intelligence division, out of the New York field office. Not someone you expect to find in Indiana.

"What's the deal? Why am I here?" I ask.

"To uphold the law and serve justice."

Oh yeah, and he's wound a little tight.

We climb into the Charger and I look longingly back at the Gulfstream. They're already spinning up the engines. I'm going to be here for a while.

"Burke told me there was a murder."

"Correct," says Decker stomping on the gas. The Charger leaps away from the hanger. "Victim is a white male, forty years old. A souvenir vendor at some kind of Comic Con thing that's going on this weekend."

A Comic Con? Sweet. I wonder what the guest list is like. Seems like even small Cons are able to get some decent screen talent these days. Maybe being stuck here won't be so bad after all.

"Security found the body at 04:30 in one of the washrooms," Decker continues. "Head cracked open. Blood all over the place. COD looks like the blunt force to the head, but waiting on the autopsy to confirm. Should have that by noon."

Noon? Definitely political. Even in LA, autopsies take longer. Someone's really put the heat on this case.

"Witnesses?"

"None. It happened sometime in the night, after the Convention Center was closed.

"And they didn't find him until 4:30 a.m.?"

"Security patrols every few hours, but mainly they just walk around," Decker says, shaking his head in disgust.

"Fine. A Con vendor gets his head bashed in sometime overnight. Why the Federal case?" I lean back in the seat, pulling on a pair of Maui Jims as the Charger gets onto the highway. I'm still on LA time, and in LA it's early.

There's a pause as Decker chooses his words. Here we go. The smoke screen. These Counter Intel guys are all the same. Spy hunters, shrouding everything they do in secrecy. Even from other agents. He'll tell me only what he wants me to know.

"The guy behind this Con thing is a prominent businessman in the community. When local PD wanted to close down the event, he lost his mind. Made some calls."

"Must have been some big calls to get an Assistant Director of the FBI out of bed."

We drive on in silence for a bit as Decker concentrates on traffic. Eventually he pulls off the freeway and navigates through crowded rush-hour surface streets. He stops at a red light.

"Who is this guy? How's he connected?" I ask.

"From what I can tell, he went to high school with the Attorney General."

We're here as lap dogs for some old puberty buddy of the AG? We aren't your run-of-the-mill violent crime guys. Where's the tech angle? And Decker? Unless the dead guy was a spy, there's no reason for him to be here. He's not telling me everything.

"Why not someone from the local field office?" I ask.

Decker looks over at me, trying to read me, but my eyes are covered by the reflective blue Maui Jims lenses. The light turns green and he hits the gas. Decker drives hard, direct. A habit, I suspect, he picked up overseas and not de-programmed during Warrior Transition training.

"Okay, so he's got some weight." I prod further. "Why the FBI? Why me? Why you? You're still Counter Intelligence, right?"

"I could tell you, but then I'd have to kill you," he says with a smirk, looking at me out of the corner of his eye.

"So that's a yes. Come on, Decker. A New York Agent from Counter Intel and an LA Agent from Spec Ops, Cyber. Because a guy got his head bashed in at a fan convention?"

Decker tilts his head and doesn't say anything else, pulling into the drop-off area of a downtown hotel.

"We aren't going to the crime scene?" I ask, frowning.

"This is it."

"You said the vic was killed at the Convention Center."

"There's a secondary here," he says, getting out of the car and handing the keys to a valet.

I roll my eyes, climbing out after him. Never the whole picture with him. Just dribs and drabs. It's a pain in the ass.

CHAPTER THREE

When we get into the lobby, Decker heads straight for the elevators. The hotel is surprisingly upscale with a mahogany front desk, polished marble floors, and a well-furnished lobby. A few people sit around waiting for whatever it is people wait for. A stand-up sign invites me to check out the coffee shop, promising Kona's finest coffee. This is the best news I've had all morning.

I peel off across the lobby.

"Parker, where are you going?" I can almost hear his eyes rolling.

"Fuel."

He follows me in to find a corny little affair with Tiki idols and barn board walls. Hawaiian cowboys. Well, it's the right island for Kona coffee. I'm feeling good about the chances for a decent cup right now.

"You need to know something," Decker says.

"Like why Agents from Counter Intelligence and Cyber are consulting on a murder, and not an Agent from Violent Crime?"

"There's more to it."

"I bet."

There's no line when we walk up to the counter. A girl holding up her phone lifts a finger for us to wait. Teenager. No tats. No piercings. She turns slightly and flicks from the bottom of the screen.

"You're hunting in here?" I ask, taking out my phone. "Anything rare?"

"Nah, just Pidgeys," she says looking up at me. "But that's okay, I've got a Pidgeotto I'm trying to evolve so I grab them when they wander in."

"Pigeons? I don't see any birds," says Decker looking around.

"They're Pokémon, Decker." I wave my phone.

"I thought you wanted coffee."

The girl puts her phone back into her pocket with a sigh.

"What can I get you?"

"Peaberry. Biggest you have," I say.

She looks at me blankly.

"From Hawaii? Kona?"

"Oh, we don't have that," she says. "But we've got a Tropic Blend. That's pretty much the same thing."

Pretty much the same thing? So much for that. I'm now certain whoever owns this coffee shop has never actually been to Kona.

"Coffee is coffee," says Decker. "It's all better than what I drank in Kandahar. We'll take two."

"You're killing me, Decker."

Cups in hand, we make our way to a table by a window overlooking the street. No one nearby. It's sunny. Warm.

"Upstairs is the vic's hotel room. Local PD checked it out after they finished with the murder scene," says Decker.

"What did they find?"

"A new state law came in last year. All crime scenes have to be swept for evidence of WMDs."

"Weapons of Mass Destruction? Seriously? Here?"

They don't even scan for WMDs in New York or LA without a specific reason. What the hell could they have found? I hope it's not biological. Gross. I don't want to go up there.

I take a sip of the Tropical Blend. Against all odds, it's actually drinkable. Or, I'm just that desperate.

"Maybe some of the detection gear is made in-state. I don't know why," continues Decker. "What I do know is they got a hit on an empty case. Nuclear."

The cup of Tropical Blend freezes halfway to my lips.

"Nuclear?"

"The radiation signature doesn't match weapons, but it's identifiable. The reading was consistent with an object exposed to the 2011 Fukushima-Daiichi nuclear accident in Japan."

I put my cup down on the table hard enough that hot coffee splashes out of the lid. The scalding pain in my hand barely registers. He can't be suggesting what I think he is. It isn't possible.

Closing my eyes for a moment, I'm taken back to the night of the tsunami. I remember Ace delivering the news. I also remember Sterling's grin of anticipation as he held that knife to Kate Mason's neck. CNN flashing "Nuclear disaster" and "meltdown" beneath scenes of destruction. My stomach lurches just as it did then.

"That got your attention, didn't it?" Decker smiles.

Manipulative bastard. He's enjoying this. He knows the deal for Fukushima Semi fell apart that night, and I left CastorNet shortly after. He knows it's important to me, and now he's making sure *I* know who's in charge. But he doesn't know about the rest of that night. Watching someone die because of my mistake.

Decker doesn't know that I went to Fukushima and bribed TEPCO workers to let me search the radioactive hot zone in a hazmat suit. He doesn't know that I followed up on every rumor and lead for months, no matter how sketchy. He doesn't know that when I finally admitted it was over, I didn't have the heart to come home for an entire year.

Salvaging the Fukushima deal became my way to make amends for the colossal fuckup that got Kate Mason killed. Something so good for the world, it would make up for what I'd done, even if I was the only one that knew it.

"The Fukushima Unicorn." The words feel thick coming out of my mouth. Like a foreign language.

"It looks that way," he says, nodding.

It isn't over, after all. My mind races with the possibilities, thoughts colliding until I can't keep them straight anymore. I force my breathing to steady. In and out. Find the calm.

We tried to keep the deal secret, of course, but a company as large and high-profile as CastorNet couldn't keep a lid on it. Word leaked out that we were on the verge of acquiring quantum computer technology, representing a giant leap forward, from a small company in Fukushima, Japan. During the tsunami and nuclear disaster, it disappeared. In the absence of details, people started calling the missing technology a Fukushima Unicorn because no one left alive had seen it. Except me.

"How do we know this isn't another wild goose chase?" I say. "People have been claiming to have known someone, who knew a guy, who saw it, for years. It's become an urban legend. That's why they call it a Unicorn."

"How many urban legends do you know that are radioactive? The lab confirmed it," says Decker, shaking his head. "It's legit."

The initial shock fading, I force myself to confront logic and reason. When I'd finally managed to get to Fukushima, everything was gone. Cleared out. The building empty; the people vanished. It was like they'd never even existed. I checked every evacuation center, *ryokan*, and *minshuku* for two hundred miles. Nothing. All I ever found were rumors.

"Confirmed what?" I ask, shaking my head. "That something that *used* to be in that case was exposed to radiation from the Fukushima-Daiichi accident? Do you have any idea how big an area of Japanese countryside was irradiated? Everything in the exclusion zone got hot."

I let Decker get to me, and that's not good. I don't want a guy like that knowing how to push my buttons. In my defense, he ambushed me. He acts all friendly, but to him I'm just a pawn in his game. Best to let him think that, for now.

"Can you take that chance, Will?"

I can't, and he knows it. Bastard.

"Tell me about this empty case." I pick up my coffee and take a long sip.

"Pelican case. Hard shell, foam padding inside with a cutout the right size and shape for a Unicorn."

A good sign. It sounds right. The genuine Fukushima Unicorn would be bleeding rads. If someone had made it out with the Unicorn, I would have found them. Which meant the Unicorn had to have been left behind when the radiation hit the area. In addition to providing protection for the Unicorn itself, a lead-lined Pelican case would contain the radiation, protecting whoever carried it.

"They found it here? Vic's hotel room, I take it?"

"Correct."

Decker takes a drink from his coffee, quick, despite the temperature. He sucks in air to cool the coffee in his mouth. No retreat. Push through. His eyes dart around scanning every face in the coffee shop, and those on the street he can see through the window.

All Decker's looking around is making me paranoid. Who does he expect to find in this little slice of middle America? I suppose if you chase shadows long enough, you start to see them everywhere.

"What else is in the room?" I ask.

"Right now, a local crime scene tech and a homicide detective. They're waiting for Uncle Sam's experts. That's us."

"They don't know who we are yet, do they?"

"No, they don't, and they don't need to. We're Special Agents, that's it."

"I don't think you understand," I say with a laugh, drawing his attention back to me. "I'm kind of a big deal. They're going to know who I am."

Decker frowns at me in confusion. I'm not surprised. He's a guy that spends his life blending in. In the Valley, you spend your life trying to stand out, and stand out I did.

"Whatever," Decker says finally, swilling a big gulp of his coffee and sucking more air in through his teeth. "Time we headed upstairs."

There's another aspect to this, one that he doesn't mention, and I wonder if that's because he doesn't know or because he doesn't want to say. I suspect the latter. Not only am I an expert on the Fukushima Unicorn, I'm also the legal owner. Or at least CastorNet is.

He stands up, straightening his jacket.

"Not just yet," I say, holding up a hand. "The Fukushima radiation match explains me, but it doesn't explain you."

"No, it doesn't," he says, stiffly.

"Stuff giving off gamma rays would go straight to Counter Terror, with an inter-agency notification to Homeland Security. But that's not who they sent. They sent you."

"And?" he says.

"Why?"

"I'm also here because of the Unicorn," says Decker.

Because of. Not for. Then it clicks. I clench my teeth in irritation. My emotional response to news of the Unicorn caught me off guard. It distracted me. I hate that. Clearly, I wouldn't be the only person interested in it. And the other types of people that would be interested are people that Decker would very much like to find.

"Who is it?"

He doesn't say anything. Just stands there, hands in the pockets of his inexpensive, but perfectly pressed, G-Man suit. Classic pissing contest. The kind I'm certain he's accustomed to winning. But he's never played them with me, a guy with little to lose to a guy like him. My worst-case scenario at the FBI ends with me walking out the door to lead the life of a retired one-percenter of a one-percenter. He knows that, but he also knows the Fukushima Unicorn is something I can't walk away from.

I roll my eyes at his silence and pull out my giant iPhone. This little train can't leave the station without me, and something tells me Decker won't be tolerant of delays.

I know he can see the screen from where he's standing. I open Facebook and start skimming through my news feed. Sarah went out to Chan's restaurant last night. Gary got a new rescue dog. By the time I'm reading the meme that Ashraf posted, Decker breaks.

"He goes by Dragoniis."

"No shit." The words slip out of my mouth.

"You've heard of him."

"Hello? Cyber?" I say, shaking my head. "He's the most skilled and prolific hacker in Asia. Supported by the Chinese government. Word is he waltzed in and out of Sony Entertainment like it was Sunday shopping at the mall. Another rumor had it that, for a fee, he removed some of the most notable names from the Panama Papers before they went public. He's breached every major bank on Wall Street at one time or another."

I pause. We also believe he wrote the core code for the secret chips in servers that went into all the big tech companies, government, and intelligence agencies. Which means he knows the location of all the back doors, including the ones we never found. With what Dragoniis knows, the Chinese could be cut off, or even better, fed disinformation. No wonder Decker's so wound up.

"But he rarely travels," I continue, "and when he does, it's always a non-extradition country. We don't even know his real name."

"We got chatter that he might be headed here," Decker answers, "and when the locals reported the radiological alert, it all came together."

My eyebrows pop up. I can't contain my surprise. He doesn't just mean the United States. He means here. Right here. There's only one thing that would make Dragoniis take the risk of someone like Decker getting his hands on him: he's after the Unicorn.

"That's right," Decker says with a nod, when he sees I've sorted it out. "And if you want a chance at getting the Unicorn first, we best be getting upstairs. Shall we?"

"Give me one second—I need to check in with LA. I'll meet you at the elevators," I say, unlocking my phone.

"Do I need to tell you this is classified?"

"Only if that makes you feel better."

"It does."

As Decker walks off to the elevators, I consider something else. We were called here on a murder. That's one dead body because of the Unicorn. How many more will there be before this is over? Given what the Unicorn is worth, my gut says a lot.

CHAPTER FOUR

Me: Where are you?

Bradley W: Café Cenfor. Peruvian Gold. You want?

Me: Late night?

Bradley W: Club Emerald. J-Lo and Leo were there.

Me: Still hacking VIP lists?

Bradley W: How else do I get in on a government salary?

Me: Get to office ASAP. Need you at your desk.

Bradley W: You're not there?

Me: Indiana.

Bradley W: WTF? When did that happen?

Me: Middle of the night. Call from Burke. Caught a high-profile.

Bradley W: Crap. OK, Boss. At desk in 15.

Bradley White is my chief technician in the LA Field Office. Formerly NSA, he's now a civilian Specialist for the Bureau. Not an agent, which is good because he's not a field man. Too excitable. But I trust him.

Now that I've put Bradley on standby, I step into the elevator to follow Decker upstairs. On the way up, my thoughts are pulled inexorably to the past.

After Sterling murdered Kate Mason, I doubled down on our efforts to *protect privacy,* and *transform the way we communicate,* and all that other great stuff from company promotional videos. The truth is, I didn't want to confront what I'd done and being consumed by work left me little time to think about it.

Even better than being consumed by work at home was being consumed by work abroad, avoiding questions about Kate Mason's murder. Not that there ended up being any. I was right, of course, the pop-up message disappeared without a trace when Sterling started the livestream. The FBI never asked any questions about what happened on the tech end. They assumed the plan had gone off properly because we gave them Sterling's location. They never asked about the message, and we never told them. But I knew what we'd done. So did Jack.

My trance is interrupted by the elevator door opening. Decker's waiting. I follow him down the hall, thoughts of my Japanese partners and their invention tugging at my conscious mind.

When we turn the corner at the end of the hall, I see a uniformed local police officer standing guard outside a door. Well, sitting to be precise. They brought him what looks like a banquet room chair and he's slouching in it, legs crossed, doing the crossword puzzle in a newspaper. Where did he get a newspaper? They still make those?

Decker struts up. Chin held high. Back straight. A force of nature. I have to admit; his size alone is imposing. When he flashes his FBI badge, the uniform jumps to his feet.

"Special Agents Decker and Parker, FBI," he says.

The uniform looks over at me and I see surprise on his face. While Decker looks every inch an agent of the Federal Bureau of Investigation, from his clean-cut hair to his G-man suit, I do not. I'm wearing jeans and a t-shirt with an X-wing fighter on it, underneath a blazer whose sole purpose is to conceal the badge and gun I have to carry. I grab my ID and flip it open for the uniform, who shrugs.

"Hold on, sirs," he says, turning around to slip a key card in the door. It opens, and he sticks his head inside. "Excuse me, Detective, two Agents from the FBI are here."

"Are they? Already?" says a female voice. Strong, decisive. "All right, let them in to join the party."

He opens the door wide enough for us to pass. The room is huge by New York standards, but average for the Midwest. King-sized bed. Sitting area. Refreshment station. Desk. Bathroom next to the door.

The first thing I notice is that it's oddly tidy for an occupied room. The bed is turned down, a card with the following day's weather written on it placed neatly between a bottle of water and a clean glass. No one slept here last night.

The key card envelope is on the counter in front of the TV, a room key still in it. On the desk a white cable is plugged into the lamp, next to an empty box of donuts and a small mesh pouch containing a gaggle of extra computer cables. A roller bag sits on the luggage rack. Carry-on size.

Industrial LED lights on tripods cast bright light in pools on the wall and floor. Someone on their knees, dressed in white coveralls, holds a digital SLR camera. Black watch on their wrist. The forensics tech.

By the desk is a woman. Average height, jet black hair tied in a ponytail, tanned complexion, wearing a gray pantsuit that doesn't quite hide her athletic figure. She's leaning on the desk, right hand on her hip, holding her jacket back to reveal a gold badge and a Smith & Wesson.

"Detective Dana Lopez, Homicide," she says, holding up a hand and then pointing to the man on the floor. "And that's Keith Miller, Crime Tech. You are?"

"Special Agent Thomas Decker, FBI."

"Special Agent Will Parker. Call me Will."

She looks at me with that evaluating cop gaze. "Seriously?" she says.

"No shit, are you really?" Miller scrambles to his feet.

I smile and wave.

Miller holds out a hand, but I don't respond. He's wearing latex gloves and he's been crawling around the floor of a hotel room. No thanks. Dana gives him a look, but before she can say anything, Decker moves on.

"I read your report, but it was brief," says Decker.

"And Parker here is just getting up to speed," he continues. "Why don't you fill us in?"

"What report?" I ask. There he goes again. Dribs and drabs. Never the full story.

"It was just a one-pager," says Decker. "Not much detail." I recognize the warning of impending machismo, like the first rumbles of thunder before a storm. Storm Decker.

Dana stands up straighter. "The blood's not even dry. Reports aren't the top priority, even if they do end up at the FBI."

"That's okay. Why don't you just tell me now about the radiation?" I say. If I'm going to have a shot at finding the Unicorn, I don't have time for dominance displays.

"Sure," says Dana, turning away from Decker. "When we arrived here at Caplan's hotel room, we did a preliminary search and found a black Pelican case under the bed. Empty."

"State regulations say that we have to sweep for chemical and radiological traces," says Miller. "When I booted up the radiation detector, it alerted right away on the open case."

Miller pauses, face flushed.

"Then what happened?" I ask. "Can we please keep the show moving, people?"

"Miller told us to get out," says Dana. "Urgently."

"I was being cautious," Miller says, crossing his arms and looking down at the floor. "I might have overreacted."

"First time it's ever gone off?" I ask.

"Yes," says Miller.

I walk over to the bed and bend down to take a look. The height underneath is right. There's plenty of space to fit a Pelican case large enough to hold a Unicorn. Even a case with sufficient internal padding. There's also another white cable connected to a white power brick plugged into the wall.

"Where's the case now?"

"Back at the lab," says Miller. "In safe storage."

I stand up and look at Miller. He meets my gaze hesitantly.

"Are you sure you did it right?"

"I'm sure." He nods, face flushing an even brighter red.

"I ask because that's the whole reason I'm here. That test result." I look back over at Dana, standing still at the lamp, watching me, evaluating. "Who's Caplan?"

"The victim," she says. "Roger Caplan. Forty. Caucasian male. Souvenir vendor from Boston."

"Collectibles," I correct her on the way to the closet.

"I'm sorry?"

"Collectibles. That's what they're called at a Comic Con. Not souvenirs. Souvenirs are things you buy at Times Square with 'I *heart* NY' on them. Vendors at Comic Cons sell collectible items associated with a particular fandom, or genre."

"And you know this how?" Dana asks, putting her hands on her hips.

"Doesn't everyone? Miller knows." I point at the tech before sliding open the closet door.

Dana glares at Miller who shrugs his shoulder and nods. I made Miller for a sci-fi fan the minute I walked in the door. And he recognized my name right away, which means he's a techie. Pure geek.

"He does?" Dana lifts an eyebrow.

"Check out his watch face. The symbol for the *Star Wars* Rebel Alliance." I turn to Miller. "You in the 501st?"

"Maybe." He never takes his gaze from the floor, awkwardly covering his watch face with the camera in his other hand.

"The 501st? I don't know that unit," says Decker.

"Of course you don't," I answer. "The 501st are cosplayers."

"Cos-what?" says Decker.

"Have you processed the laptop yet?" I ask Dana, ignoring Decker.

"We haven't recovered one," she says.

"Good, so it hasn't been compromised."

"There wasn't one at the scene, and there wasn't one on the desk when we came in," she continues, ignoring my commentary. She's not easily rattled. Intriguing.

"Well, then, it's still in here," I say, tapping on the metal safe on the upper shelf of the closet. It makes a muted ringing noise. Like most hotel safes, it's not very thick metal.

"How do you know that?" Dana asks, narrowing her eyes into little slits. She's got a hell of a stare, and I lean back under the weight of it.

"Because under the bed is a white power cable plugged into the wall. Apple, USB-C, 60W. So, there's a MacBook. Caplan also had an iPhone, based on the lightning cable plugged into the lamp."

Miller's under the bed. "He's right," he says. "It must have fallen down off the nightstand. I didn't notice it before."

"So where would the laptop be?" I ask, spreading my arms wide. "Wherever he went, he didn't take the Pelican case that would protect him from the radioactive contents. If he doesn't take that, he certainly wouldn't take his laptop."

Miller pops his head back out from under the bed looking like a meerkat in his white overalls. Dana's still squinting at me, but she's stopped frowning. Decker's grinning. I'm doing exactly what he wants, which is mildly annoying, but it's also what Burke sent me here to do, so I have to suck it up. For now.

"If it's here, where?" I continue. "I assume Miller's checked the desk and dresser drawers. The TV cabinet won't fly because there's a mini-fridge on one side and a coffee machine on the other, leaving no space."

"Which brings us to the safe," interrupts Decker. "You opened it yet?"

Dana looks at Miller.

"I can't," he says with a shrug. "I've asked hotel security to come, but they haven't yet, so I've been processing the rest of the room."

I wave my hand at him. "You go ahead with that; I've got this."

Inside my jacket pocket are two devices. My hardened Bureau Android, and an iPhone. I use the Bureau phone for official communications. Everything else is the iPhone. Of course, it's not an *ordinary* iPhone, it's *my* iPhone.

I take it out now and search for the app I want. When I find it, I hold my phone up to the safe.

"What are you doing?" asks Dana.

"Opening it," I say.

"How are you going to do that?" asks Decker. "Are you going to make a call?"

Oh, Decker. You sound so old. It may be called a phone, but it's really a pocket computer. And like any computer, its power comes from the apps running on it. And I've got some great apps.

This particular app goes about its work. Technically it doesn't have to touch the safe, just be close, but I'm tired, and the Tropical Blend wasn't enough jet fuel, so I rest it on the front.

"You may have noticed there's no key hole," I say to Decker. "Without the four-digit code, hotel safes open up via a wireless connection on the right frequency. Miller's still waiting for hotel security to open it because, right now, they're charging the device they use to override the lock. It doesn't get used all that often, and undoubtedly sits in a desk somewhere until the battery is dead."

"But you're using the phone antenna to scan and search for the right frequency," says Miller. "Damn, that's clever."

"Yes, it is." I'm rewarded for my patient leaning by an electronic whine and the grinding of gears. The display on the safe lights up and says "OPEN." I reach out for the handle and pause. "You dust this already?"

"Yeah," says Miller.

Dana crosses the room. Her frown is gone, the squinting eyes showing curiosity now, rather than suspicion. Decker catches my eye. The Unicorn. Could it also be in there with the laptop? What if Caplan put it there for safekeeping, damn the radiation?

"Wait," says Decker to Dana and Miller. "This could be dangerous. What if there's something radioactive in there, too? Maybe you should wait outside."

"What, are you Feds somehow immune to radiation?" Dana huffs. "We're fine here."

My hand hovers over the pull handle. How many years has it been? How many sleepless nights trying to piece together what happened to the Unicorn? And now it could be on the other side of this thin metal door. This isn't how I imagined our reunion. By trying to get Dana and Miller out of the room, Decker's revealed himself to be a problem. If it's in there, he's going to take it, giving the United

States government a terrifying power. Is that something I'm prepared to let happen? Too late now.

I swing the door of the safe open wide, standing on my tiptoes to see all the way to the back. Inside is a sleek gray laptop. The MacBook. But nothing else.

I let out a sigh of relief and disappointment.

CHAPTER FIVE

"**W**ell, is it in there?" Decker asks behind me.

He and the locals are gathered in a tight group around the closet. They can't see past my head into the safe I just hacked. I hear Decker's bulk shifting around trying to get a glimpse.

"No, there's just the laptop."

"*Just* that? What else are you looking for?" I can feel Dana's breath on my neck, she's so close.

"A Fukushima Unicorn." I step away, backing them off while reaching into my pocket for a pair of nitrile gloves.

"Stop, that's classified," says Decker.

"No, it's not. Everyone knows he had a deal to buy it," says Miller. "It's on Will's Wikipedia page."

"You have a Wikipedia page?" Dana's eyebrow goes up again. She stays close, hands on her hips.

"Of course, he does. Agent Parker, can I get in there to take a picture?" Miller asks, angling in with the camera.

"What's a Fukushima Unicorn?" Dana asks, but I'm too focused on the laptop to answer and Decker doesn't want to.

When Miller finishes with the camera, he gently lifts the laptop out of the safe and puts it on the desk, pushing the empty donut box out of the way. I lift the screen up and it comes to life showing the standard macOS login screen. Caplan's used a picture of Han Solo as his user avatar.

"Hey, what are you doing?" Dana demands. "He shouldn't do that here, should he?" She looks at Miller who lifts his hands and shrugs.

She's right. Normally I'd take the laptop back to a lab and get my techs working on it in a controlled environment. But my lab is thousands of miles away, and we're on a time crunch. If Dragoniis got his hands on the Fukushima Unicorn, every second that ticks by takes them both further away.

"For what I'm going to do, I can."

"And what's that?"

"I need to get this laptop to my technician."

"Then why do you need to open it?" Dana asks, her hand on my arm in caution.

"He's in LA."

She looks at Miller who says, "I'd let him do whatever he wants. His company wrote the book on security and encryption."

"Company? I thought you were an FBI agent," she says to me, the grip tightening.

"*Special* Agent," I say with a grimace. Why does no one remember the Special? "Miller's talking about the company I founded before."

"Before what?"

"Before I got to the FBI. Now listen, we're on a countdown here. Caplan's from out of town. So, unless this is some random hotel robbery gone wrong, his killer is going to be connected to him or why he's here."

"The Comic Con," Dana says.

"Right, so if he isn't gone already, we have . . . " I check the time on my smartwatch . . . "just over fifty-four hours to solve this. After that, the Con is over, and everyone associated with it, and with Roger Caplan, leaves town."

I watch as she evaluates my logic. She locks eyes with me. Gives me the penetrating cop stare, but I'm used to it now. Her eyes are dark brown. Soft, yet intense.

She lets go of my arm. "I hope you know what you're doing," she says.

"If anyone does, it's me," I say.

Miller's right. For our secure messaging, CastorNet developed and deployed some of the most advanced encryption on the planet. Certainly better than what the FBI is capable of. Don't know about the NSA though; Burke won't let me talk to them. But the Unicorn would change everything.

I need to send the contents of the laptop to Bradley. I could analyze what's on it, sure, but that's not the best use of my time.

Before I can do anything though, I need to unlock it.

"It's got a password," Dana says. "How do we get past it?"

"Me."

I sit still for a minute, thinking. Dana and Decker look over my shoulder. Miller's around somewhere, and I'm sure he's watching me, too. But it doesn't bother me. I've been in a fishbowl all my life.

The simplest way to hack a password is to guess it. There are other ways, but they're all more complicated, and take time. If I can guess it, we can keep moving. To have a chance at guessing, you need to know the individual. You have to use all the data you can. And hope to hell he didn't use a strong password.

"Is Caplan married?"

"Divorced," says Dana.

"His birthday?" Miller asks.

"It won't be his birthday. Too obvious. This is a guy that takes the time to put his laptop in the safe."

"So what?" says Decker. "Maybe he just doesn't want the hotel staff to lift it."

"Maybe," I say, "but it shows he's security minded. He took the time to change his avatar. He thought about it."

"What if it's a strong password?" Miller asks.

"Then we'll have to try something completely different. Let's hope it's not."

"How can you tell if it's strong?" asks Decker.

"You can't," says Dana. "Not until you crack it. Strong means a combination of numbers and letters, maybe punctuation, that doesn't spell a word or portion of a word."

I lift my hands away from the desk and turn to look at Dana in surprise. I hadn't expected her to answer that question. Usually, I try to keep greasy *n00b* fingers as far away as possible from the tech. When I look at Dana's fingers, I see neatly manicured nails. No colors or shiny coatings.

Wait a second. Fingers. Shiny. Images collide in my mind, clicking into place.

I lift the laptop, angling it under the light. I rotate it around, studying the keys carefully.

"Oh, come on," says Decker. "Even I know you can't see it."

"On the contrary," I say, "you can see it perfectly clearly. Especially if you just ate a box of donuts. Look, some keys are shiny with grease, transferred there from the donuts by Caplan's fingers, but most aren't. The trackpad's shiny with donut grease too, in a little circle. Looks like Caplan logged in and then did some surfing."

"I'll be damned," says Decker, leaning over my shoulder.

"Now we simply decipher the password from these letters."

"What letters do we have?" Dana asks.

"Looks like E, U, I, L, N, M," I say looking at the keys in the light of the desk lamp.

Not a great list if you're playing Scrabble. Short on the most common consonants, but that's good for me here, it limits the opportunities. Four words jump out at me.

I try them all, starting with "ileum" and ending with "lumen." No luck. The little login window shakes at me in disapproval each time.

"Try shorter words?" asks Miller.

I sense their breathless awe at my greasy keys discovery starting to fade. They're thinking this isn't so simple after all. They're thinking this whole idea is flash with no follow-through. They're thinking I can't do this.

I already know shorter words won't work, so I ignore Miller to focus on the problem. People live their entire lives in their computers. Even more so their phones, but I assume that's with the body, and I'll get to it later. I need to get into the laptop now. Bradley's waiting and the Unicorn is on the loose.

Is it possible that Caplan went strong? A random combination of those letters? Usually numbers and punctuation make up strong passwords and there's no grease on the top row. Maybe it's strong but not random. Maybe I'm thinking about the wrong language. The guy's here at a Comic Con. Maybe it's Klingon or something.

While I'm thinking over options, I roll the letters around in my head. What do they feel like? What could they be connected to? What could make them complete? There's something about them, on the tip of my tongue. I mutter combinations. The others wait and watch. Decker shifts back and forth, restless. Dana is tapping her fingers on the desk. Slow and steady, thinking, not impatient. A nervous tick. Ritualized behavior brought on by anxiety. Not even aware she's doing it. Her fingers move subconsciously, repeating the same rhythm.

That's what's missing. Repetition. Each greasy key could be pressed more than once. I need more coffee. I should've seen that quicker.

The separate pieces in my mind fit together and become one. The words, the sounds of them, combine in my head to form bigger words made from the same letters, now that I can use each letter as many times as I want.

I type in another attempt, hoping it's the last. If I fail now, they'll think they can do this too, and want to take turns. Then this whole process slows to a mind-numbing crawl. We can't afford to lose any more time. I have to be right.

I press ENTER.

The screen opens, revealing Caplan's desktop.

"Whoa!" says Miller.

"How did you do that?" Decker demands.

"Nice work," says Dana, patting me on the back. "What was it?"

"Millennium. We're at a Comic Con, but they're not just about comics. You get all the fandoms from anime to horror, video games to graphic novels, and of course, sci-fi. The avatar was the giveaway."

I push back from the desk and dial my phone. It's been fifteen minutes.

"I still don't get it," says Decker.

"Millennium," says Miller, louder, as if that makes it obvious.

Decker shakes his head, looking vacant. It doesn't mean anything to him.

"Caplan's a *Star Wars* fan," says Miller. "His avatar was Han Solo. The *Millennium Falcon* is Han Solo's ship."

I have a split second to enjoy the sour look on Decker's face before the call connects and is immediately answered.

"I'm here, Boss," says Bradley accompanied by a loud staticky noise on the line.

"What is that? A wrapper? Are you eating?" The trash at Bradley's desk routinely looks like the bin in a food court, filled with fast-food containers.

"Your texts stressed me out. And I'm still a little rough from last night."

"I need you to dig deep for me, Bradley."

"I know, I know. I got it. I grabbed two Egg McMuffins to go with the Peruvian Gold. I'm good, I promise."

"You're sure?"

"As sure as I am about a date with Ryan Reynolds."

I shake my head. Like many in LA, he's obsessed with celebrity. Totally different from where I grew up in Silicon Valley. Bradley has it worse than most. If there's a chance of his favorite celebs turning up at any given club, he'll be there. The current object of his devotion is Ryan Reynolds. Can't fault his taste.

"I've got a laptop that belonged to a Roger Caplan from Boston, in town for a Comic Con. He was a vendor. Someone murdered him last night."

"Interes-ing," says Bradley, his mouth full of McDonald's breakfast, obscuring his words. "You wan' me 'o do a full worku'? Any-fing special?"

"Everything. We're on the clock here. In fifty-four hours, it's over. Drop everything else. Get me quick hits first. Online profile. Then get into details. I want to know where he shops, what forums he hangs out in, what social media he uses, and what kind of porn he likes. What does he read, watch, or listen to? All of it. But right now, only you, Bradley."

"What? You want all that, but I don't get any help?"

"We need to keep this on the down-low."

"Why?"

"There could be a Unicorn here."

"What, you mean like a My Little Pony?"

"No. What? Where did that come from?" I pull the phone back in dismay.

"You're at a Comic Con, you said. Right? I thought maybe you're a Brony." I hear his voice from the speaker. "Sorry, just leapt to a conclusion."

"A Fukushima Unicorn, Bradley."

"Holy shit! Seriously? Okay, yeah, I'm on it, Boss."

I hang up the phone and Dana bends down so that we're eye to eye before she says, "I think it's about time you tell me what a Fukushima Unicorn is."

CHAPTER SIX

"We can't talk about the Fukushima Unicorn," says Decker.

Dana never takes her eyes off me. She knows the Unicorn is my thing, not Decker's.

"Well, you can talk about some of it," says Miller. "Wikipedia, remember?"

"I will, but first I have to set up this transfer to my lab."

She waits for a second. That frown of hers flickers across her face.

"All right," she says, "But we're not leaving this room until you do."

I know she wants answers, and the investigation will be better off when she has them. Getting the copy up and running gives me a few minutes to decide what to tell her about the Unicorn.

Turning back to Caplan's laptop, I open a browser and enter an IP address manually. When I'm prompted for credentials, I log in and a small application automatically downloads. When it installs, it gives Bradley complete remote control of the laptop, fully encrypted, all the way. A chat window pops up.

Bradley W: Got it. I'll start the copy.

Will P: How's the connection? How long?

Bradley W: Average. Looking at a couple of hours.

Will P: In the meantime, start on the online profile.

Bradley W: Will do. What's going on with the Fukushima Unicorn?

Will P: Not now.

Bradley W: Okay. TTYL.

I push back from the desk. Dana's waiting with her arms crossed. She's smart. She's local. She could help me find the Unicorn. That is, if the Unicorn is actually here. The radiation and the case are a good sign, but it could still be faked by someone with access to the Fukushima exclusion zones.

"Hey, Miller," I say, crossing to where the white-suited crime tech is standing next to the bed. "Do you have any pictures of the case?"

He fiddles with the back-panel controls of the camera and brings up some shots. It's a black case. Pelican. Interior padding is composed of gray foam pillars you peel out one by one until you've made an opening the size and shape you want. And the shape, in this case, is a narrowing series of rectangles like the Empire State Building.

Advancing through the photos, I see that Miller's done his job right, saving me time. Bravo, Miller. In some pics he placed a small yellow measuring T-square adjacent to the opening. The cutout looks to be about eight and a quarter inches long.

The last time I saw the Unicorn, it was hooked up to wires on a bench at Fukushima Semiconductor. Surrounded by larger machines, it seemed tiny, but up close you could tell it was roughly the size of two fists. I remember it was hot outside that day, but frosty cold inside, with that mild fishy smell that seemed to be everywhere in the village.

I turn back to Dana, now tapping her fingers on her crossed arms. What do I need to tell her? How much is enough?

"What do you want to know?"

"Why don't you start by telling me what it is? I assume it's not a horse with a horn in its head."

This is the closest I've come to the Unicorn since the tsunami, and I may never get this close again. The more I tell her, the better the chance I have of finding it. But the tenser Decker's going to be. I decide I'll deal with that later.

"The Fukushima Unicorn is a fully functional, miniaturized, and portable quantum computer."

"A computer?" Dana asks, rolling her eyes. "You want me to believe the FBI's here for a lost computer?"

"It's not an ordinary computer."

"How so? Explain it to me."

Most of the time, when I talk tech to non-technology people, they nod their heads and make noises like "uh-huh" and say things like "exactly" or "absolutely." But not Dana. She doesn't seem to think that asking questions makes her look foolish. No hesitation, no break in her confidence. Nice.

Before I can answer, Miller jumps in, eager to impress his detective.

"A normal computer uses binary, cycling the circuits between their two states, on and off, very quickly. Quantum computers are different. According to particle physics, quantum particles can exist in more than just two states, and they can be in those states simultaneously, opening up the ability to perform calculations faster. A lot faster."

Miller looks at me for approval. I nod. Simplified, but enough. I glance over by the door where Storm Decker is brewing, his lips pressed into a thin line. He doesn't like opening the kimono like this. It's also bugging him that it's Miller doing the explaining, which means I'm right: it isn't secret. This amuses me.

But when Miller continues on into the various states of quantum particles, Dana's eyes glaze over.

"Don't worry about the technical details," I say. "That's not what you want to know."

"You're right," she says, blinking. "What I want to know is why someone would kill for it."

"For starters, it's worth a lot of money."

"How much money?"

"My company, CastorNet, was in the process of buying Fukushima Semiconductor, inventors of that computer," I say, settling back down into the chair at the desk. "Any company able to commercialize it would be worth over a billion dollars, which is one of the reasons they call it a Unicorn."

"You were buying this company for a billion dollars?" Dana asks, raising her one eyebrow again.

"My company was, yes."

"You had a billion dollars?"

"CastorNet had that leverage, yes."

"What about you?" she asks.

"As the largest shareholder, let's call it almost." Back then I obsessed over how close I was to that goal. Now I try not to think about it.

"Why sell to you?"

"Because I was the one that discovered what they were up to." I glance at the laptop screen watching a little blue line move millimeter by millimeter across the screen. "I saw the pattern when no one else did. A handful of the most brilliant computer engineers in Japan quit their jobs and dropped out of sight, walking away from universities and high-paying corporate jobs. All under bizarre circumstances.

One fell in love with a Maid Café girl and they ran away together. Another had unpaid gambling debts to the Yakuza, who killed him for it. Stories that kept anyone from going looking for them.

"But I saw through it. My parents loved the country and I spent time there growing up, so I knew the language and culture. I went there and dug around. Eventually, I found the truth in an industrial building next to the Fukushima-Daiichi nuclear power plant where a tiny little computer chip company had set up shop. Low and behold, here were all these engineers with something to change the world. I had a software company; they had a hardware company. A match made in heaven. We became friends. Eventually, I convinced them to sell their company to me."

"How did you do that?" asks Dana.

"I'm very persuasive."

It's true. I laid down all that "for the people" and "transformational" promo material and told them we'd change the world together. They believed me, so they agreed to sell.

"What happened to the deal?" asks Dana.

I hesitate. Memories of the night my life was torn apart roar to the forefront of my mind. But I can't give in to them. Not now.

"Fukushima? The nuclear accident, right?" Miller says.

I nod. "Fifty minutes after getting hit by a tsunami, the Fukushima-Daiichi nuclear plant lost four reactors to meltdowns. When the radiation leaked, everything nearby got a lethal dose. Fukushima Semi was in a village right next door to the plant." I sigh, shaking my head. "They got fried."

Dana opens her mouth but seemingly changes her mind and closes it again. Something on her face softens.

"Your friends, what happened to them? Did they get out?"

"I don't think so." I stop again, clearing my throat. "A member of the Board of Directors in Tokyo got a text message that they were packing to evacuate. That's the last he heard. They, and their proto-type, vanished. This time without a trace. The people. The equip-ment. Everything. CastorNet ended up buying the company for the intellectual property rights, at a fraction of the price. The design of the quantum computer was too sensitive to have in the cloud, and was stored on-site. The Board was eager to salvage anything out of the deal when the data backups disappeared with the people."

I pause, remembering the destruction I saw in the aftermath of the tsunami.

"Best guess? There's a bridge they would have crossed on their most likely route. By the time rescuers got into the area, that bridge was gone. A lot of people disappeared along with their vehicles that day."

Dana leans back in her chair, looking over at Decker, then back at Miller. "And this thing was never seen again?"

"A car belonging to one of the staff washed up on a beach hun-dreds of miles away. But it was empty. Beyond that, only rumors on the internet," I answer with a shrug. "None of them ever panned out. That's the other reason it's called a Unicorn."

"A mythical creature no one has ever seen," says Miller.

"But you saw it," Dana says, ignoring him.

"Yeah."

"And now it's here."

"Looks that way." I point to Miller's camera.

"I'm sorry," she says after a thoughtful pause. "It's a fast computer, I get it. But that was years ago. Computers get faster all the time. Are you sure this is still worth killing for?"

"Dead certain. Bend your head around the fact that at the quan-tum level, the circuits actually exist in multiple states simultane-ously," I explain, holding up my hands and interlacing my fingers. "On *and* off. That means it doesn't have to finish one calculation before moving on to the next.

"For example, to break encryption, a binary computer calculates every possible combination of keys, one at a time, until it finds the right one. But there are trillions, so even at thousands per second it could take years before it finds the right key. A quantum computer can calculate all of them at the *same time*, and simply picks the right answer. Breaking encryption goes from years to seconds."

"Encryption, as in messages?"

"Messages, stored data, anything. Private, corporate, government, military . . ."

"Careful," warns Decker.

The wave of understanding washes over Dana's face, starting with amazement and ending with her deepest frown yet.

"And that's just the warm-up," says Miller. "With the right software, it could read your mind and predict the future."

"Come again?" asks Decker, pushing off from the wall. Apparently, his understanding of quantum computing begins and ends with security.

"That's impossible," Dana says, leaning back.

"Miller's right," I say with a nod of my head. "Collect enough data, feed it to artificial intelligence software, running on a quantum processor, and it would know what you're going to do before you do it. Imagine the system watching you shop at a grocery store. You walk down the ice cream aisle. It predicts what flavor of ice cream you will think of, so that at the critical moment of decision, it recommends a brand and flavor to tip you over the edge and swing the sale."

"That's creepy," she says.

"Now scale it up." I lean forward, locking eyes with Dana again. "Imagine that same computer system in the hands of government. It collects all the data it can about a person, private or not, because nothing can keep it out. It raids phones, tablets, computers, even your car. Feed all that into the AI, so it knows what you're going to do before you do it. Including a crime. Now imagine that government has a different definition of crime. They'd know who's going to speak out against them, attend a protest, or post a social media link they don't like, *before* they do it. What if it's a government that routinely ignores human rights? What comes next?"

"Oh my God." I see her physically shudder.

"Can you think of a country that would want that power?"

"That's enough," says Decker.

"Think they'd kill for it?" I push on.

"I said that's enough," says Decker, raising his voice. He's blasting me with the warning glare I'm sure he gave his soldiers when they stepped out of line back in the day. But I'm not one of his soldiers, so I glare right back.

"I think I'm starting to see why the FBI is here." Dana looks from me to Decker, sucking in her cheeks between her teeth. "What are you going to do with it when you find it?"

Decker stays silent, shaking his head in my direction. For once I agree with him. I shrug and say nothing.

"Uh-huh," she says, standing up, her hands on her hips. "Tell me, is this thing dangerous?"

"Define dangerous," I say.

Dana holds up a hand, cutting me off.

"This thing is radioactive. Is it dangerous to the public?"

Decker and Miller look at me.

"Not if it's kept in a shielded case," I answer.

"Like the one that was under the bed, and is now empty."

I see her point. How many lead-lined cases can there be around Indiana to store this thing safely?

"How do we find it?" Miller asks.

"We start by going to the Comic Con."

"You're thinking we find Caplan's killer, we find the Unicorn," says Dana.

"Bingo."

"Just like that?" asks Decker, looking at his watch.

"It's a start."

Dana holds up a finger, swinging it between Decker and me. "Before you two walk out of here, let me be clear. My priorities are the safety of this community and finding whoever murdered Roger Caplan. In that order. If for one minute, I think you're working against those goals, we're going to have a problem." She waggles her finger for emphasis.

The determined set of her face leaves little doubt as to how bad that would be.

"Are we going to have a problem?" she asks.

"Not at all," I answer. "Right, Decker?"

His nostrils flare. He sucks air in through his teeth. "Nope," he says in a tone that, to me, says anything but.

Looking over at the laptop, I see the copy is moving well. In an hour and a half, Bradley will begin to pore over its secrets. Thoughts of Fukushima crash around in my head. I need something else to focus on. Like a murder. Suddenly the hotel room seems too small.

I stand up and walk out the door.

CHAPTER SEVEN

The security office in the hotel is typical: small, out of the way, and filled with boxes of other stuff. Kitchen supplies from the looks of it, and extra linens stacked around two desks, one of which holds a computer, phone, papers, and a little gold sign that says, "Head of Hotel Security."

But it's the other desk I'm most interested in. It's dominated by a wall of monitors on extendable aluminum arms. Three screens wide by three screens high. Neat bundles of blue cables connect the hotel security system to the network. It's neat and tidy. Professional. Probably hasn't been touched since it was installed, but at least it was done right in the first place.

In the office is a crisply dressed guy with a shaved head, likely to avoid the embarrassment of male pattern baldness if my glimpse of the stubble line is correct. He's short, so it's easy to catch it. If I were him, I'd shave my head too.

"Everything's here," he says. "The whole hotel network can be accessed from this desk."

"The Wi-Fi too?"

"Yes, sir," says short and bald. I think he introduced himself as Dwayne. "All the manuals are on this shelf over here."

To get to the shelf, he clears away a stack of cardboard boxes. They must be heavy because he's huffing and puffing quickly, despite looking like he's in shape. I wait until he's moved the last box and then look at the binders. I recognize them all. Good quality products, and if the software installation is as good as the hardware, we're in business.

Assuming at one point the Fukushima Unicorn was in the Pelican case in Caplan's room, the first step toward knowing where it is now is knowing when it left.

There's a knock behind me. When Dwayne opens the door, Storm Decker surges into the room with Dana hot on his heels.

"Here he is," says Decker.

"You just took off," Dana says.

"He does that," Decker grumbles, then to me, he asks, "What have you found?"

"So far, manuals," I answer, sliding the first one off the shelf. I flip it open to the cover page. Yup. The Administrator login ID and password, as left by the contractor that set it up.

Plopping the manual down on the surveillance desk next to the keyboard, I settle into the chair and log in to the system with my purloined credentials.

"You mind if he does that?" Decker asks.

"Not at all, Agent," says Dwayne. He leans into Decker, lowering his voice. "Can I ask you a question? How was Quantico? You know, I visited once."

So, Dwayne's a Fed Groupie. An Agent wannabe, working a security job he thinks might one day lead him to the Bureau. That's good, they're always eager to please. Though they tend to be chatty. As if on cue, Dwayne starts to pepper Decker with questions, keeping them both out of my hair.

I start exploring the computer. There are icons on the desktop for the three main security applications: surveillance cameras, key card system, and Wi-Fi administration. Perfect.

"Checking surveillance footage?" asks Dana. "Caplan was murdered hours ago. And we don't know how long before that he arrived at the hotel. This could take a long time."

"It could," I say, opening up the key card system.

It's a good one. The hotel paid for the right options. Most important of which, the system logs every time a guest room door is opened, whether the key card is swiped or not. Useful.

Next, I open the surveillance program.

"I've already talked to the hotel manager," says Dana. "They've only got cameras in the main public spaces. The front lobby, elevator lobbies, front desk, and the outside perimeter."

"Are you surprised?" I ask. "This isn't a Vegas casino."

"Maybe," says Dana. "But more is always better."

Can't argue with her there.

Knowing the software well, I run through the configuration quickly. She's right. Nothing in the guest hallways. Ditto the stairwells. Even the coffee shop and restaurant are blank spaces.

Finally, I look at the Wi-Fi system, diving right into the reports. The system automatically captures a massive volume of data, typically used in troubleshooting. I have other uses.

"It can't have been *that* tough for you," says Dwayne, looking up at Decker. "If you were Spec Ops before the Bureau, you must have aced the Academy."

"Some of it was familiar ground," admits Decker. I didn't think it was possible but he manages to stand up even straighter, shoulders back, chest out, puffed up like he's on parade.

"What are you going to get out of the Wi-Fi? What he was surfing?" asks Dana.

"Better than that, if we're lucky," I say, turning my attention back to the computer. I scan through the reports until I see one that says "Handoff." Perfect.

Now that I know what's in each system, I can really go to work. Flipping through the screens, I grab snippets of video. I must be making a bit of a racket on the keyboard because Dwayne stops talking followed by Decker's heavy presence looming over my shoulder. I don't slow down. I'm in the middle of the hunt, closing in on my quarry. A picture is forming, a framework first, followed by the details. Eventually, I push back from the desk, rolling a couple of feet in the chair, and stretching out.

"There it is."

"There's what?" Decker asks

"Caplan entered the hotel at 10:55 p.m. last night. He's on video here," I say, gliding back to the desk and cueing it up on screen.

The video is bright and clear. Caplan enters through the main lobby doors and makes a beeline for the elevator bank. Average height and build. He's sporting a t-shirt with Captain America's shield on it and floppy cargo shorts. Brown hair peeks out the back of a white ball cap. Possible mullet. Ouch.

"Wait a second. How did you know what Caplan looks like?" asks Dana leaning forward.

"Simple. I found his phone, and there he was holding it."

"How did you do that?"

"I looked at the last entry to his room on the key card system." I flip screens and point. "From there, I worked backwards, cross-referencing with the Wi-Fi."

"What does the Wi-Fi have to do with it?"

She must have caught my eye roll because then she says, "Help me out, I want to get this right."

The delay irritates me, but it's a respectable question. She's determined to get the job done, not wasting time by pretending to understand what she doesn't.

"Every gadget has a device name. Most people never change what the operating system assigns when it's set up. When they connect to

Wi-Fi, they're identified on the network with that name. Here at the hotel, if a device leaves and returns within the same twenty-four-hour period, the Wi-Fi automatically reconnects, using the same name."

"Why twenty-four hours?" asks Decker.

"Guests are charged by the day," answers Dwayne. "Even the rewards club members who get it for free have to say yes every day to the terms."

"Still don't see how you found Caplan specifically," Dana says. Suspicious. Challenging. Is she interrogating me?

"Because when I look at the logs, I found an entry for 'Roger's iPhone.' It connects to the main lobby access point four minutes before Caplan's room is opened with the key card. So, I pulled up the lobby camera from the time the phone connects to the network, and there he is." I rest my hand on the mouse. "Now, can I get back to the timeline?"

"By all means," says Dana, holding up her hands.

"Caplan comes in at 10:55 p.m. His phone connects to the hotel Wi-Fi in the lobby. He makes a beeline for the elevator, but he's not the only one. Look here."

Backing up the video to just before Caplan enters, the lobby camera shows a family at the front desk with three kids. The biggest kid is chasing one of the other ones around. There's no sound, but they must have been screaming, because everyone in the frame is looking at them. All except one.

A big guy in a suit isn't distracted by the demonic children. He's sitting on one of the sofas reading a newspaper, folded down so it doesn't block his view. Another newspaper? Seriously, where are people finding these things?

I point him out to Decker and Dana.

"While the little hellions are running around like a prison riot, this guy just sits there, watching the front door. Calm."

The main lobby door slides open and Caplan walks in. He glances at the infant banshees, then makes for the elevator. The man with the paper stands up and follows him.

"Care to guess where Mr. Newspaper's going?"

"Caplan's floor," says Dana. "He was waiting for him."

"Who is he?" asks Decker.

"No idea," I say, grabbing the mouse.

I play a succession of clips. The two men waiting in the elevator lobby, followed by the ride up. Inside the elevator, Caplan doesn't seem to notice he's being watched. When the doors open and he steps off, Mr. Newspaper follows. The elevator lobby camera on Caplan's floor shows them walk off down the hall in the same direction.

"Now we go dark on the surveillance footage."

"That's it? We lost them?" says Decker.

"No." I rub my forehead. "We just don't have video. But his phone is still connected to Wi-Fi, so we can use the access points to follow where he goes. Here in the logs you see 'Roger's iPhone' connect to two access points in the fifth-floor hallway, one after the other, and then to the one in his room. Key card logs show his room door opens with the key at 10:59 p.m. He stays there until the door is opened, without a key card this time, at 11:17 p.m."

"Did he leave the room?" asks Dana. "How do we know he didn't just open the door to let someone in?"

"Because Wi-Fi has the phone on the move again."

"When he gets back on the elevator, is he alone?" she asks.

"This time he doesn't take the elevator," I say, holding up a finger. "He takes the stairs."

"I thought there are no cameras in the stairwells."

"There aren't. The third Wi-Fi access point on each floor is located by the stairs. 'Roger's iPhone' connects with each one, in order, from the fifth floor all the way down to the main floor, where he goes out a side door, avoiding the lobby. That's where we get our last shot."

I start the last video clip. The screen shows a small surface parking lot next to the building. A door opens, blocking the view. Whoever installed the camera put it on the wrong side. When it closes, you can see the back of someone that looks like Caplan walking off into the dark.

"Well, that's interesting," says Dana.

"I know, right?" I say, nodding my head.

"What is?" asks Decker. "He left the building."

"First, he left alone," she says. "That guy with the newspaper—I don't even know where he got a newspaper—is gone. Second, he's wearing a jacket."

"So?" says Decker.

"It was ninety-five degrees last night," says Dana. "Way too hot to wear a jacket."

"Unless?" I say, rolling my hand in front of me.

"Unless you need to hide something under it," she says, "like a Fukushima Unicorn."

CHAPTER EIGHT

Dwayne leads us to the same door Caplan used. If he had the Unicorn with him when he left, retracing his last steps is our best chance of finding a clue to where it is now. Dwayne stands awkwardly in the door behind me, blocking the way, to ask Decker for his contact info. Having left Miller behind to finish processing the hotel room, Dana's following somewhere behind them. Tapping commands into my watch, I take off down the street. Well, the maps app calls it a street, but it's more like a wide alley, closed in by towering buildings on both sides.

"Where are you going?" Decker shouts after me.

I glance back to see Dwayne with a big smile on his face, cheerily waving around a business card.

"Comic Con!"

"How do you know where to go?"

"Technology!" I wave my arm in the air. My watch is already vibrating in a specific pattern to tell me I need to make a turn at the end of the alley.

The Convention Center is a short walk away, and the nav takes me by the most direct route. That's how Caplan would have gone. Unlikely that he'd dawdle while carrying something radioactive under his jacket.

At the entrance to the alley, I look down at my watch to confirm the direction I'm supposed to go. The high-pitched whine of a sport bike engine revving up tears into the quiet morning. I jerk my head up, just in time to see a red motorcycle bearing down on me. Jumping back to the safety of the curb, I get a glimpse of the rider, dressed head to toe in red leathers with white accents. They turn to face me as the bike passes so close, I can feel the heat of the exhaust. The reflective film on their visor catches the rising sun, blinding me.

As the bike zooms off up the road, I hear footsteps behind me. Two sets. Storm Decker's heavy marching is easy to pick out. The other must be Detective Lopez. Tighter, but quick, and in a perfect rhythmic cadence. Athletic.

"Are you all right?" Decker asks.

"I'm fine," I say, rubbing my eyes.

"Sorry about that. We have a problem with those crotch rockets every time the weather gets hot. This way," says Dana, turning left.

Restaurants with sidewalk patios are all over the busy street. There would have been a lot of people here last night, despite the late hour. A glance at the watch tells me it's almost a straight shot to the Convention Center from here. If he knew or suspected he was being followed, Caplan would have felt safer in a crowd.

A block away, Decker points at an older couple walking down the street wearing brown hoop skirts with gold balls glued to them, flashlights bolted to brown army surplus helmets on their heads. In their right hands they carry bathroom plungers and in their left, paint rollers.

"You've got some strange folks in this town, Detective Lopez. What's up with them?"

"They're cosplayers, Decker," I answer.

"Cos what now?"

"People that dress up in costume for the Comic Con. That's all hand-crafted."

"Costumes? What are they supposed to be?"

"Daleks," I say. "A robot race from *Doctor Who*."

"It's weird."

"It's interpretive."

What else can I expect from Decker? A lifetime of living within rigid rules. No imagination.

"Over here," says Dana. She's found a clutch of uniformed officers by an entrance.

"They won't let us in the front, Detective," says one of them as she approaches.

"What do you mean *they won't let you in*? It's a fucking crime scene." Dana transforms before my eyes, raising her voice and waving her arms around. "What bullshit is this? Since when do we need permission to investigate a goddamn crime?"

The uniformed officer responds to her frustration with a smile, immediately at ease.

"I know, I know, Detective Lopez. Crazy, right? But he's insisting that if we're in uniform, we have to wait outside, now that the doors are open. Said he's already talked to the mayor and if I had a problem with that, I could take it up with him."

"He *who*?"

"The guy in charge of this thing, Charles Farber."

"For fuck's sake. Wait here, I'll take care of it," she says, and then to Decker and me, "FBI, you're with me."

She pivots and makes a beeline for the nearest door, but Decker is closer and gets there first. A security guard checks the wristbands of convention goers as they enter, "Leroy" embroidered on the front of his yellow shirt. A line of people twenty deep, some in costume, some not, are politely waiting their turn. Storm Decker walks to the front of the line, chin up, back straight.

"FBI," he says, flashing his badge and moving to cut around the guard.

"Yeah, right," he says stepping in front of Decker. This guy's even bigger. "Nice costume, bro, but you'll have to wait your turn like everyone else."

"What?" stutters Decker. His jaw bounces up and down but no more words come out. His eyes are wide as he tries to process what just happened. This is definitely a first for him.

"*X-Files*, right? Looks good. But I have to ask you to go to the back of the line," he says, pointing.

Before Decker can recover, Dana's maneuvering around him. "No cosplay here, Leroy," she says with a tight smile, lifting her badge. "Police. And these two are real-deal FBI. We're here on business, and I'm sure your boss doesn't want a scene. So, step aside."

"No, ma'am, he does not," agrees Leroy. "I wasn't expecting the FBI. My instructions are to send uniformed officers around the back, but you can come in here." He steps aside and waves us through, lifting a handheld radio to his face. Decker shoots him a glare.

"This guy in charge of the event, Farber? He's got some real juice to flirt with obstruction like this," says Decker disapprovingly.

I'd never seen anything like it before. Then again, I've never been called in the middle of the night by an Assistant Director of the FBI either. A strange day keeps getting stranger.

"Farber's a local developer. Owns half of the buildings in the downtown. Big money, even bigger ego," says Dana.

Decker snorts.

Inside the main hall, white marble floors glisten under a soaring glass wall and ceiling. A set of escalators in the middle leads up to a mezzanine. Pretty decent for a small city.

A harried-looking young woman with a clipboard runs toward us, waving her free hand to get our attention.

"Please, Mr. Farber sent me to meet you. You are police, yes?" she says as she reaches us. I recognize her accent right away. Korean.

Decker and Dana reach into their blazers for their IDs.

"No, no. Please. No need to show identification," she says, waving at them to keep the badges hidden. "I am Sally Park, Mr. Farber's assistant."

Dana introduces us without showing our IDs. Ms. Park nods politely at each of our names.

"Please, follow me," she says, leading us away into the crowd.

"I don't see why you couldn't just open late," says Decker.

"I'm sure Mr. Farber will answer all your questions," she says.

Decker looks unimpressed and I get the feeling he's about to go aggressive on her, so I head it off at the pass. I've been up for too many hours, without enough caffeine, to watch a full Storm Decker assault. Wait, caffeine, there's a thought. I look around for a food court while answering Decker's question.

"Because people were already lining up for hours before the doors opened, weren't they, Ms. Park?"

"Yes, Agent Parker."

"A lot of them will have taken the day off work," I continue. "They've been planning on being here for weeks."

"So, let them wait," says Decker. "Murder takes priority."

Sally Park looks pained when Decker says the word "murder" out loud.

"Does it? The big studios spend millions promoting product in the pipeline for the coming year. A superhero movie that costs two hundred million to make could earn a billion in worldwide ticket sales if it's a hit. And these are the people that determine if it's a hit," I say opening my arms wide at the crowds around me. "Ms. Park, what's the expected attendance this weekend?"

"Forty thousand," she says immediately. "We are sold out at capacity. We could sell more, but this is the largest venue in city."

"And how much is a ticket?" I say.

"It depends on the type of ticket. One-day pass. Weekend pass. VIP pass. Plus, there are special tickets for special events."

"On average," says Dana, a frown on her face.

"Average entrance revenue per guest is seventy-five dollars for the weekend."

"So, there you go," I say, waving at Decker. "Three million in three days, direct revenue."

"Plus, sales of photos and autographs. And vendor fees," Park adds.

"Probably another million there?" I look at Park who nods.

Decker lets out a low whistle. Commerce is everywhere. Throughout the hallways people pull purchases out of plastic bags to show off newly acquired treasures. A clutch of girls looks at a picture in a large glass frame and giggles.

Some guys dressed up as characters from one of my favorite shows, *The Double Limit*, are holding up glossy 8x10s of Jerry Oldham, the time-traveling-cop star of the series, and comparing what he wrote when he autographed them.

"Everything here costs money, Decker. Every photograph, autograph, and, of course, collectible has a price tag on it. Ms. Park, including tourism, what's the total economic impact to the city?"

"Ten million dollars," she says without hesitation. I bet Farber drilled her on that number when it got political early this morning. "It's very important for our city. A big deal."

"I'll be damned," says Decker.

"Mr. Farber is very concerned about disruption," says Ms. Park. "He doesn't want to lose attendance. We are telling people only that an accident happened. A slip and fall. Here we are."

We've followed her past the main entrance, down a side hallway to a set of double doors near the back of the building. She opens them wide, ushering us into the main vendor hall. The typical wide-open space of a Convention Center, stretching the length of a couple of football fields, is filled with thousands of people. Chattering away, they create a roar of white noise like the rush of a river cascading over a waterfall. Painted white cinder-block walls around the perimeter support the steel beams of a ceiling thirty feet overhead.

Lined up in the huge space are row upon row of vendor booths in neat, rigid aisles. Throngs of people shuffle along in all directions, occasionally bumping together in traffic jams. Standing two stories tall in the middle of the hall is a wire-frame tower, every square inch covered with t-shirts celebrating all things geeky.

I feel a familiar thrill. An anticipation of what new things there are to find, and celebrities to see. I wonder if I'll get to see Jerry Oldham. I'm not here for fun, but the sights and sounds bring back memories of better times.

"Holy shit," says Decker, raising his voice above the cacophony.

"This is a slow day," I shout in response. "Twice as busy on Saturday."

"You think somewhere in here is the person that took out Caplan?" Dana shouts.

"And the most powerful new technology since the atomic bomb," I add.

"This is bad," says Decker, scanning the crowd with a grim expression.

I know what he's thinking. There's a lot of people here, sharing a large and yet confined space with something dangerously radioactive. Plus, someone who's already killed once to get it.

I lean in close to Decker's ear so only he can hear me. "And we've got fifty-two hours to find them."

The crowd thins out as Ms. Park leads us to a row of tables on a long platform backed by fabric-covered scaffolding at the back of the vendor hall. Hung on the curtain behind each table is a sign with a celebrity's name in huge letters next to their photo. Autograph alley.

As Park points out a sign for the washrooms, I notice that nobody's here, except for a few of the handlers. Each one sells glossy 8x10 photos to fans, writing down their names on a Post-it note so it gets spelled correctly. In between signings, they let fans know when the object of their adoration will be returning.

"Will Parker, is that you?"

I don't expect to find many admirers this far from the Valley, but it wouldn't be the first time. Our products had a loyal following.

Turning around, I find it's not an admirer. Not at all.

A middle-aged guy with wavy gray hair and a neatly trimmed beard that's nearly white holds out his hand. Martin Hicks. He's wearing the standard uniform of corporate IT workers: tan khakis and a golf shirt, royal blue this time, with a corporate logo on it. Stretching wide above his head is a banner with the same logo on it. Pyntel, the chip manufacturer. Behind him is an open-corner display space, covered with plush carpet and a forest of slick black towers displaying an array of desktop and mobile devices powered by their processors.

Last time I checked, Hicks was a senior vice president of something or other. I knew him back in the Valley days. A smarmy corporate Yes-Man begging and pleading his way up the ladder.

"Martin," I say, breaking out in a wide smile. "What are you doing here? So good to see you, man." I take his hand and shake it warmly.

"Good to see you too, Will. I never thought I'd run into you here, not in a million years. How have you been? Didn't I hear you left the life?"

"Yeah, I did. Totally. Whole new gig now."

Gross. Two seconds in front of someone from the Valley and it's like I never left. The whole thing's an act, of course, but that's how the game is played. Hollywood celebrities and their petty backstabbing have nothing on tech workers when it comes to frenemies. Everyone in Silicon Valley is an ally, an asset, or an enemy.

"You're a cop or something, right?" Martin asks, cocking his head to the side.

I nod, putting on a serious face to match my serious role. "FBI as a matter of fact. Special Agent."

"No way! That's terrific, I mean, to be able to follow your passion like that. I admire you, man, taking that bold step. Chasing your dreams. Do you ever miss it? Think about coming back?"

"Well, you never know, Martin."

The only dreams that motivated me to join the FBI were nightmares, but Hicks doesn't know that. People I worked side by side with for years, like Ace Prior, don't know. Only Jack knew the full story, and he's gone now.

The memory of Jack triggers a pain in my side. He was a good man. He didn't deserve what happened. I'd take one Jack Walton over a room full of Martin Hickses, wide-eyed and grasping my upper arm in a phony gesture of encouragement.

What a farce.

"Right now, I'm living the dream," I say. The words are sour on my tongue. Time to change the topic. "What about you? Still at Pyntel, I see."

"You know it. I'm a lifer."

"What are you doing at a Con?"

"Well, I've got marketing under me now," he says with a sigh, suggesting that the burden of increased responsibility is a noble sacrifice he's taken on. "Co-COO with Jordan Grant. You remember Jordan, yes? Well, I like to get out here on the front lines from time to time. Meet our customers. Get some feedback on a new product coming out, you know, hear their thoughts firsthand."

Complete and utter bullshit. It's a job for a product manager.

"Of course, of course," I say. "That's where the real innovation happens, isn't it? Well, listen, I've got to jet, but it was awesome catching up. Ping me sometime. Good luck with the show."

"Thanks, Will, I'll do that. Great to see you, man. It's not the same in the Valley without you. But, onwards and upwards, right?"

I'm already walking backwards and I pivot to make my escape.

"What was that all about?" Decker asks when I catch up with the group outside the bathroom entrance.

"Someone I used to know from back in the day."

"From *back in the day*? You mean when you were 'considered one of the hottest young tech CEOs?'" Dana asks, waving her phone at me. I see my own face. My Wikipedia page. "Good photo."

I hate that picture. Taken when I was younger and launching CastorNet, you can just make out the corner of our old cheesy banner in the background. The clear glasses I'd affected at the time made me look older rather than smarter. Terrible. For a while I tried replacing it, but another editor kept putting it back. I gave up.

Status in the Valley comes from having the fastest-growing, hottest product. Bonus points for being a young age. Money is the official scorecard.

What I did, walking away, confuses guys like Hicks. On one hand they're convinced that I've lost my mind, the only possible explanation for dropping out of the race. On the other hand, they're glad I'm now one less voice they have to drown out for attention.

"Is he an almost-billionaire like you?" Dana asks.

I snort. "Not like me. I invented something, founded a company, and built it. He's a corporate drone; he never invented anything. I don't know if he's ever even written a line of code. But he's rich, sure. Second from the top at Pyntel."

"Really? What's he doing here?" asks Dana.

"He said he was getting in touch with his customers," I say, looking over her shoulder. Hicks has disappeared into a swarm of twenty-year-olds in Pyntel t-shirts handing out swag.

"Do you believe him?"

"Not for a second. It's a pretense for him to be here."

"Think it's connected to Caplan's murder?"

"Caplan?" I look back at the corporate flunkies in their khakis and team shirts. "Not directly. But the connection to the Fukushima Unicorn is too much coincidence to ignore. If Pyntel managed to get their hands on it, they'd monetize it into products worth hundreds of billions."

"You think he knows it was here," says Dana.

"Show me what happened to Caplan, and I'll tell you."

She squints at me again, evaluating. Finally, she looks me in the eye and says, "Brace yourself."

CHAPTER NINE

There's blood. A lot of it.

Caplan's body has been taken away by the coroner, but the bathroom where he met his end has been left as is. Probably because they think the FBI would want to see it for ourselves. As I hold my hand to my face to try and filter out the coppery smell of blood that's sprayed or smeared on just about every surface, including the ceiling, I think I really could have done without.

Try as I might to avoid it, that smell gets deep into the back of my throat and I cough, barely managing not to gag. Thankfully, there's nothing but Tropical Blend in my stomach to make a repeat appearance if I did.

"You all right?" Dana asks, looking at me, a frown creasing her forehead. I suspect she's afraid I'm going to contaminate her crime scene.

Not sure I can speak without vomiting, I nod, hoping it comes off as more confident than I feel.

"Haven't seen a lot of gore, have you?" she says.

I shake my head. No, I really haven't. We saw photos of violent crimes at Quantico, but since then I've been in Cyber where most of the crime takes place online, at a distance. Sure, I'd seen some fuel for nightmares: child pornography, tortured victims of human trafficking. But not messy murders, and definitely not in person.

One side of the room is stalls. The other is split in half with a partial wall between the urinals and a handful of sinks, set into a granite countertop with a dark grain. One of the sinks is completely soaked in blood; everywhere else has been sprayed.

"Let me run it down for you," says Dana, snapping her gloves into place. She looks over at me. Do I see a flicker of sympathy in her eyes?

"The blood trail starts here," she continues, pointing at the sink soaked in blood. "Spatter is consistent with his head striking the edge of the counter. Caplan was most likely hit from behind, smashing his head down. There's a corresponding wound on his forehead."

She draws an imaginary line across her forehead with one finger of her nitrile gloved hand. The Tropical Blend churns. Ugh.

"After that, there was a struggle. It's going to take Miller and his team some time to work out the sequence of events from the spatter patterns. They cross over each other all over the place. Suffice it to say, Caplan didn't go right down. Whether he fought or was just flopping around, we can't tell yet."

One of the stall doors has a smear on it. He surely went in there at one point. I look at the floor in front of the toilet. Smudgy footprints in the blood are swirled around in a circular pattern.

"Someone tried to disguise their tracks," I say, pointing at the footprints.

"Good eye," says Dana. "There are at least two distinct sets of prints so far. One belongs to Caplan, the other to the unsubs."

"Unsubs? There was more than one?" asks Decker. He's leaning up against the door, hanging back and watching, trying to look casual. I'm not buying it. He's rigid, muscles tense. I wonder how many crime scenes like this he's seen, but then, he was in the Army, so he's probably seen worse. Maybe it's his natural uptightness. Maybe you never get over seeing this stuff.

"We can't tell, so we're assuming the possibility of multiple suspects at this point," Dana says. "Whoever made the tracks went back and smeared them out to hide the tread patterns. Could have been one, could have been half a dozen. No way to know until the techs go over every one of them."

"How long is that going to take?" Decker asks.

"Too long," I say. "Any sign of the Unicorn?"

"There's a void on the counter," she says. "Miller caught it. The dark pattern of the countertop hides it well, but there's definitely a line to the right of the sink. Something was up there. But it wasn't a hard case like the one in the hotel room."

"How do you know?" asks Decker.

"Wavy line?" I ask Dana. She nods. "Something soft. A bag?"

"Miller can't say for certain, but that seems likely."

"Radiation?" I ask.

"Inconclusive. Miller said nothing rose above background levels, but if it was only in here for a few minutes it wouldn't leave much of a trace."

"Did he check the rest of the building?"

"Yeah, nothing."

I sigh. Did I really think it would be that easy to find?

"Anything else left behind?" I ask. "Anything on him?"

"Wallet, hotel key card, the usual," says Dana.

"Phone?"

She pauses, unsure. She takes out her phone and looks something up. "No. Miller's report doesn't list a phone. Not at the scene, none on the body."

"What about his hands?"

"His hands?" Dana asks, pinching her eyebrows together.

"Were they covered in blood?"

"Wait a second," she says, scrolling through the report. "Yes, they were bloody. Except for the right index finger. That was wiped clean. That's weird."

"It's obvious."

"How did you know about that?" asks Decker, unfolding his arms and cocking his head to the side.

"His phone. We know he had it when he left the hotel. It isn't here now. So, the killer, or someone else, took it. If it's locked, it's useless."

"The fingerprint scanner," says Dana. "Would have been easy while the blood was still wet, before it got sticky. Definitely happened after someone cracked his skull open."

Gross. That's enough. I'm out of here.

I walk back out onto the Con floor, thankful to get away from that smell. Looking down at my feet, I remember I'm wearing my favorite pair of Converse. Just my luck. I should have known better. I lift them up to look at the soles. At first glance they look clean, but the sole is dark and—

"What are you doing?"

Standing there on one foot, the other pulled up to examine the sole, I look up to see a short, portly man scuttling my way. He's got a receding hairline but thick, bushy eyebrows over dark brown eyes that are glowering at me. His olive complexion is flushed and he's puffing.

"Take off those gloves," he says, pointing a meaty finger. The thick gold rings on his hand sparkle in the bright lights of the vendor hall.

"What?"

"You look like a cop; take off those gloves."

"I am a cop. FBI," I say, reaching into my pocket.

"No badges," hisses the portly man.

Sally Park pushes through the crowd and hurries toward us. The portly man must be Farber.

"All right, settle down," I say, dropping my foot back to the ground.

"Don't tell me to settle down," he says, balling his hands into fists. "You're supposed to be keeping this out of sight."

Park arrives, clutching her clipboard to her chest, tiny beads of sweat on her brow.

"These are the FBI, Mr. Farber. They have no uniforms, and you said to let them in if they have no uniforms," says Ms. Park.

"I said not to let them in if they looked like cops, *like* wearing uniforms. Cops around the entrances look like security. Cops wearing gloves and gathering in groups inside looks like there's a problem. Smarten up. Details, Sally!" he says, waggling a finger at her. She lowers her head quickly, murmuring an apology. I don't think this is the first time he's cut her down.

"It's all right, Ms. Park," I say, taking off the gloves and balling them up inside out in my fist. "I'm finished anyway."

"You're finished?" asks Farber, wheeling on me. "Good, so I can get that room cleaned and reopened? That's supposed to be the bathroom for the celebrities. They're going to be pissed if they don't have their own bathroom away from the weirdos."

"Hold on, I didn't say we're finished with the room. I'm just finished with the gloves."

"Are you messing with me?"

"You'd know it if I was."

"So, when are you going to be finished? I need that room."

This guy's on fire. I get that he wants his Con to get back to business as usual, but this Caplan guy had his lights snuffed out just a few hours ago. The blood is barely dry. Probably still sticky in some places. My stomach lurches.

"What's going on out here?" says Decker, coming up behind me.

Good. Let Decker handle him. My stomach flops over and I remember I still haven't eaten anything. Maybe food would settle it, unappetizing as that is after what I just witnessed. I start walking away.

"Ahh, now we're getting somewhere. That's right, walk on out of here, public servant. There's business to be done here."

"Easy," says Decker. There's a warning in his tone. The storm is brewing. "A man's dead here."

"Yeah, well, it's one guy. Business goes on. My business."

It's not the first time I've heard someone so callous about another life. I worked human trafficking cases, after all. But there's something different today. I wish it was the way Caplan was killed, or anxiety about the Unicorn, or a lack of sleep. If I'm honest with myself, I know what it is. The last time I saw blood like this was the night Sterling killed Kate Mason. When he sliced her throat, the blood spraying down her chest, I turned away. I couldn't watch. I didn't want to see what I'd done.

My face burns with the memory of my mistake. I clench my hands into tight fists, fingernails digging into my palms. My breathing is ragged. I spin and I'm back in front of Farber. Close. Invading his personal space, but not touching him. I loom over him, forcing him to look up at me.

"Look, Farber, I don't think you know who you're talking to."

"Sure, I do," he says, poking a finger at my chest, but stopping shy of making contact. "Just another cop. We've already got too many here. One phone call and I can have you removed."

"First, one question," I say so close I know he's smelling Tropical Blend. "Where were *you* last night, Mr. Farber?"

He stops abruptly, like he just ran into a wall. His mouth flaps open and shut.

"At home, not that it's any of your business," he says, but his voice wavers, a crack in the bluster.

"I decide what's my business. And I'll tell you who I am. I'm the guy that can put out one Tweet to a million followers and have this place emptied out within the hour."

"Bull." But there's no conviction. This isn't going at all like he expected. He's thinking it over, trying to figure out if I'm bluffing.

"Oh, I'd listen to him," says Decker. "He's got his own Wikipedia page."

"Suit yourself." I take my phone out. At first, Farber just stands there glaring at me as I type. Soon enough he starts to look nervous, biting his lip and shifting his weight before he relents.

"Fine. But I told you, no gatherings of cops," he says finally, leaning over to look around me at Decker and Dana. "You're not wearing gloves, but you look like cops."

"What about him?" Decker asks, pointing at me.

He glares at me, his eyes settling on my X-Wing fighter t-shirt.

"He's fine, he looks like one of them," he says, pointing a thumb over his shoulder at the crowd.

"They're fine, too," I say. "They're cosplaying *The X-Files*. Mulder and Scully."

Farber's eyes dart back and forth between Decker and Dana. His mouth opens and then closes again. He has no idea what I'm talking about.

"Whatever," he says finally. "But stop standing around."

Farber turns and storms off, Sally Park chasing along behind him.

"Wasn't Mulder a white guy?" asks Decker.

"He doesn't know that," I answer.

"He's going to call Chief Wilmont," says Dana. "Then Wilmont's going to call me."

"We're going to get a call from Burke," says Decker.

Still in my hand, my phone buzzes with a message.

"Well then we'd better get moving."

CHAPTER TEN

Bradley W: Got something, can you talk?

Me: Not right now. Tell me.

Bradley W: Caplan into Dark Net.

Me: Seriously? Doing what?

Bradley W: Still working on details. Looks like marketplace.

Me: Buying or selling?

Bradley W: Selling.

Me: Fukushima Unicorn?

Bradley W: Yup. Auction.

Me: Who won?

Bradley W: You'd really better call me.

Me: FaceTime in 5.

I need to find someplace quiet enough to talk to Bradley, and it isn't out on the main floor of the vendor hall. Making my way through the crowd, it seems like the flow is always going the other way, so I'm left sliding around the masses, dodging people left and right.

"Where are you going?" Dana asks. I hadn't even realized she was following me.

"I need to make a call."

"You went a little hard back there, don't you think?" she asks turning sideways to pass between a Wookie and a zombie.

"Farber's an asshole," I reply, reaching the end of the aisle and breaking out of the crowd.

"No disagreement here," she says, catching up and walking beside me. "You always this blunt?"

"I don't like to waste time."

She shrugs her shoulders. "Where are we headed?"

"We?"

"Listen, I didn't get saddled with two FBI agents because a collectibles vendor got killed in a bathroom," she says, keeping her eyes on the crowds ahead. "Whatever you're here for, it isn't to catch a murderer. That's on me, even after you leave. But whatever case you're working is connected to my homicide, so we're either in this together, or getting in each other's way. In my years on the job, I've learned that together leads to closed cases and getting in the way leads to cold cases. I prefer closed. You?"

She's not wrong.

"A panel room. That's where we're headed," I answer.

"What's that?"

"Where they have presentations, talking about your favorite show, or books, or get cosplay tips or whatever. They're quiet."

"Who are we calling?"

"My technician in LA. He's got something."

She waves me on with a smile, and we go back to working our way through the crowd.

The panel rooms are on the other side of the main entrance. In each, a podium at the front faces about fifty chairs arranged in rows. Small for a Con, but with four walls and a door, perfect for me.

In the first one we come to, a young woman in a Kawaii maid café outfit with bright pink hair is setting up wigs and costume pieces on a table next to the podium.

"FBI," I say, holding up my badge. "We need the room. Now. Out."

The young woman looks put out, but she leaves quickly. I close the door behind her.

"Give me a hint," says Dana.

"Our vic's been a bad boy online," I say, taking out my phone and setting it on the podium. "He's been on the Dark Net."

"The Dark Net? Like where you can find a hit man? How did he do that?" Her jacket is pulled back again and she's resting her hand on her hip. This is what I've come to coin her "investigator" pose.

"Hit man, or bulk drug shipments, or child prostitutes. The Dark Net's invisible to search engines like Google. But if you have the right software, it's wide open."

"What was a guy like Caplan doing there?"

"Looks like he was trying to sell the Fukushima Unicorn."

Concern crosses her face like a cloud. Elements of a much larger, darker world have arrived in her city. But she doesn't look surprised or fearful, like this is something she's never seen before. Mostly she seems disappointed.

"You're not from around here, are you?" I ask.

She shakes her head. "Miami."

The call connects and Bradley's clean-shaven face appears. He's a youthful thirty with a jaunty, hipster hairstyle. Normally it's coiffed high above his head, but today it flops over on its side, a casualty of the late night before.

"Will, can you speak?" he asks, seeing Dana over my shoulder.

"Go ahead. This is Detective Lopez, local PD. Caplan's murder is her case."

"Sure, Boss," he says, turning to his left. There's some clacking of keys as he brings up notes on his second monitor.

"Caplan was deep into the Dark Web," he continues. "I'm still trying to catalogue it all. But it seems he started going there after finding some threads on Reddit about sketchy celebrity stuff. At first, it was limited to things like fappening-style nudes and, I kid you not, a lock of George R.R. Martin's hair. Basically, anything he thought he could make a buck off of."

"Most of that stuff's fake," I interrupt. "How did he get from there to a Fukushima Unicorn?"

"I think he figured that out, too," says Bradley. "He started looking at stuff from Japan about a year ago. I haven't been through it all yet. In the more recent history, he got into Fukushima stuff the way people got into the Chernobyl stuff. Forbidden, possibly dangerous.

"I also found a partially deleted cache with snippets of text. Looks like message logs. He was talking to someone who had 'radioactive stuff' to sell. Some local near Fukushima. They're really cagey."

"That's because the government strictly forbids removal or possession of radioactive artifacts," I say.

"So, people turn to the Dark Net to trade it?" asks Dana.

"Exactly," says Bradley turning back to the camera. "Apparently there were pictures, too. I haven't been able to find them yet, but whatever was in them clicked for Caplan. The seller didn't know what it was, but I think Caplan had a guess. There was a search for 'Fukushima Semiconductor' which led him to the famous Reddit thread on the regular web, and then the trail ends. He started getting as cautious as a cheating husband: browsing privately and deleting histories."

"How would he know what this computer looked like?" Dana asks.

"The famous Reddit thread Bradley's talking about was started by someone claiming to be a former employee who published a detailed description. I could never find out who it was; they posted once and never again. The description was bang on, and people have used it for years to attempt to sell fakes."

"If there are so many fakes, why would he suddenly think it's the real deal?" asks Bradley.

"The message snippets," I say, raising my voice to be sure Bradley hears me clearly. "How much was this person selling? Just one item?"

"No, he was selling all sorts of stuff," he answers, typing rapidly. "But Caplan zeroed in on the one thing."

"Then we've got two reasons," I say. "First, it's supposedly radioactive. That's easily tested, and it's really tough to fake. Second, someone selling a fake Fukushima Unicorn, says it's a Fukushima Unicorn."

"Oh my God," gushes Bradley. His hand appears with a handful of colorful sugar candy, which he pops in his mouth. "But if this guy's selling rando radioactif jun," he says around the confectionary. "*not* saying it's a Unicorn, makes it more likely it *is* one."

"So he gets his hands on this thing, how?" asks Dana.

"Check with CBP and DHS," I tell Bradley. "Look at his email, his credit cards. See if he's been to Japan."

"Will do, Boss," he says, typing notes on the second screen.

"And once he does get it . . ." starts Dana.

"Then he's got to sell it," I finish. And then, to Bradley, "Was he using an auction site?"

"No, he did it all using message boards. Looks like he blundered around until he found a forum where they took him seriously about having a Fukushima Unicorn. But when he did, he struck gold. He took bids in private messages. There were a lot at first, but it narrowed down quickly to four serious players."

"He isn't covering his tracks anymore?" I ask.

"Not for two weeks. He had to go in the open to draw the bidders and things have been happening quickly since then."

"Who's bidding?"

"All we have are handles," says Bradley, typing rapidly.

My phone pops up a message. A screen capture from Bradley. There are four message headers and four handles: reap495; jforce80; DarkRiderX; and Kaiju2k.

"None tagged in the cyber unit database," says Bradley.

"Which doesn't mean anything," I muse. "Likely all fresh burners just for this."

"How long will it take to find out who's behind them?" asks Dana.

"I'll do my best," says Bradley. "But don't hold your breath."

"Why not?" asks Dana. "If they're leaving messages, can't we track their IDs?"

"On the Dark Net, people cherish their anonymity above all things, and it's set up for that," says Bradley.

"How did he convince the bidders he had a legit Unicorn?" I ask.

"He had the correct description," says Bradley, crunching a single M&M. "And there was one picture I did find. Of a radiation detector screen. Like you said, it's hard to fake, and the levels match the Fukushima accident. Beyond that, I don't know."

"Is there a winner?" I ask. "Which handle?"

"That's the thing—the auction's not over."

"Caplan's dead, the Unicorn's gone, I'd say it's over," says Dana.

"Well, no one told the bidders," says Bradley. "All four of the finalists have posted within the last few hours. The music may have stopped, but they're still dancing; I don't know how much longer."

"They'll hang around as long as there's a chance that this is real," I say. "When was Caplan's last post?"

"Lemme check. Uh, yeah, here it is," he says, pulling up the information. "Last night. Via mobile, tagged by the app."

"Mobile? We can't find a phone. Not at the scene, not on the body."

"Okay, I'll see if I can find it," Bradley says, adding it to his checklist.

"Wait," says Dana. "If they're still posting today, that means . . ."

"It's still in play," I say, running my hands through my hair. "If any of them had it, there'd be no reason for them to post again on the message board."

"Then where is it?" asks Dana.

"That's the question, isn't it?" I say, leaning forward. "When's the auction supposed to end?"

"According to Caplan's last post, tomorrow," says Bradley, lifting a handful of M&Ms to his mouth.

I turn to Dana. "Can we keep it going that long?"

"I don't see why not," she says slowly. "If this is all as anonymous as you say, there's a good chance they don't know Caplan was running the auction. And even if they did, Farber made sure we kept the murder quiet. No one outside of law enforcement knows he's dead. My department's tight. We can keep a lid on it."

I start pacing up and down the rows of chairs. One of the four bidders must be Dragoniis, the legendary Chinese hacker that drew Decker here. If he realizes Caplan's been murdered, and along with him any chance of getting the Unicorn, he'll disappear back into cyberspace.

"How much is the bid?" I ask Bradley.

"Ten million," he replies.

Dana's mouth drops open and those expressive eyebrows reach for the sky. "Who would spend ten million dollars for this?"

"People who wouldn't think twice about killing Caplan or anyone else in the way to get it. Innocent or otherwise."

"Terrorists?" Dana asks, swallowing firmly.

"Doubtful. Don't let the radiation distract you," says Bradley. "Religious radicals who set off bombs in public spaces don't need an omniscient supercomputer to do it. Just an endless stream of angry young men."

"Think bigger," I say, dropping into a chair. "Corporations. Drug cartels. Nation-states. They have the resources not only to buy it, but to put it to work, too. If they're bidding, the people they send will be ruthless."

It's a big risk for Dragoniis to come to the U.S. One wrong move and he's spending the rest of his life in an American prison. Or even worse, if Decker gets his claws into him. But for the Chinese, it's worth the risk. They'd be able to level-up their game from corporate and political espionage, to target the Pentagon's Cyber Warfare department, CIA headquarters in Langley, or even the NSA.

Martin Hicks isn't a thief or a spy, as far as I know, but I'm certain he's here for the Unicorn all the same. Bringing it back to Pyntel, the chip company he works for, would make him a corporate superstar. Right now, quantum computers are the size of a closet, nowhere near as sophisticated as the Fukushima Unicorn, and require heavy-duty cooling systems, thus limiting their use to research. Before what Fukushima Semi had done, enabling real artificial intelligence, on your desk, or in your hand, was nothing more than theory.

Made real and brought to market, they'd make a traditional computer, even one powered by Pyntel's flagship processor, look like an abacus. My deal for Fukushima Semi was a near miss for them. It would have put their primary business on the fast track to bankruptcy. After the accident, they poured millions into R&D but never produced a working prototype. If the Fukushima Unicorn reappears, so does the threat. Unless, of course, Pyntel are the ones to commercialize it.

"No question Caplan was in a dangerous game," says Bradley. "But why kill him before the deal is done? Ten million dollars is a fortune to Caplan, but a drop in the bucket for an MNC, or a government. Why risk losing the Unicorn altogether by trying to steal it?"

"Because you weren't going to win the bid," I say. "Or maybe you were, but you didn't think your competition would accept it. With what the Unicorn is worth, these organizations will pay anything, or do anything, to get their hands on it."

"But how would you know if you were losing?" asks Dana, "And if the Dark Net is so anonymous, how would they find Caplan?"

"Caplan made a whopper of a mistake," says Bradley.

"He didn't use his name, his actual email, or anything that foolish, did he?" Dana asks.

"Oh God no, he wasn't that much of a newb," says Bradley. "But you know what I always say, Detective? You write it, someone can read it. He set the pickup location."

"Once he did that, the list of possibilities got a whole lot smaller," I say, running my hands through my hair.

"What's the location?" Dana asks.

"I'll give you three guesses and the first two don't count," says Bradley.

"Here." I wave my arms expansively. "The Comic Con."

Ending the call with Bradley, I walk out the door.

CHAPTER ELEVEN

Decker: Where did you go?

Me: Talking to Bradley. Caplan auctioning Unicorn on
Dark Net.

Decker: Dragoniis? Probably one of the bidders.

Decker: More than one?

Me: Yes.

Decker: That's a problem. What are you doing now?

Me: Going shopping.

Decker: ?

I look up from my phone to find I've wandered back out to the
main entrance hall. The light is bright here and I squint.

Beside me, Dana says, "You know you just walked up a corridor
full of people with your head down and you didn't run into anything once?"

Of course I didn't. I would have noticed that. "Did I?"

"How do you do that?"

"Practice. Where's Caplan's booth?"

"I'll show you." She sets off through the crowd toward the vendor hall.

"One more thing," I add, chasing after her. I try to make it sound casual, like I'm asking where to get a good cup of coffee. "I need to see the Pelican case the Fukushima Unicorn was in."

"When we're done here, I can take you back to the station."

"I need it at the hotel."

She stops and pivots around to face me so abruptly, I almost crash into her. Instead, we're toe-to-toe. There's an aura of energy around her. I really feel it this close-up. She's a person of action, ready to run, jump, or fight at a moment's notice. Her muscles are always tense, ready to spring.

"I need to examine it, and see how legitimate this is. I need to see the size and shape of the cutout," I say.

"You know what the dimensions are. Miller measured them."

"I'm the only one left alive who saw the computer before the nuclear accident. I'll know for certain by seeing it, not from a photograph."

"You want a radioactive case in your hotel room? You know, most people would want to get away from something like that."

When she says it out loud, it does sound like a bad idea. But bad or not, it's something we can do. She's got a crime to solve, and the case is evidence. But Decker and I have other goals, and to us the case is a tool. If the bidders are still active, then they're here. And if they know what the Fukushima Unicorn is, then they know who I am, and they've surely seen me by now. If one of them killed Caplan, failed to find the Unicorn, and then sees me with the specialized travel case, it could draw them out.

But I don't want to tell her that and risk her saying no, so I settle for, "Exactly. Yes."

"I'm not letting you put a radioactive object out where it can hurt people. That includes you."

She doesn't want me to get hurt? I knew I made an impression.

"It's not that hot," I reassure her. "The radiation's transfer from an original source. If we keep it closed, it should be fine."

"It's evidence, and potentially dangerous."

"Trust me."

"Trust you? I don't even know you," she says, holding up her hands.

"But you know I'm an expert. You read my Wikipedia page!"

She takes a calm breath. "I don't know how you normally do things at the FBI, but I have a community to protect. One person's already dead. I'm not about to take chances with public safety."

"Fine. Have Miller close it, and scan it. When he confirms it's safe, bring it to my hotel room. I'll keep it closed; it'll be fine."

She turns her head and narrows her eyes. Her jaw slides back and forth almost imperceptibly. She's thinking. Running down the risk-reward. Analytical. I respect that.

It doesn't take her long to make a decision. "I'll have Miller get on it."

Sharp vibrations from a phone in my pocket form a familiar pattern. FBI headquarters.

Checking my watch, I see Burke's face in the call display. A picture I snapped while he was giving a speech. His face was all scrunched up like a giant pug. It's how I like to think of him.

I know I'm only delaying the inevitable when I tap the ignore button. He'll be back. But before I talk to him, I need a favor.

Noting the clock, I mentally add the hours to Tokyo time. How the Unicorn got here, and into Caplan's hands bothers me. There's nothing wrong with the collectibles business, but I've never met anyone in it that struck me as capable of fencing the world's most valuable goods. How it got into America is one question, but how it got out of Japan is equally important. Maybe even more so.

(In Japanese)

Me: Han, old buddy.

Han: Parker-san. How are you?

Me: Very well. In the middle of something. Need some help.

Han: Name it.

Me: Need info on passenger.

Han: Stuck on puzzle 42. Big Fish Pyramid.

Me: I'll see what I can do.

Han: Send me the details.

Me: Will do.

Han: Big Fish!

Han's a good contact in Japan. For some reason, he thinks that because I worked in Silicon Valley, I know how to beat every video game ever produced. Try as I might, I've never been able to break him of that belief. So now, whenever I ask him for a favor, his preferred currency is hints for whatever video game he's currently stuck on. Since he has what I need, what Han wants, Han gets.

"What language was that?" Dana asks as we make our way back to the vendor hall.

"You were looking over my shoulder?"

"It was hard to miss," she says without elaborating. I consider being indignant, but one glance at her expression tells me it would be a waste of time.

"Japanese."

"Who were you talking to?"

"An old friend."

"About the case?"

"Why would you think that?"

"Fukushima? Japan? You're texting someone in Japanese? You don't have to be in the Bureau to suss that one out."

A fair point.

"I can accept the fact that some random collectibles vendor has the Fukushima Unicorn," I explain. "It also makes sense that he was trying to sell it. Most of these vendors are buy-low, sell-high types and clearly he knows what he has."

Also bothering me is that Roger Caplan, purveyor of geek culture, found what I couldn't. But Dana doesn't need to know that.

"What I want to know is: How did he get it into the country? Something radioactive enough to spook Miller into evacuating the crime scene?"

She shrugs, holding her hands in front of her and biting her lip. "No idea."

"Exactly. Han can help me with that."

We arrive at Caplan's booth. Black wire framework walls, supporting shelves of collectibles, form a miniature store, the entrance covered by a gray tarp. As we approach, the fabric rolls back and there's Decker, looking unhappy, even for Decker.

He holds out a Bureau phone in my direction. "For you."

Decker opens the tarp further and waves me in, dropping it back in Dana's face, cutting her off outside.

Reluctantly, I lift the phone to my ear. "Parker."

"Parker, where the hell have you been? Why don't you answer your goddamn phone? It's basically attached to your fucking hand." Director Burke, and he's main sail to the wind. Farber's been busy.

"Chasing down leads, Sal." He hates it when I call him Sal.

"Is one of those leads someone named Charles Farber?"

"Not clear yet. Possibly."

"Well, you'd better get clear, Agent, because he's banging the drum, damn hard and loud, to have you fired."

"*Am* I fired?"

"Not clear yet. Possibly," says Burke.

I do believe that was humor. A little black, but it's something. I've always suspected Burke is happier when he's mad.

"Listen, Farber says he wants this convention back on the road again but it's not that simple. We've got a body here," I explain.

"You've got a job to do there, Parker, and it isn't to antagonize a prominent local businessman," Burke cuts me off. "Solve this murder without lighting fires that I need to put out when the Attorney General calls."

"In fairness that's not why you really sent me, Director. I'm here for the Fukushima Unicorn."

"What is it with you people? Decker keeps calling this thing a Unicorn too. It's a quantum computer. Why can't you say quantum computer? And yes, that's why you're there. And Decker's there to track down a foreign agent. Quickly. On both counts."

Burke's a someone-pissed-in-my-Corn-Flakes kind of guy at the best of times, but he's especially testy whenever he's talking to me. Sure, my methods are different, but my close rate is higher than his ever was as an Agent. I know. I looked.

"Farber's obstructing," I say. "He won't let us walk around."

"He what? He won't *let* you? Is this goddamn preschool? To my continued dismay, you're an FBI Agent, Parker. Start acting like one. You hear me?"

"I do." The crescendo washes over me.

"Good, so cut out the shenanigans. Play it straight. No more confrontations."

"Even if he's a suspect?"

Burke sighs. "Is he a suspect?"

I want to say yes. It would be easy to say yes, and it would take Burke off my back. But in all honesty, I can't. Not yet.

"No."

"Then stop lighting him up!" Burke shouts.

There's a pause while Burke collects himself and I give him the minute. If I let him get it all out, I can get back to finding the Unicorn.

When he speaks again, he's quieter.

"But if that changes, the moment it changes, let me know," he says evenly. "I want this case solved. I want to know who killed Caplan, where the quantum computer is, and I want this Chinese hacker found."

I like Burke and this is why. Despite being an uptight rager, one good blowout away from a coronary, he believes in what he's doing here. He's a man with a passion for truth and the consequences that flow from that. In fact, that's probably why he's so uptight in the first place. The twin concepts of truth and justice are too often replaced with expediency and compromise in Washington.

"Fine, I . . ." he says in a fatigued warning.

"Sorry, Assistant Director Burke."

"Just get it done."

The call with Burke over, I pull back the curtain to let Dana inside. There's room for all of us, but it's tight. With the tarp around us, it feels like we are alone in a small room. Hearing thousands of voices blurring together around us is disconcerting.

I look over Caplan's stuff for a while.

"What is all this? It looks like junk," says Decker, pointing at a row of vintage '80s action figures.

"One man's junk is another man's treasure, Decker." Barbarian. I'm staring straight at an original Kenner R2-D2 from 1977.

"It looks old," he says.

"Not all of it," says Dana. "These look new."

She's leaning in close to a row of bronze sculptures of *Star Wars* characters. They're beefy, the size of a loaf of bread or bigger, and all from the original trilogy, no prequels. A blue tag with Japanese writing hangs from each of them, attached with a white ribbon.

"You know," she continues, moving on to a rack of autographed photos. "I noticed most of the other vendor booths have a particular theme. Like, one place was t-shirts, another was all toys, and one looked like all stuff from a single show, with a blue rectangle on everything."

"A lot of people find a niche and delve into it."

"Well, what's Caplan's niche? I don't see anything that ties it all together."

Frowning, I look around. I see what she means. He's got action figures, fan art, autographs, and even a few stuffed plush characters. To the inexperienced eye it's a little of this and a little of that. To an educated eye like mine, there's a unifying thread.

I point at the row of action figures. "The common theme is quality. Those are original Kenner figures from 1977, and only the rarest characters."

"If you say so," interrupts Decker, picking up a Pikachu wearing a blue shirt, "but I see these stuffed animal things all over the place."

"These stuffed Pokémon are all officially licensed. The one you're holding is a special edition from the 2014 World Cup. Pikachu was the official Japanese team mascot. He's wearing the team jersey."

Decker shrugs and tosses the Pikachu back on the shelf. "They all look the same to me."

"Take another look," I say, walking over to the sculptures by Dana. "These pieces are hand-crafted, original works of art. The proportions are perfect. Museum quality."

Taking out one of my nitrile gloves, I use it to pick up one of the sculptures. A magnificent, and heavy, Jabba the Hutt. His tongue sticks out and his bulging eyes seem to look right at me. I flip the tag over.

"What I thought, Japanese." I point out the writing on the tag.

Decker leans over for a closer look. "I wonder what it says."

"It's the artist's name, 'Tokyo, 2015,' and then 'Sail Barge Jabba' at the end. $500." I lower the tag and reexamine Jabba's head. "Oh yeah, look at that, there's the chain around his neck."

"You read Japanese?" Decker asks.

"I spent a lot of time there when I was young," I answer.

Decker grunts and turns his attention to Dana. He's getting restless. It's tight quarters, and he's the biggest person in here. "Have your people canvassed the other vendors around here? Talked to them about our victim?"

"Not yet," she answers, shaking her head. "Farber wouldn't let us set up checkpoints for people coming in. You saw it, he wouldn't let any uniforms in here. I talked to a few people. No one saw or heard anything unusual."

"Video surveillance?" he asks.

"None in the bathroom, obviously. For the rest of the building, we've been waiting for a supervisor to get here with the playback password." She looks at her Fitbit. "They should be here by now."

"The guard from last night?" Decker asks, tugging at his collar.

"Told a uniform he didn't see anything."

"You take his word for it?" I ask.

"No. That's why he's still here. We made him wait."

"Now we're talking," says Decker. "I'll go check out the security office. You two go talk to the weirdness peddlers around here."

He doesn't wait for a response before slipping out of the booth. I hear him take a deep breath once he's past the curtain.

"He really doesn't like small spaces, does he?" asks Dana.

"You noticed that, too."

"Hard to miss."

As much as I appreciate the opportunity to dig on Decker, something else has caught my attention. Peeking above the top shelf of Caplan's booth, on the other side of the wall, is a white plastic cylinder with a black glass circle on the front.

"Know what that is?" I ask, pointing at it.

"Yeah. It's a camera," she says. The "duh" at the end was silent, but I picked up on it. I'm good like that.

One successful internet security camera campaign on Kickstarter spawned an industry of copycats. They all look similar, a blob in white or black plastic, with a couple of lenses.

The one's pointed right at the victim's space. And since it's a good bet that Caplan came here last night, it's bound to have seen something important.

"Let's take a walk."

CHAPTER TWELVE

The vendor with the security camera turns out to be a guy named Gordon Webb, proprietor of "Spider Webb's."

Where Caplan's booth was precisely ordered, Webb's is a hot mess. As I poke around the stuff stacked everywhere, Webb's common theme seems to be "whatever struck his fancy that day." There are vintage *Star Trek* phasers from the '80s, and current, BBC-licensed Sonic Screwdrivers next to a handful of humorous t-shirts, polyhedral dice, and *Christmas Vacation* eggnog mugs in the shape of cartoon moose's heads. Boxes of even more stuff peek out from under the tables.

Webb himself is hirsute to the point of a roly-poly bear. His graying-brown hair is curly and wild, surrounding his head like a soft halo. His bird's nest of a beard is an extension of his mane. The frames of his glasses are enormous, drawing attention to his dark blue eyes. He's clean though, well groomed, which isn't always the case at these things.

"Listen, Farber's got Chief Wilmont's number on speed dial," says Dana. "If we go in there and ask questions about a murder, the word is going to get around, and we're going to get more calls. We're investigating a theft."

"Go ahead." I shrug. "I want to take a look around the place first anyway."

Webb smiles broadly when Dana approaches, inviting her to call him "Gordo." At first, he's happy to talk to her. She flashes him a wide smile, showing off the product of some top-notch dental work. His eyes dart over her figure, and I swear I see him lick his lips before he invites her to look around his booth.

When she produces her badge, and asks where he was last night, his eager-to-please attitude dries up like a snail in the sun. His eyes narrow behind the substantial lenses.

"I was at Klingon Karaoke, of course."

"Excuse me? What's that?" Dana asks.

"I would think it's obvious," he says with a sigh. "Karaoke facilitated by members of the Klingon Empire."

She shakes her head and shrugs her shoulders with a look that says, "You'll have to do better than that."

"Karaoke where people dress up in costumes," he says with an exasperated sigh.

"Right," says Dana. "Do you wear a costume?"

"Of course, I have a vintage screen-ready Starfleet uniform from *The Wrath of Khan*."

"Sounds impressive."

"It is. The ladies, especially, admire a man in uniform."

"Is that so?" says Dana, with a tone that says *Absolutely not*. "Can anyone confirm you were there?"

"Ask around. I'm known as The Commander."

"What time did you leave?"

"I don't remember. Talk to the organizers if you're interested in what happened at the Karaoke."

"I'm more interested in what happened here last night."

"Does that mean you caught him?" Webb asks, crossing his arms and resting them on his generous belly.

"Caught who?" says Dana.

"The thief. It's about time."

Dana catches my eye over Webb's shoulder, frowning. That was supposed to be our line. This is the first we're hearing of a theft. How many people were in here last night?

"What thief is that?" Dana asks taking out a black notebook. An actual, paper, cop notebook. Cool. I wonder if she uses shorthand.

"The one who's been stealing from the vendor booths overnight, of course. That *is* what you're here for, isn't it? There's losses at every show, but this Con is the worst. Every year a whole bunch of us get hit, and every year we complain about it. I told Farber if it doesn't stop, I may not be back again. I think he's finally listening to me." Webb waggles his finger at Dana as if she were Farber standing there in front of him.

"What can you tell me about Roger Caplan?" Dana asks, ignoring Webb's gesticulations.

"Roger? He's the thief?"

"Why would you say that?" Dana asks.

"Everyone knows how he is."

"I'm new, why don't you explain it to me?"

Webb thinks about it for a second and shifts his weight from one foot to another. His eyes dart up and to the left.

"How should I say it? Greedy? Maybe that's too strong. He sure doesn't cooperate with the rest of us. He knows what we've got. We go to the same Cons. But if he doesn't have what a fan is looking for, he won't send them over to us. More likely he'd buy it from us on the cheap and sell it to the fan for more."

"How is that not greedy?"

She hits him an open question. Rita Kapinsky, an instructor at Quantico, once told me an interrogation is just a conversation with a purpose. Dana's keeping this conversation flowing well.

"Well," says Webb pulling his glasses forward and looking over the top. He's going for professorial, but coming off as awkwardly shortsighted. "Greed is really about intent, isn't it? And I don't think Roger's intent is to harm anyone. He's in a bad way. Ex-wife." He pushes his glasses back up and nods sagely.

Dana perks up. Stats say the majority of violent crime is perpetrated by someone known to the victim, and as the probability of being the doer increases, the closer the relationship gets. Spouses are always number one on the list.

"So, you know him pretty well?"

"Not really, but when you're on the circuit, you tend to run into the same faces city to city."

"How long's he been divorced?"

"A few years now, I think."

"Does she come to these things? Is she on the circuit, too?"

"His ex? No. Never. All she wants to do is bleed him dry."

Webb lunges suddenly to his left, his face twisting in anger. Dana shoves her left hand out in front of her, reaching instinctively with her right for her hip. She's too close, she won't be able to draw in time. I fumble under my blazer for the Glock at the small of my back. But it doesn't matter. Webb isn't even looking at her. He's got eyes on a kid at one of his tables, holding up a Pop figure of Rick Grimes from *The Walking Dead*.

"Hey!" he shouts at the kid, his face immediately shifting to crimson. "You want to buy that? No? Then don't open it. You open it, you bought it."

The kid drops the Pop figure and walks away. I'm getting a gut feeling that Webb isn't the most successful entrepreneur. I don't know. Maybe I'm wrong. Maybe yelling at your customers *is* the way to go?

"These damn thieves," Webb continues, watching the kid wander off. "And he's here every year. To tell the truth, with what he had at home, I think he liked going on the road."

"Who, the thief or Caplan?" asks Dana.

"Yeah, Roger."

"You're here every year, too?"

"Me? What? Are you calling me a thief?" Webb puffs up like some kind of hairy blowfish. His shoulders square and he puts his hands roughly where his hips would be if his girth didn't keep him from finding them.

"*Are* you a thief?" Dana looks him in the eye, pen poised over her notebook.

"No!" Webb says, turning red in the cheeks.

He starts to list off all the stuff that he's had stolen. Sounds pretty petty, actually. Small stuff, bright shiny things that look like jewelry. A time turner from *Harry Potter*. Or an amulet from *Supernatural*. Flashy but worthless.

As he continues to prattle off the list, I make my way behind him to the back of the booth, directly below the security camera. Perched next to it, out of reach of the casual browser is a bronze sculpture of Han Solo encased in carbonite from *The Empire Strikes Back*. It's a tall rectangle with the smuggler's well-known pose: face rising out of the solid material, mouth open in shock, or maybe agony, hands held up defensively—even though he went into the chamber with his hands bound, but the final prop is so cool everyone forgives that. This sculpture's the size of a bookshelf speaker, and being made of metal, it must weigh a ton.

There's a tag on it. I reach up and flip it over to discover the same Japanese writing as the metal sculptures in Caplan's booth.

"That's not for sale!" Webb bellows behind me.

I turn around to find him waggling one chubby finger at the Han Solo sculpture. His face has become an alarming shade of crimson. His breathing comes in puffs as he waddles over.

"This is my associate," says Dana. "Will Parker, FBI."

"Oh, uh, I thought you were looking to buy that."

"No, but it's a great piece," I say.

"Yes, it is. Handmade by an artist in Japan. He makes a small run of a single design each year. Very rarely seen in North America."

"Roger Caplan had some other pieces by the same artist, I think." I twirl the tag with my fingers. It's clear that this is some prized possession to Webb, so I keep touching it, which is stressing him out.

"Did he?"

"If it's not for sale, why is it on display?" Dana asks.

"Because I like to look at it." Webb crosses his arms, tucking his hands into his armpits, and shrugging his shoulders. "I've got more Solo stuff. It doesn't hurt to leave a showstopper piece like this on display. Drives the prices up. Making money in rare collectibles is all about timing. I'll wait until interest in Han is at a peak, and maybe I'll sell it then for top dollar."

And he says Caplan was greedy? Jeez. Looking around Webb's booth, I didn't see anything rare enough to fall into the "command the top dollar category" except for the statue. Not like Caplan's booth where everything was a quality item.

"Tell me about that camera," I demand, changing the subject.

"The which?" says Webb, still flustered by my touching the sculpture. I drop the tag and point at the white cylindrical web camera.

"Oh that," he continues. "It doesn't work. I mean, it does work when I plug it in, but I don't plug it in here."

"Why not?"

"Too much hassle. The Wi-Fi isn't reliable in the Convention Center, so you'd need to connect it to a laptop. And for a laptop you should have a power source, which they don't give us here."

"So then why put it up there?" asks Dana.

"Well, it's like those plastic owls you buy for your balcony."

"I wouldn't know, I live in a townhouse," says Dana.

"You know, to scare away birds," says Webb, looking at me for agreement.

"I don't have a balcony either. I live in a mansion on the beach."

Webb just looks at me, trying to figure out if I'm joking and why. I glance over at Dana who rolls her eyes. I shrug. What? It's true.

"You're talking about scaring pigeons away," I continue. "Think that would work with seagulls? I have seagulls."

"Probably," says Webb, stroking his beard. "The camera is the same thing. It scares away thieves. Birds see a predator and stay clear. Thieves see a security camera and they leave my stuff alone."

"You just finished telling me about all the stuff you had taken," says Dana.

Webb shrugs, turning red again. "I don't think the owls work all that well either, but it's worth a try."

He barks abruptly at another potential customer who's picked up some other thing from his table. When he lumbers over to try to close the sale, I find Dana right up close to me.

"What do you think?" she asks.

"I think something's fishy."

"Me too."

"I'm certain there are some fakes in here. The stuffed Pokémon look particularly sketchy."

"I'm not talking about the stuff. I'm talking about him." She scrunches her face up in a scowl.

"Aside from his questionable business practices? Well he's right about the Wi-Fi. It's often bad in places like this, especially when the crowds roll in. I checked it out and saw a cord dangling from the camera, not connected to anything. But some of the cameras have battery backups and a slot for a memory card, so you don't need a laptop at all. So that's a big maybe."

She bites her lip in thought, leading the way out of the booth and down the aisle. I follow along, looking around at the other vendors. No security cameras at any of them, disconnected or otherwise.

"There's something I don't like about the guy," Dana says.

"Aside from the way he was looking at you?"

"Aside from that." She curls her lip in disgust. "He's got a short temper."

"Which isn't a crime. Farber's got a short temper, too. And have you met Decker?"

"It was a pretty violent act," she says as we reach the end of the aisle. "Let's split up. I'm going to talk to more people. See if the story on Caplan's consistent. You do the same; meet me at the other end."

A gaggle of preteens giggling over a poster swarms around us. By the time they've cleared, Dana's disappeared into the crowd.

There could be more to be learned about Caplan by talking to the others. But doing a bunch of knock and talks about the same thing over and over again is not my idea of a good time.

A cheer rises from the crowd somewhere off to my left. Something's happened to get them excited. When I look over that way, I see the familiar logo for a big video game retailer.

Han. The idea of sorting through walkthroughs of Big Fish Pyramid online for hours doesn't appeal, and I bet there's someone over there that already knows the answer. This seems like a better use of my time, so I decide to leave the interviewing to Dana.

Before I get underway, I fire off a message. She is right about one thing—there's something sketchy about "Gordo." So, I add him to Bradley's list to look into, after Caplan.

My phone buzzes. Decker needs me. The message says he has a lead, but he needs my technical expertise in the security office. First though, I need that game tip.

CHAPTER THIRTEEN

Game Planet's space in the vendor hall is a sprawling, purple-carpeted empire a dozen times the size of Caplan's and Webb's little booths. A fully operational retail store at the center selling video games, toys based on geek culture, and t-shirts, is surrounded by a perimeter of the latest game consoles mounted on stands below large screen TVs. A swarm of employees wearing identical shirts that match the purple carpet work their way through the crowd of customers, signing them up for the store loyalty program on iPads clad in purple cases.

Pyntel's space is adjacent to Game Planet's, separated by a giant motor home wrapped in vinyl advertising a new game called Wasteout 3. Dirty and rough-looking men, and women, carrying improbably large weapons, face off against horrific zombie hordes. In the background, soldiers in exoskeleton suits of armor fall from futuristic drop ships.

The publisher's logo is one I recognize. It was a startup in the Valley. They had a lightweight VR engine with terrific gaming potential, but needed some serious hardware development to make it all work. They were desperate for cash, and I looked at buying them, but gaming didn't really align with our strategic direction, so I passed. They ended up getting bought out by Pyntel as another revenue stream for the giant corporation.

Around the outside of the motor home, I make out the faint outline of cutouts for enormous panels I suspect can be raised to reveal TV screens on which to demo the game. It's all closed up now though, except for the regular side door into the RV. Two people are just inside the doorway. While I can't make out their faces, I can tell something is up. One is waving their arms around, and the other is braced with their legs wide and hands on their hips.

Approaching carefully, I recognize the arm waver as Martin Hicks. His adversary is a shorter, solidly built woman with Princess Leia buns in her hair. She's wearing a Game Planet purple shirt, but it's different from the floor walkers in the retail area. They're wearing golf shirts and she's wearing a long-sleeve oxford with the company logo embroidered on the front. In the tribal world of big corporate, this marks her as higher up on the food chain.

"It certainly wasn't any of *my* people, and *your* people are the only other ones with a key. You see where I'm going here," says Hicks. His face is flushed and there are beads of sweat along his brow line.

"I understand what you're saying," says Leia Buns, "but I don't know what to tell you. That just isn't the case. None of my people were even *here* last night."

"Uh-huh. Where's the key that we gave you yesterday?"

"Right here on my key ring, where it's been the whole time." She pulls out a small bunch of keys and jangles them around in Hicks' face.

Hicks takes a deep breath and holds it, looking like a little kid throwing a temper tantrum. While he's building pressure, I climb the wobbly metal steps up to the door.

"Hey, gang, mind if I interrupt?" I ask, knocking on the doorframe. "Oh, hey, Martin."

I introduce myself to Leia Buns, who says her name is Mary Morley, a marketing VP with Game Planet.

"We're right in the middle of something here, Will," says Hicks. "I'd love to chat, but maybe we can do this later."

"Oh sure, Martin, I can wait," I say.

And then I stand there, watching. Mary looks confused and Hicks looks annoyed. After a few beats of uncomfortable silence, Hicks scratches his chin.

"Maybe you didn't understand me," he says. His jaw is tight and his words strained. "I really need to finish this up, so you should go and come back later."

"Oh, I understand, Martin. But I'm not going anywhere. I've got a question for Ms. Morley here. Official business." Hicks is only full of self-importance until he meets a bigger dog. Before I carried the badge of a federal agent, I accomplished more in the Valley than Hicks can ever dream of. Unless he gets his hands on the Fukushima Unicorn. The thought of it makes my teeth clench.

Morley casts a glare at Hicks before turning to me. "What do you need, Mister . . . or is it Officer?"

"Agent. Special Agent, actually."

"Fine. Special Agent Parker, what can I do for you?" Any residual irritation from her conflict with Hicks dries up. It's replaced with the curiosity mixed with nervousness I've come to expect when interviewing people for the Bureau.

"Do you have anybody who's really good at Big Fish Pyramid? I need some help."

"Big Fish Pyramid? That's a mobile-only game. We mainly do console and PC games." She looks even more confused now and, entertainingly, Hicks looks even more irritated. "There are a few guys and gals on the team that I know play mobile, too. I could ask around for you."

"That would be great, thanks," I say, flashing her a smile.

"Is there anything else?" asks Hicks.

"I'm so glad you asked," I say, tapping my lips with a finger. "I overheard you talking about something that happened last night? Which is interesting, because I'm also looking into something that happened last night. What's the deal with the key? Is it for the RV?"

Hicks and Morley look awkwardly at one another.

"Someone got into our mobile display vehicle last night," says Hicks.

"Mr. Hicks seems to think my staff had something to do with it. But as I was just telling him, they were all gone for the night. I was the last person to leave, and I had the key with me."

"So, if your staff weren't in the MDV, what about you? Where were you last night?" asks Hicks.

"I believe that's my line," I say, leaning in to look around at the interior. "What's in this mobile display vehicle anyway? What are you displaying? Was anything taken? Let's take a look."

Climbing up the steps to the inside of the vehicle, I slip past Hicks and Morley. The interior isn't the wood paneling and bolted-down La-Z-Boy of a regular RV. It's all business. The walls are bare metal with thick bundles of wires routed neatly to the backs of the TV displays I rightly guessed were in here. But there are far more wires than needed for screens and some game consoles. A server rack is mounted on one side of the RV, filled with commercial networking hardware. Fans whir loudly and dozens of green lights flicker on the front of network switches. Next to the server rack is a long cabinet with metal drawers that looks like it belongs to a race car mechanic.

"Nothing was taken; they just rooted around," says Hicks. "But it's what they *could* have seen."

"And what's that?"

"Wasteout 3, of course. Didn't you see the banner?"

"Not up on the latest games. Never heard of it."

"It's the biggest game launch of the year," explains Mary while Hicks rolls his eyes. "It should make a record quarter for us. Lots of merch tie-ins."

"It uses the Peregrine engine, and I think you've heard of *that*," says Hicks, crossing his arms.

He tosses that out like it's a dig. Like Peregrine is the one that got away. Nope. If I wanted it, it would have been mine. By the time Pyntel was sniffing around Peregrine, I was already talking to the guys in Fukushima about their quantum prototype.

There could be a connection between whoever was rooting around in their network on wheels and Caplan's murder. If letting Hicks think he outflanked me on the Peregrine deal will keep him talking, it's a game I can play.

"VR toolkit, right? Pyntel developed the hardware?"

"That's right," says Hicks. "We developed and manufacture the headsets and cameras that make the system work. Plug and play. No complicated measurements and setup like the old stuff."

"Has anyone seen the hardware before?"

"Prototypes of the headsets? Sure. We've shown some big development shops so they can start planning their own games using the Peregrine engine. All under nondisclosure agreements."

Hicks' annoyance with me is vanishing. He can't help talking up their new gear. This is a project he's attached to, and in his vanity, he wants to make sure I know it.

"Do you have them here?"

He opens a drawer in the mechanic's cabinet and shows me rows of what look like wraparound sunglasses. They have unusually thick arms, but nothing worse than the chunky style of sunglasses that come in and out of fashion. What I notice right away is that there are no wires.

"Wireless?"

"You bet."

"Onboard processing then."

"Yup." Pride is evident in his raised chin.

"In *those*? They're very slim." Of course, I knew all this, but I'm baiting him, leading him on. "What about the software?"

"It's not here. I didn't want to leave it in my MDV and I'm glad I didn't."

"It's not *your* display vehicle," says Mary, "it's *ours*. I paid for 33 percent of it."

"Right, and I paid for 66 percent, so it's *mine*."

"And it launches this weekend?" I ask.

"A week from now," says Hicks. "This is the preview weekend. It's the first time anyone's going to see the game's VR integration. We've released some 2D gameplay video, and screenshots, but this is the debut with the full setup."

"You didn't beta test it?"

"No, we wanted a big bang. We kept it under wraps, which should be fairly easy to do when you have physical hardware. We just keep it under lock and key. That only works until you give the key to someone who's going to stab you in the back," he says casting a snide sideways glance at Morley.

"That's it, screw you, Hicks. I don't have to stand and listen to your bullshit, and I don't have to explain where I was last night or what I was doing. Certainly not to you."

"Whoa, whoa, whoa. Settle down," I say, holding my hands out in front of me. Morley's face is scrunched up into an angry ball, her hands clenched into little fists at her sides. "There were some thefts here last night. My partners are out interviewing people now."

"See? I told you it wasn't my team, Hicks," she says.

"Thefts? Since when does the FBI investigate thefts?" Hicks scoffs.

"Since whenever we want to," I answer.

"You didn't say what was stolen," he says.

"No, I didn't."

"Hicks, you owe me an apology!" Morley shouts.

"Fine, it *possibly* wasn't your people that broke in."

"*Possibly?* You're such a dick, Hicks." She pauses for a second. "Oh, that's funny," she says. "Dick? Hicks?"

"Really, we're making fun of names now? Mary Morley? Now there's a stripper name if ever I heard one."

Alliteration and rhyming in a name don't mean stripper. But calling her one is the cheapest, fastest way for a guy with Hicks' limited creativity to fish for a rise out of Morely. What I don't know is whether his dominance-posturing is for her or me.

"Dial it down, both of you," I say, raising my voice with a warning tone.

"Stripper? You only wish, Hicks," says Morely, narrowing her eyes.

"Believe it or not, seeing you naked isn't something I would wish for. In fact—

"Shut up!" I shout at them both. Morely seems capable of handling Hicks, but there's one more question I need answered. "I've been up since before dawn and I'm way low on caffeine. Unless you want my local buddy to put you into one of her cells, cut it out and answer my questions."

Thankfully, they both stop their caterwauling. Peace is restored to the RV. My head is throbbing. Whether from their noise or a caffeine deficit, I don't know. But I do know I want out of this metal echo chamber.

"Hicks. The software. Where is it?" I ask.

"It's right here," he says pulling a small external SSD out of his pocket. "That's what I came in here for when I found the door ajar and the drawers opened. I'm loading the software today for the launch tomorrow. It's the latest patched version."

"So, whoever was here last night, all they saw were the goggles?"

"That's right," says Hicks. "Why?"

"Where were you last night?"

"In my hotel, working. In fact, I have more work to do and this is wasting my time."

Hicks storms to the door forcing Morley to jump back out of the way. He stomps down the hanging metal stairs and disappears into the crowd.

"What a prima donna," says Morley casting a glare out the door.

"Prima donna?"

"Yesterday he was all smiles and chuckles. He spent ten minutes explaining to me how this game was going to ring up high sales for GP, and I'm like, 'Yeah, I know all that; that's why I paid for a third of the thing,' and it was like he barely heard me. Just kept rambling on about the 'new frontier.' Today he's storming around like we kicked his dog. Then he discovered the MDV break-in and lost his mind."

"That's not normal for him?" It certainly wasn't how I remembered Hicks, and it wasn't consistent with the schmoozy hello he gave me in the morning.

"Not at all. I mean, he's mildly annoying. He's always going on about how great Pyntel is, you know, towing the party line. But I've never seen him raise his voice, let alone lose it like this. Something flipped his switch."

"You've worked with him a lot?"

"Off and on for a few years now. GP and Pyntel have done a lot of co-promoting. Haven't seen as much of him since he got the COO job. Then, a couple of weeks ago he jumped right into the Wasteland 3 launch. He insisted on being here for the preview." Morley makes a face like someone just passed gas. "You don't think he's the thief, do you?"

I don't know for certain what Hicks is up to, but I doubt he's the trinket thief that had Webb's fur flying.

"Probably not," I say, walking away and adding, "Let me know about Big Fish Pyramid."

Something put a bee in Hicks' bonnet. But was it murder? I have little time to ponder that before I get another text message from Decker, telling me to hurry up.

CHAPTER FOURTEEN

An hour later, after helping Decker in the security office, I'm back at the hotel taking my first sip of round two of Tropical Blend along with a ham sandwich on a surprisingly decent croissant. Yeah, I know, fool me once and all that. But sometimes you go with the devil you know, rather than the devil you don't.

Decker felt the security guard from last night wasn't being completely honest with him. By the time I got there, Storm Decker had reduced the guy, a grown man with a wife and two kids, to tears.

Keeping tabs on a building as massive as a convention center is impossible to do without a good security system, and the owners of this behemoth had invested well. The large, tidy office contained an array of decent security tech. Aside from berating the guard, Decker reviewed the surveillance footage from last night and found something unusual.

Decker's not without his gifts, and one of them is a staggering attention to detail. Hideously annoying if he's reviewing your paperwork, it's a critical talent when it comes to things like watching boring video on high speed. It's a skill he would find very useful in Counter Intelligence where they'll watch targets for days, weeks, and months on end.

One of the external cameras catches a view of the intersection at the corner. Playing back footage from the middle of the night revealed more people around than you might have expected, but nothing out of the ordinary to me. Not Decker. He caught something in the traffic. A city bus. At 4:00 a.m. by the time stamp. In a city this size, that's long after transit's been shut down. Unless someone stole a bus and took it for a joyride last night, the video's been tampered with.

Whoever altered it was good. Me good. A brief hiccup in the building Wi-Fi after midnight didn't disrupt the hardwired cameras, but it did temporarily drop the connection to the workstations in the office. Sometime after that, the looped video began.

When I last saw Decker, he was leaning even heavier on the guard to tell him who tampered with the system. There's no way he'll know anything about that, but with Decker's attention focused on him, I slipped away.

Now that I'm back at the hotel with the first sips of coffee already easing my headache, I check in for the night. Also, something I'd rather do without Decker looking over my shoulder.

The front desk already has a reservation under my name. It appears Decker made it when he arrived in the morning.

I slip a folded $100 between my driver's license and credit card before handing them over. How this plays out depends on geography. In a big city like New York, they check the amount openly, thank me, and then offer free Wi-Fi, breakfast, or a stack of coffee coupons. Here, the bubbly young clerk with a name tag that says Loretta slides the bill away quickly under the keyboard and hits me with a broad smile.

Typical Decker; embracing Bureau modesty has reserved a "traditional" something or other. I ask if she has a suite available. I left the

Valley behind for a greater purpose, but that doesn't mean I need to leave the comforts behind too. She glances at the $100 bill peeking out from under her keyboard, then taps around on the computer for a while.

"All we have left is the Presidential Suite. And with the hotel booked, the upgrade cost is pretty high, Agent Parker."

Special Agent. Why is this so hard?

I ask her how much, and she drops a big number for being outside a big city. Waving it away, with a warm smile of my own, I tell her the rate is fine, and she can keep it.

Her face lights up like a ray of sunshine after a day of rain. From under the counter she produces a box of brand-new yoga mats. "These are from the wellness weekend package, but you can have one, if you want!"

Yoga sounds like just what the guru ordered. I pick a green one.

Loretta's finishing up the paperwork when Storm Decker rolls into the lobby. He spots me immediately at the counter and blows over my way, arriving just in time to hear Loretta just explain where to find the Presidential Suite. It's a measure of how tired he is that he leans on the counter. In order to lean, you have to bend your back. I wasn't sure he could do that.

"Presidential Suite?" says Decker. "Bureau won't pay for that."

"Bureau doesn't have to. I travel on my own dime."

"Must be nice."

"Yes. It is. Anything else from the guard?"

"Nothing," says Decker with obvious disappointment on his face.

"Too bad," I say, lifting up my brand-new roll of green foam. "I need to recharge my chakra. Loretta here just gave me this sweet new mat, so I'm going to do some yoga."

This isn't about my chakra, but some part of me can't resist the urge to poke Decker.

Decker looks at me in horror as if I'd said I was going to rob a bank. "Did you say yoga? We're on the clock, Parker. You're the one that said this is over on Sunday."

"The physical calm of yoga enhances clarity of mind," is all I say to Decker. "It only takes a few minutes."

My dad was an engineer at Hewlett-Packard. When I was really young, he told me the reason people often fail at a task is because they don't place a high enough value on thought. He said one of the best things I could do to succeed, at anything, was to schedule time to think. This is that time.

"Where are you going to be doing this?" he asks. Good question.

"We've got a small gym," offers Loretta, "but you know what? It's a really nice night, and there's a park right across the street that runs along the river. There's plenty of room on the lawn, and the view is great. I go there after work sometimes." She twirls her hair around her finger.

"There you go," I say looking at Decker. "Problem solved."

"Yeah, well, while you're sitting on the lawn," he says, "I'm going upstairs to fill out our daily report."

"Give my regards to Burke."

"I'd really rather not."

*   *   *

The park Loretta pointed me to overlooks a wide, shallow river. The water sparkles in the late afternoon sun, reflecting hints of green from beneath the surface. There's enough current that you can hear it burble around large rocks in between the sounds of traffic.

A white railing follows the edge of the water, adjacent to a black tarmac path. To my right is a wide paved area, filled with concrete benches currently being attacked by kids on skateboards. There are a couple of food carts at the side: hot dogs and ice cream. A dozen or more people enjoy their snacks as they mill about, taking in the view. A few of them are from the Con, still dressed in their costumes, but there are a fair number of people in street clothes as well. To my left, the path disappears from view behind a stand of mature trees and neatly manicured greenery.

It's a warm late-summer evening and while the sun is well past its peak for the day, it's still shining brightly. In the center of a patch of lush green grass, I sit with my legs crossed on the yoga mat, dressed in a pair of loose Lululemon shorts and my favorite Under Armor t-shirt. I've just finished a yoga routine I've practiced many times before, and settle in to meditate, allowing my mind to relax, focusing on my breathing.

I believe my mind capable of doing just as much work subconsciously as consciously. When I reach a state of calm, new ideas and insights flow around me like the water in the river. First come the questions. Who killed Caplan? Where is the Fukushima Unicorn? Is it even really here? What if Dragoniis did get his hands on it? Is Hicks just a bidder or something more? How is Farber tied into the murder and theft? Who hacked the security system? For now, I push all of it from my conscious mind, trusting my subconscious to churn through it.

I breathe deeply. In. Out. In. Out. The traffic calms behind me, waiting at a red light. I hear the river flowing. A child's laugh wafts into my ears from the direction of the ice cream cart.

My phone vibrates with a staccato pattern on my thigh. Something's wrong. It's unfamiliar; it's just rapid short vibrations that don't stop. That shouldn't be. I always set my phone to do not disturb while I'm meditating. I know all the numbers allowed to pass through and their vibration patterns. This isn't one of them.

Opening my eyes, I'm momentarily blinded by the afternoon sunlight. When my vision clears, I see a notification on my phone. The sender is "Caplan, R" followed by a phone number, and the message says, "DON'T LET THEM GET IT."

Caplan? I'm about to reach down and unlock it when I hear a woman scream. For the length of a heartbeat I think of Kate Mason and the way Sterling silenced her.

Snapping my head toward the sound, I spot Loretta from the hotel. She's dressed in casual clothes now, one hand covering her mouth in terror, and the other outstretched. A few yards ahead of her on the path from the road are Miller and Dana, headed my way. Miller's holding the black Pelican case. Dana is pointing at me.

A tall, broad-shouldered man in a shiny gray suit and a black open-necked shirt is coming up behind them. Loretta's finger points at the black semi-automatic in his right hand.

Miller and Dana don't see him coming.

They're turning toward Loretta's scream, but too slowly. He'll get to them first. I can't stop whatever's going to go down from happening. All I can do is be ready for what comes next. I scramble for the Glock I brought stashed in my hotel laundry bag, at the same time rolling up onto my knees.

The gunman grabs the handle of the Pelican case with his free hand, driving his shoulder into Miller's chest. To his credit, Miller doesn't let go. He jerks the case backwards, pulling the gunman with it. Dana pivots, taking a step back, reaching for her pistol.

The gunman doesn't hesitate. He raises the semi-automatic and fires two rounds into Miller's chest at point blank range. Miller lets go of the case, collapsing to the ground. The gunman slides his aim over to Dana. Her hand grasps her Smith and Wesson, but too late. He fires a single round into her chest.

Dana goes down.

I leap to my feet, leveling my Glock at the gunman, but I'm too far away. There's movement behind him. Cars. Pedestrians. Too many people. I can't fire. I'll miss. I'll kill someone.

"FBI, freeze!" I shout as loud as I can without letting my voice slip into a scream, just as I've been trained. I run toward them, pistol in front of me.

The gunman jerks around and looks in my direction, lifting his arm. I can't return fire, so I dodge, diving and rolling to my right behind a steel garbage can.

Two rounds slam into it, the sharp sound of their impacts followed by a reverberating gong. When no more shots follow, I lean out to look around. The gunman's broken into a sprint, racing toward the path that disappears downriver, beyond a stand of trees. I still have no shot. There are just too many people around. If I couldn't hit him before when he was standing still, I'm definitely not going to hit him now.

I take two strides in pursuit and then stop. Miller and Dana.

Do I help them, or do I go after the case and the shooter? This is why I wanted the case. This is the lead I was looking for. The closest I've been to the Unicorn since the tsunami.

I can't leave Lopez and Miller.

I shout an obscenity, lowering my gun and running toward where Dana and Miller lie on the ground. Already a pool of blood is forming under Miller. A bad sign. But Dana is moving, rolling over onto her stomach and propping herself up on her elbows. She sees me coming and waves me off. I can't hear her, but I see her mouth the word "go."

I pivot again, and take off full speed toward where the gunman vanished down the path. I'm fast and it only takes me seconds to reach the tarmac. Spotting him ahead, I put the hammer down, running hard, gun at my side for safety. The tall man isn't as fast, especially not with the bulky case swinging off his hand.

He glances back, seeing me on his tail. The path is crawling with people taking in the clear weather and scenic view. He shoulders his way into a group of soft, middle-aged men, knocking one of them down. The others stop to tend to him, blocking the path.

I shout at them to get out of the way, but they don't move, braying like donkeys until I yell "FBI!" That, combined with the gun at my side, convinces them to part, clearing a path for me to leap over the one on the ground.

The gunman cuts left into the woods, disappearing quickly into the dense brush. I lean in, bringing out every last ounce of speed I have, my bare feet pounding the pavement.

Reaching where he turned off, I plow right in after him. This is a mistake. The ground is old leaves and spiked twigs covering sharp rocks. My bare feet immediately betray me, throwing off my balance.

The gunman's waiting for me behind a tree. Fortunately, I'm already mid-fall when he fires and I feel the shot go over my head. Hitting the ground, the Glock slips out of my hand.

I'm not out of surprises yet. After giving up on the Fukushima Unicorn, fate led me to the dojo of an old grand-master of Okinawa-te karate. For the next eight months, I trained all out, every day. I may not have found atonement, but I did learn how to fight. Hand-to-hand is my wheelhouse.

From a coiled position on the ground, I leap up at the gunman, raining a rapid flurry of blows on his head and shoulders. Instinctively, he raises his hands. Exactly what I wanted. I grab the hand holding the gun, adjusting my grip as I wrench it to the side. When I find the right place, I squeeze as hard as I can, my fingers clamping down like narrow vice-grips on a nerve center. Opening against his will, his hand drops the semi-auto to the ground.

I lower my attack, slamming my open hand into the side of his rib cage, following through with my shoulders, to put my entire upper body weight into it. But he's a big guy, and he takes the punch with a stoic "oomph," raising his knee to kick. Turning my hips, I lift my leg to block, but it never connects. His knee was a ruse, and he stomps down instead on my bare foot, crushing it between his boot and a rock.

The pain is intense. The shock of it distracts me for a second, and that's all he needs. He leans forward, slamming me with his chest. My foot still pinned under his, I can't readjust my stance and I fall. Pulling my shoulder in, I manage to roll without hitting another of those sharp rocks. I brace for a follow-up attack that never comes. Instead, he makes a run for it with the case. Scrambling up, I chase after him.

Using his size and brute force to clear a path, he crashes through the brush. Branches, some as wide around as my wrist, snap back behind him, slapping me in the face. I dodge and weave as best I can, but he still breaks out of the trees ahead of me.

A horn blares as we emerge down the street from the hotel. A big black Mercedes idles at the curb, back door open. A man leans out, waving to the gunman, shouting something I don't understand. I recognize his face from the hotel security video. It's the man that followed Caplan up to his room.

Normally I'd have no trouble chasing down this guy on open ground. But my crushed, bare foot is roaring in pain with each stride. I can only ignore so much. The limp slows me down. He's going to make it to the car.

A figure streaks in from the left, blindsiding the gunman with a flying tackle. As they tumble to the ground, I realize it's Dana. Having followed the commotion of our chase from the street, she must have anticipated his escape route.

"Out of the car, now!" I shout at the Mercedes. "FBI! Get out of that car!"

The man from the video reaches forward and shouts something else I can't make out. With a roar from the V8 engine, the Mercedes leaps ahead, door still open, tires chirping on the pavement as the traction control kicks in. I catch a glimpse of one of those tinted plastic covers obscuring the license plate before the car shoots off down the road, weaving around a city bus and vanishing from view.

Dana is wrestling with the gunman, who's still trying to get to his feet. I drop my knee into his back, and with our combined weight, he stays down. Dana grabs his arms, producing handcuffs and snapping them into place with the smooth grace of someone who's done it hundreds of times before. She grabs a handful of hair at the back of his head, jerking it back and eliciting a choked cry from her captive.

"What the fuck is your deal?" she demands. "You're under arrest."

The gunman is gasping, like he's trying to say something. Dana eases her grip.

"Lawyer," he coughs out.

"Eat shit," says Dana, releasing her grip and letting his head slam forward into the ground.

CHAPTER FIFTEEN

At the police station, faces are grim, including my own, as the consequences of the shooting by the river unfold. My reason for getting the Pelican case was to use it as a decoy, but I hadn't expected the response to be that immediate, or violent. I should have had Dana keep it under wraps, but if I'd told her my plan, she might not have let me have it. Now Miller and Dana have paid the price for my mistake.

Miller's one lucky dude. Crime techs in this city, like most, don't wear body armor in the field. Why would they? They don't show up until the shooting's done.

Three factors put him in the ICU instead of the morgue: the shooter missed his heart; the round was a non-expanding, full metal jacket; and the first person at his side was an Emergency Room doctor who'd been at the food carts enjoying the river park after work.

Dana, on the other hand, was wearing a vest, which stopped the bullet. Even so, there's enough energy in a 9mm to bruise ribs, despite the armor. Word from the hospital is that she popped a couple of Tylenol before forcefully insisting on getting back to work.

If I'd been able to warn them even a few seconds earlier, things might have been different. But there wasn't time, even with the mysterious message appearing on my phone.

The message came in with Caplan's name. Since I don't have Caplan in my contacts, that means it was sent with SMS spoofing. Whoever sent it has strong tech skills. They must have been there, watching me as I went through my yoga routine in the park. When they saw the gunman arrive, they sent the warning.

Any serious bidder for the Unicorn knows its history, and knows I'm connected to it by the deal at CastorNet. I'm not exactly a low-profile person, but it makes me uncomfortable to know someone was following me. For the moment, I don't have to worry about that, here in the station.

It troubles me that the message came in on my iPhone. How did they find my number? My Bureau phone number's out there, printed right on my business cards. My personal number, on the other hand, I only share with known contacts.

Until I know how that happened, I'm not going to say anything about the message. The last thing I need is Decker not letting me out of his sight, even if it's for my own safety. Though, I am going to have to keep looking over my shoulder.

When Dana comes in, I'm trapped in a conference room with Decker, on the phone with FBI Headquarters in Washington. She's wearing the same shirt she had on this afternoon, complete with a bullet hole and scorch marks. She looks pissed. Cops part in front of her like a school of tuna in front of a shark.

I want to hear her say for herself that she's going to be okay. Whether that's out of concern for her well-being, or so she can forgive me, I don't know. That will have to wait. Right now, Peter Griffon, from the Organized Crime task force, and Rena Nassar, from Counter Intelligence, are filling us in on just how fucked we are.

I sent Griffon the gunman's photo before he was even booked because I had my suspicions. Russians aren't known for their subtlety, and a broad daylight attack on two police officers is the sort of thing they would do. Besides, the guy just looked like a Russian with that shiny suit.

As usual, I was right.

"The shooter's name is Vasily Petrov," says Griffon. "A highly ranked employee of Vladimir Golovchenko, head of an organized crime syndicate. Golovchenko's small by Russian standards, not part of the 'Moscow Circle' as we like to call them, but he's an especially nasty customer. Known as 'The Reaper of Vladivostock' because coming up through the ranks in his hometown, his preferred method of execution was decapitation using a scythe.

"Within the last year, he's become increasingly volatile," Griffon continues. "I'm not surprised at a public shooting by one of his men."

"We've got Petrov in holding now," says Decker. "Do you want us to wait for someone from the task force, or can we have a go at him now?"

"By all means, have a crack at him," says Griffon. "But we're not sending anyone from the task force."

"You just said he works for this Reaper of Vladi-something," says Decker.

"Precisely," says Griffon. "Which means it's pointless to talk to him."

"He lawyered up on the spot," I say, leaning toward the phone. "He didn't say a word after the shooting. An hour after booking, he's got a big-time defense attorney at his side."

"Forget about the lawyer," says Griffon with a wry chuckle. "He's just window dressing to speed along the process. When you sit down with him, I'm certain he'll be ready to plead guilty."

"Guilty? There's no way the DA's giving this guy a plea deal," says Decker, "even if he's willing to roll."

"He's not interested in a plea deal," says Griffon. "Pleading guilty cuts off the investigation, keeping anyone from digging into Golovchenko. If he turns informant, Golovchenko murders Petrov's family, his friends, and basically anyone that didn't think he was a total dick. Hell, he'd probably have a few of them killed, too. No way Petrov says a word about Golovchenko."

"So, we won't get anything," says Decker. I think he may be the master of understatement. He leans back in his chair, lacing his hands behind his head.

"Beyond his name, an admission of guilt, and a statement of regret? Nope. Not a damn thing."

"The locals aren't going to like that much," I say, watching Dana through the glass wall.

"The locals? Let them worry about it, Will. We've got bigger things on our plate," says Decker. "Don't let yourself get distracted."

"Get distracted?" I look back at him. "By what?"

"You've been awfully friendly with Lopez."

"She's a good detective. You do realize that after getting shot, she got up and went after Petrov."

"And it's a good thing she did," says Decker. "Because if she didn't, then Petrov would be in the wind. With the case."

He's insinuating that I should have taken the shot and put Petrov down. He may be right, which is especially annoying. I had a shot and I didn't take it.

Decker wouldn't have hesitated, and that's where the friction is coming from. Decker's a former solider, comfortable with action and skilled with firearms. I'm not. The truth is, I'm a lousy shot. Every year when I certify at the range, I only pass by the skin of my teeth. And that's on a range, shooting a paper target. In the real world, in a split second? It's just as likely I would have shot some civilian by accident.

"What I want to know is why Golovchenko wants this computer thing so bad," says Nassar, her loud, clear voice reverberating through the phone.

"Think about what Russian criminals have done online," I say, pausing to let them consider it. "Ransomware attacks. Election tampering. Every cyber warfare tactic they've employed would be elevated to unstoppable with a quantum computer. And with it portable, by the time we track down their location, they've packed up and moved. Just like the Cold War."

"Cold War?" asks Griffon. "I'm from Organized Crime, not Intelligence. Help me out."

"It's called *maskirovka,* the art of tricking your enemies," explains Nassar. "Knowing we were watching with satellites, the Soviets mounted their nukes on trains and kept them moving around the country so we couldn't target them. They also had fake nukes on identical trains so we couldn't tell what was real. Today they use inflatable tanks and jets good enough to confuse our drones."

"Hold on, you guys are talking about stuff way outside of Golovchenko's league," says Griffon. "He just isn't that sophisticated. Think blunt instrument, not a scalpel. The surveillance hack at the Convention Center, for example. Beyond his capabilities."

"Couldn't he hire those skills from the Dark Net?" Decker's frustrated. He wants a target to go after and Griffon's not letting him have it.

"For the Convention Center hacking?" I interrupt. "He could outsource that. But using the Unicorn is completely different. It isn't like an iMac. You don't just plug it in and it works. You need to build artificial intelligence software around it. That's cutting-edge stuff. You need deep resources."

"I might be able to make that connection," says Nassar with a sigh. "This would explain some of the chatter we've been hearing lately out of Eastern Europe."

"What chatter?" Decker asks. "You didn't say anything about chatter."

"Wasn't relevant yet," she answers.

"Well, it's relevant now. What's the intel?" asks Decker scowling at the phone.

I struggle to keep from laughing. How do you like those dribs and drabs now, Decker? Ordinarily, I wouldn't bother restraining myself, but I suspect Decker's close to losing it, and I don't like the idea of being in the room if Storm Decker reaches hurricane force.

My phone vibrates. Seeing it's Bradley, I hit DECLINE. I'll call him back in a minute.

"Word is that Golovchenko's been doing work for the Russian government abroad, in exchange for favors at home," says Nassar.

Decker pounds his fists on the table.

"That actually makes sense," says Griffon, ignoring Decker's ruckus. "We know Golovchenko spent time in East Berlin in the 1980s, the same time the Russian President was there with the KGB. We've long suspected there's a relationship between them. Golovchenko doesn't have the resources to utilize the Unicorn, but you can bet the Kremlin does."

"I'm with you, Agent Griffon," says Nassar. "From where I'm sitting in Counter Intelligence, I can tell you Russia couldn't use the FSB to go after it themselves. Not on American soil. Hawks in the White House would demand a response. It's too dangerous. But by using a criminal like Golovchenko, they stay at arm's length. They can deny everything."

"So you've got a hacker contractor for the Chinese government and Russian criminals with links to the Kremlin," says Griffon. "And this Unicorn is still on the loose?"

"Yes," I answer, running a hand through my hair. My phone vibrates again.

"Well then, good luck, gentlemen. You're going to need it," says Griffon.

I'm wrong. Griffon is, in fact, the master of understatement. My phone is still vibrating, messages coming in rapid succession.

Bradley W: Will. Heard about shooting. Know you are busy, but this is urgent.

Bradley W: Seriously. Ping me ASAP. 911.

Bradley W: Will!!!!

Me: Sorry. You are right, busy. On phone with HQ. What's up?

Bradley W: Caplan refers to "associates" online.

Me: Witnesses didn't mention anyone else with him. No one else in room. Bluffing for cover?

Bradley W: Daughter. Amanda. Arrived this morning.

Me: WTF? Where?

Bradley W: Checked into different hotel. Missed it on first pass.

Me: OK. I'll go get her.

Bradley W: Too late. New message in Caplan's Dark Net account.

Me: What message?

Bradley W: Subject is "New Bid."

Bradley W: Content is image.

Bradley W: IMG attached

The room swims around me. In the space of a heartbeat, every nightmare I've endured since the night of the tsunami has become real. I can't get a breath; my lungs are frozen. I want to run, but I can't move. I drop the phone on the table. Decker asks me what's wrong, but I barely hear him.

Staring up at me from the screen is a picture of a young woman, no more than eighteen, long brown hair swept back behind her ears, horn-rimmed glasses standing out against her smooth, youthful skin. She's thin, almost waif-like. Pretty. An innocent middle-class American girl.

She's also gagged and bound to a chair, just like Kate Mason.

CHAPTER SIXTEEN

Before Decker can ask me again if I'm all right, Dana walks into the conference room for the next call. Her arrival gives me momentary reprieve. Desperately, I seize the seconds to process this development. It isn't Kate Mason in the picture, but the similarity is threatening to tear down the delicately constructed peace treaty I have with my past.

Since joining the FBI, I've diligently avoided kidnapping cases to avoid confronting my role in what happened the night of the tsunami. There were always plenty of other crimes to solve without going there. Now, I have no choice.

I haven't talked about my mistake with anyone, not even the highly paid therapists. I would have talked to Jack—I should have talked to Jack—he was my partner and best friend. But I never got the chance.

Despite the glass walls, the room feels like it's shrinking around me, suffocating. I want to get up and walk out, and I could. I could walk out of this room, straight out of the police station, and just keep on going. What good is being an almost billionaire if you can't do that? But where would I go? Already, I tried the other side of the world and I couldn't escape my past. I abandoned my life in Silicon Valley, and still it's found me.

"What's wrong with Parker?" asks Dana. "He looks as pale as I do. You'd think *he* was the one that got shot."

She's got her hands on her hips. In the center of her torso, the bullet hole and scorch marks stare back at me, dark nylon fabric peeking out from underneath. A new vest. That's my fault. So is Miller in the hospital. Caplan's daughter is being held hostage, and if we don't get her back, that'll be my fault too.

"Snap out of it, Will," says Decker. "We need to talk to Burke. He's going to want to send an army of agents down here. I know you don't want that any more than I do."

I find my voice, but it's slow and thick, like I'm only half awake. "No, I don't."

The city cops are already wound up, and if Burke sends swarms of FBI down here to join them, it'll surely spook the bidders off. We'll lose the Unicorn, Dragoniis, and who knows what will happen to Caplan's daughter.

The phone, already dialed into the conference bridge, comes to life. Opera comes through faintly in the background. It's Friday, it's late. He's at home. I've been there. A homey, modest place that always has a DIY project on the go. Italian opera and building things is how he manages his stress. Burke doesn't wait for greetings and introductions, launching directly into his erudite assessment of the situation.

"All right, I just got off the phone with the local chief. You may not have started it, but you're in the middle of a shit storm now," he says. "He's pulling in every cop in the city down there. Understandably, he wants to track down anyone connected to this shooter, Petrov. Detective Lopez? Impressive takedown. Agent Parker, what's this I hear about you being disrobed?"

"It wasn't disrobed, sir, I was in yoga wear," I reply. "Lululemon."

"Lulu who? What were you doing in yoga wear?"

"Yoga."

I'm not trying to aggravate him this time; my mind is occupied with more important things. It races through all the permutations of what happens next, in each scenario assigning a probability to getting Caplan's daughter back unharmed. It isn't looking good.

Burke sighs deeply and the sound is momentarily muffled as his hand passes over the mouthpiece at the other end. I'm guessing he's not a yoga practitioner.

"Whatever, good collar, both of you."

Burke doesn't ask about why the case was there at all. If Burke suspects I used the case to draw out dangerous bidders from the Dark Net, he doesn't say anything.

Hungry for more data, I look at the picture again. Amanda Caplan's wrists are bound to the legs of a chair. A ball-gag strapped around her head fills her mouth so she can't scream. Her eyes are red and puffy, her cheeks streaked with tears. On her knees is a laptop, turned to face the camera. It's powered up, and the screen shows the Google search page. But it's not the Google logo. It's a Google doodle. A drawing Google puts up for one day to celebrate something unique about that date.

I pull up Google's search page on my phone. It's the same doodle.

The picture was taken today.

"There's been a development," I say, closing my eyes and swallowing.

My body vibrates like a tightened wire in the wind. I struggle to keep my breathing even.

"Roger Caplan had a daughter," I say, turning the phone around for Decker and Dana. "One of the bidders has taken her."

Even Decker is stunned into silence, reaching out to take my phone as if holding it would dispel what I said. The muscles around his jaw ripple as he clenches his teeth together. Dana's brow darkens into a frown so deep it threatens to swallow her eyes completely as she looks over his shoulder.

After I explain how Bradley located the photo in Caplan's Dark Net private messages, Burke outlines a plan to send reinforcements our way. He wants to assemble a task force with the locals. Freeing Amanda Caplan, capturing the Chinese agent, and finding the Fukushima Unicorn is too much for two agents to handle. He's not wrong, but a flood of bodies is not what we need.

"Sir, could we discuss this approach?" Decker's leaning forward toward the conference phone again. His hands grip the edge of the table, knuckles white. "If there's a foreign asset on the ground here, it's possible a ramp-up of agents might cause him to run."

Of course it will cause them to run. For a chance to buy the Fukushima Unicorn, it was worth the risk for Dragoniis to come here. But he didn't figure on facing down an army of G-Men. He won't stay.

"Dragoniis is no fool, Director," I say, pulling myself together and raising my voice from the end of the table. "Cyber's been aware of him for years. He's kept his identity a complete secret, and moved frequently, always avoiding countries with extradition to the U.S. Decker's right—if he's on U.S. soil, this is a once-in-a-lifetime opportunity."

"I understand the value of discretion, Agents," says Burke. "That's why I sent Decker in the first place."

He doesn't mention me. Yeah, okay, discretion isn't my thing. But I haven't been bad at all this time around. So far, I've only pissed off Farber, and he doesn't really count because I've got a dollar bill that says he gets out of bed angry every day anyway.

"This is bigger now," Burke continues. "A girl's been kidnapped. And we have public safety to consider. Petrov shot cops in broad daylight, in public. What's to say his cronies don't do it again? There needs to be a public response to maintain order."

"I understand, Director. The city is already losing its mind. Chief Wilmont is being bombarded by media," says Dana. "But the kidnapping isn't across state lines. It's still our case, unless we ask for FBI assistance."

"Are you saying you don't want our assistance? Do we need to have this discussion with Chief Wilmont?"

Decker and I exchange a glance. We recognize the warning in Burke's tone. Dana's pushing the envelope, but Burke hasn't shut her down because this is still her town, and she's the top detective on the force. I checked. While Petrov was being booked, I talked to some people in the building who told me Dana's close rate is number one.

"Not at all, sir. Agents Decker and Parker have been, and continue to be, invaluable to the investigation. I'd like to remind you there's a murdered civilian at the beginning of all this. He may have been from out of town, but he was killed here, and his death kicked off this chain of events, which culminated with bullets flying in the streets. Here. In my city. I took one of those bullets in the chest today. And while I appreciate the support of the FBI, if additional agents risk this investigation, possibly putting my community in further jeopardy, I believe I speak for Chief Wilmont when I say it's a risk I don't want to take."

I lean back in my chair, eyes wide. She just schooled a director of the FBI.

"For future reference, Parker, *that* is how you object," Burke says after a long pause, his tone a stone-chewing gravel. "So just how would *you* recommend we proceed, Detective?"

"There's a lot going on here, sir. We need to keep the public safe, but we can't spook whoever has Amanda Caplan. They may think they're still dealing with Caplan, or may not even know who is running the auction," Dana says. "The murder scene is in the Convention Center, and the auction for the Unicorn is supposed to end there, making it a concentration point of the case. It makes sense to keep our focus there.

"It's also the most public, along with the downtown hotels," she continues. "To protect people, we add uniformed officers to the Convention Center's entrances, scanning everyone as they come in. That creates a secure, weapon-free zone in that building where we can pursue the suspects involved with minimal threat to the public. We throw some plainclothes in the hotels, keeping a low-profile, but ready for rapid response. We've got enough cops on the force, especially with the chief authorizing OT. It's a public response, but it's an *expected* response. So, it won't spook the killer, this Chinese hacker, or the kidnappers."

It's a good plan. It's high-profile enough to show something is being done, but not so much of a barrier that it would stop the auction.

"Won't this Chinese agent be spooked by uniformed cops everywhere?" asks Burke.

"No, sir," says Decker. "In fact, it would be more suspicious if we didn't do that. He's not afraid of local cops. They're looking for common criminals; they're not spy catchers. No offense, Lopez."

"None taken."

"Okay, say for a minute I approve this. Wilmont's going to have to sign off on it, too." Burke's softening. Cautiously entertaining the plan.

Having reached a state of calm after the initial shock of seeing Amanda Caplan's photo, I can close this deal. Time to drop the mic.

"It's all about the Fuku—the quantum computer," I say. "That's why the Chinese sent their hacker Dragoniis. That's what Golovchenko's soldiers are here for. That's why the kidnappers took Caplan's daughter. Right now, they all still believe that Caplan's auction is on."

"How is that possible with Caplan dead?" asks Burke.

"No one outside of law enforcement, and his killer, know Caplan's dead. We've explained our presence by saying we're investigating a robbery," says Dana.

"Smart, Detective," says Burke.

"It was Agent Parker's idea," she says.

"My analyst in LA has been monitoring Caplan's accounts on the Dark Net," I explain. "The bidders are all still active. If any one of them had the Unicorn, they would have left and gone silent. We keep the auction going, we keep the bidders active, and we have a chance of tracking them down and bringing them in."

Something I respect about Burke: he doesn't pussyfoot around when making a decision. I just hope it's the right one. Decker, Dana, and I wait, holding our breath.

"Detective Lopez, I know you want Caplan's killer, and Golovchenko. Decker, I know you want Dragoniis. Parker, I know you want this quantum computer. But the priority must be Caplan's daughter. Life over limb."

"I agree with that, but additional agents—" says Decker before Burke cuts him off.

"Hold on," says Burke. "I worked my share of kidnapping for ransom. If one of the bidders is holding the Caplan girl and the auction is compromised, there's a better than even chance they kill her as part of their exit strategy. Because why leave a witness? Too much Bureau profile will tell them the auction has been compromised."

The three of us in the room let out sighs of relief. Decker flops back in his chair, and Dana closes her eyes, rubbing her forehead. I unclench the hands I realize were balled up into tight fists.

"But the FBI can't fail to act," Burke continues. "I'm sending you Griffon and Nassar. They're experts on the Russian connection, and they have field experience. Two agents won't be too obvious. And we still need to get Wilmont onboard."

"I'll take care of Wilmont, sir," says Dana. "I'll have him call you directly."

"Let me be clear, for all of you," Burke says, pausing to make sure he has our attention. In the background the faint sounds of an aria swell to a climax. "Amanda Caplan's life comes first. She's real. The rest of this is still theoretical."

Storm Decker is looking pained again. More Agents. Having me here poking at his mission to catch Dragoniis was bad enough. Griffon's ambitious and upwardly mobile. On the road to Supervisory Agent. Decker's afraid he's going to end up in the back seat.

Authority and I have a casual relationship pretty much all the time. But the clock is ticking. Having Decker look over my shoulder was irritating but manageable. Two more agents challenging what I'm doing could really slow me down.

"One more thing, Director," I say and Decker shoots me a glare. Dana squints hard at me. We're walking away with what we want, and it's always a bad idea to sell what's already been sold. "We're on a time limit here. Caplan's daughter is being held right now. Caplan was here for this Comic Con. The planned end-point of the auction would be sometime in the next . . ." I look at my smartwatch. "Forty-ish hours. Decker and I already have a good lay of the land. If we have to start over, we could lose it."

Silence. Burke knows what I'm saying. We need to run this. Decker's biting his lip and clenching his fists. I shrug. No sense in dancing around the issue.

"Director," I say, slowly, without any trace of my usual antagonism. "You know why I joined the FBI. I know you do. No antics. This is the best way, I promise."

"Fine," he says, finally. "You and Decker take the lead. The objective remains the same: Amanda's life over all else."

CHAPTER SEVENTEEN

There's just time to make it back to the Comic Con before it closes for the day. Dana's right, the Convention Center is a focal point of the case. The auction is still on. Caplan was killed there. Someone looped the video there. I don't know if we'll find all the answers, but I'm certain it's the best place to start. We need to know more about what happened last night, and I'm certain that if we go back tonight, we'll find someone who can tell us.

Our next best lead is the photo of Amanda Caplan. Before I go, I get Bradley to walk the photo over to the FBI's lab. Kidnapping holds a special place in the Bureau's DNA, and with a life at stake, it will go to the top of the pile.

Monsters like the serial killer Bruce Sterling can be almost impossible to find—that's why the FBI needed my help when Kate Mason was taken. Their only contact with the outside world is entirely optional, beyond when they take their victims. Kidnapping for ransom is different. Amanda's kidnappers have to communicate to negotiate payment. With every communication there's a chance to figure out who and where they are. They've given me a lot with that picture already, but once the image techs have done their magic, I'll have so much more.

Someone's watching me, and until I know who, it's better not to be on my own. I don't want Decker following me around, so I ask Dana to come with me, telling her it's Bureau policy not to operate alone. I suggest that with the image analysis underway and a team of local detectives doing the grunt work of searching the city for signs of Golovchenko, she could be doing something more productive.

"Like what?" she asks.

"How about video games?" I answer, raising my eyebrows.

She squints at me again, the way that she does when she's thinking, puzzling something out, and then agrees with a shrug.

There's something that draws me to her like gravity. She's confident and dedicated. She knows who she is and what she's doing. I've spent my life focused and goal-oriented, so I know it when I see it. And I admire it.

When we get to her car, I realize immediately that this is a bad idea.

"What happened to you in there?" she asks, pulling out of the garage. "Something knocked you for a loop."

"It was a disturbing ransom photo."

"Uh-huh," she says, turning a corner. "The thing is, the murder scene was disturbing, too. I watched you. You were repulsed by it. Almost woofed your cookies. That ransom photo is different. It frightened you. Why is that?"

"Just not something I'm used to seeing."

"Right," she says in a tone that tells me she doesn't buy my answer at all, then she changes tactics. "How does an almost-billionaire end up in the FBI?"

"Same way as everybody else. Quantico."

"That's not what you said to Burke," she says, shaking her head and pursing her lips. "You said, 'You know why I joined the FBI. I know you do.' It was deliberate, based on a specific reason that he's aware of. What does he know?"

He knows that I helped him find Bruce Sterling, and that I watched Kate Mason die. But I'm not getting into that, so I deflect her questions with my own. "Webb's alibi. Did it check out?"

"I talked to several other vendors," she says, accelerating through an intersection. "They remember seeing him at the bar."

"Where was it?"

"A place called Chico's. Three blocks from the Convention Center. It's odd. I couldn't find anyone that spent the evening with him. But they definitely saw him."

"That's typical," I say with a chuckle. "You're not dealing with the most social demographic. It's not unusual for someone to show up, parade their costume around, and then pose for people to admire, all without ever talking to anyone. Plenty of folks show up alone, drink alone, and leave alone."

"Sounds fun," says Dana wryly.

"It could be worse. Back in the Valley, socializing was a full contact sport. When you accepted an invitation to a party, you were emailed an attendance list with guest profiles."

"You're kidding."

"I'm not. That way, when you got there, you knew who you needed to talk to, about what, and how to kick off the conversation."

"'Hey, how you doin'?' didn't work?" she says with a snicker.

"Says to me that you haven't done your homework." I shrug. "So you likely don't have a goal for talking to me, and you definitely don't have the WIIFM worked out."

"The what?" she says, turning to face me, her cop frown on full display.

"What's in it for me."

"As in what you would get out of talking to me?"

"Exactly."

"No way. You're full of shit." She laughs, the frown disappearing, her teeth flashing in the gloom.

"Wish I were."

"Pardon me for saying it, but your parties don't sound like a lot of fun."

She goes silent as she concentrates, negotiating a side street partially blocked by a delivery truck. We're almost at the Convention Center, and I think she's dropped the interrogation until she asks, "Long way from the Valley to the FBI. How'd that happen?"

I dodge again, asking for the latest update on Miller because there's no way she'll redirect from that topic. I'm right, and the answer to that question brings us the rest of the way to the Con. He's still touch and go, the doctors have done what they can, now all that's left is to wait. A heavy police presence at the hospital guards his room, even though it's unlikely Golovchenko would send anyone to finish him off. The objective was the Pelican case and the Fukushima Unicorn they thought was inside it, not Miller. He just happened to be holding it. And wouldn't let go. If he had, maybe Petrov would have just taken it and left.

Leaving Dana's car at the curb and approaching the building, I see the additional police presence is already in place, standing alongside the private security guards, who are now searching everyone before entry. The uniforms all know Dana and wave us through with a nod.

Once inside, I want us to fade into the crowd. As Farber pointed out earlier, I already look like one of the fans, but Dana sticks out like a sore thumb. Especially with a neat bullet hole surrounded by black burns in the center of her chest.

I stop at the giant tower of t-shirts.

"Large, right?" I say, reaching into one of the bins.

"I beg your pardon?"

"Your t-shirt size. We need to de-policify your look. I'm guessing a medium normally when it's, you know, just you without the vest. But with the Kevlar, up one size, so large."

I hold up a Wonder Woman t-shirt in front of her.

"You're kidding, right?" she says, putting her hand on her hip and glaring at me.

"Okay. Superheroes are a little clichéd for a cop." I scan the other bins. "Does anything here leap out at you? *Lord of the Rings*?"

"Is this really why we're here?"

"Listen, your guys are screening everyone entering now, but people have been coming in here since this morning. There could be a bidder in here, and they could be armed. Since we don't know who they are, it's better if we blend in."

Of course, there's also whoever's been following me. The hair stands up on my neck, but I don't turn around. If they're watching, I don't want them to know I'm looking for them.

Dana nods, reluctantly.

"*Star Trek*?" I ask.

"Oh, please."

"*Doctor Who*?"

"Who?"

"Exactly."

"No."

Taking a step back, I look further. While I realize that it doesn't matter what shirt she wears, as long as it's fandom something, it would be better if there was something here that she was into. I tell myself that's because she'll be more comfortable, and not because I'd like to know if we have something in common.

"Do you like Harry Potter?"

"Who doesn't?"

"Ah, *Deathly Hallows* then." I walk over to the bin with the familiar symbol combining a triangle and a circle, bisected by a straight line. It's printed in white, on a plain black t-shirt.

We're the last people around inside the towering temporary structure when I buy her the shirt, handing it to her in a plain white plastic bag. She hands me her blazer and starts unbuttoning her blouse.

"You're putting it on right now?"

"You said I need to stop looking like a cop, right? I assume you didn't mean later."

It's not exactly private here. When she takes her blouse off, I turn away.

"Thanks, but no need," she says.

Out of the corner of my eye I see black body armor, covering her chest and back. Right. A padded bandage wraps around her torso underneath. Raising her hands over her head to put the *Deathly Hallows* t-shirt on, she winces, biting her lip.

"Better?" she asks.

"You look perfect," I answer, turning around just in time to see her conceal her weapon, hanging the bottom of the shirt loosely over the top.

"Well, thank you for the shirt, Will," she says, smiling.

She tosses her old blouse in the trash by the register. Catching my surprise, she says, "You may have noticed, it has a hole in it."

With a bit of time before closing, I lead us to the food court I saw earlier. We're in luck, discovering a sandwich booth still open. They're packing up for the day, but they have leftover bagels, and coffee in a thermal carafe, which they agree to leave for us. When they made it is anyone's guess, but it's better than nothing.

"I'm guessing we didn't come here for stale coffee," Dana says, putting a cap on her cup. Black. No sugar. I'm impressed.

"No, we didn't. We came here to find a witness."

"A witness? The security guard said they didn't see anyone."

"Let's count who was here last night. Caplan. Whoever killed him. And a thief. That's at least three," I say, marking them off on my fingers. "I wouldn't put too much faith in the security guard."

"A fair point," she says.

She pauses, a silence stretching out between us as I fold back the hatch in the coffee cup lid and take a sip.

When she breaks the silence, her voice is gentle but firm. "I need you to tell me why you joined the FBI."

The sip of coffee tastes bitter. But it's here, it's hot, and it's got caffeine so I swallow it anyway.

I sigh. "Why does it matter?"

She takes a moment before she speaks, considering her answer. She's not squinting or frowning at me. This is a different side of Dana. Not the cop side, constantly questioning and challenging. This is her as a person.

"This isn't your run-of-the-mill homicide investigation anymore. When I woke up this morning, I had a visitor to the city who got his head smashed in. Tragic, but that's all. Now I've got a priceless, and radioactive, piece of technology plus the spies, hackers, Russian mafia, and kidnappers, who are after it. Oh, and two FBI agents who aren't being completely honest with me."

When you put it like that, it does sound bad.

"Listen," she continues after taking a sip of coffee, "I grew up in a not-nice part of Miami. Surrounded by gangs. When I became a cop, I went back and worked the street there. I've been around some seriously dangerous people. But *this* case makes me nervous."

"You'd be crazy not to be," I answer, nodding.

"What makes me nervous is what I don't know. Too much is hidden. Like you. Why does someone give up the life of a king for the life of a cop? You changed your *entire life* for a reason. That's a big reason. And it has to be part of who you are. If I don't know what that is, I don't know you. If I don't know you, how can I trust that you have my back?"

I look away. In fact, I didn't have her back. I let her carry the Pelican case out in the open, which got her shot and Miller just about killed. I owe her for that. But how much? What she's asking, I've never told anyone, because it means talking about the night of the tsunami. Except when I was interviewed by the Bureau, but even then, I left out the mistake that gave Bruce Sterling the chance to kill Kate Mason.

"I came here with you tonight because you're smart," she says, leaning over, to put her face in front of mine. "You're a pretty remarkable investigator, and I can tell you're on to something. But there are hidden threats all around us."

She's more right than she knows. I think of the message from Caplan's phone. Is my follower still in the building, or did he or she leave with the public?

"Like it or not, we're in this together. I can't spend time second guessing you, when I need to be on guard. That puts my life in danger," she says, subconsciously putting her arm over her chest where the bullet hole used to be.

In this moment, as memories of the tsunami swirl around me, there's one face that emerges: Jack. We were in it together too, until I shut him out, and look at how that ended. In the short time I've known Dana, I've already managed to get her shot. If she wasn't wearing that vest, she'd be gone, just like Jack. Jack deserved better. Dana deserves better. Am I really going to make that mistake again too?

"I'll tell you, I promise," I say, looking into her dark brown eyes. "But first we have to get out of sight before whoever's coming gets here."

Her eyes gaze into mine, searching for honesty. She must be satisfied with what she finds, because eventually she nods and says simply, "Lead on."

CHAPTER EIGHTEEN

We find a dark, empty room across from the entrance to the vendor hall. I don't know who's coming back tonight, but I know what they're after, and it's in there. Anyone walking by the room would see only a darkened doorway, but inside, the light from the hall casts a dim pool between us. Dana waits patiently, sitting at the edge of shadows in one of the padded conference chairs as we eat the dry, chewy bagels. I've told her I would answer her questions. Now it's up to me to deliver.

"You want to know how I ended up at the FBI," I say, pausing to wash down the last bite with coffee. "Short answer, because after months of studying under an old karate master on a mountain in Okinawa, an elderly couple was murdered in the village below. After I found their killers by tracking stolen items online, I wanted to do more like that."

Dana blinks, her brow rising high and eyes widening. Likely not what she expected.

"But you want the long answer. You want to know how I ended up there from Silicon Valley."

"I want to know *why*," she says, leaning forward.

"The night the tsunami hit Fukushima, I was supposed to be on a plane to Tokyo. But I wasn't. I was in my office because Salazar Burke came knocking on my door to ask for my help."

"Wait, the Burke I know?" asks Dana, tilting her head.

"One and the same," I say with a sigh. "That's how we met, and that's how he knows what I meant. He was a SAC back then, a Special Agent in Charge in the Criminal division. The day I met him he was hunting a serial killer named Bruce Sterling, who had just lifted a college girl, Kate Mason, from her dorm."

"Did you find him?" Dana asks from the shadows.

"Yes," I say slowly, nodding. "But it went wrong. The Bureau had tracked Sterling down online, where he was using our software, but not in real life. Which meant they had no idea where Kate was being held. Our app was encrypted and they wanted us to break through that to find him. But we were launching a big marketing campaign, focusing on the security and privacy of our service. Burke knew we'd say no if they just showed up with a court order for the location. So, he came with a better plan."

I rest my elbows on my knees and she does the same, our faces just outside the pool of light but clearly visible, making me feel connected to her, and yet distant.

"He sat Jack and me down, and told us the story of Kate Mason. He showed us her childhood photos and videos, following up with the milestones of her young life: first date, senior prom, freshman year of college. Facebook posts with her boyfriend, happy and in love. Burke made her real.

"Then he showed us pictures of Sterling's last victim. Mutilated. Exsanguinated. Bled out like a cow, her pale body posed for pictures like a china doll. It was the most horrible thing I'd ever seen. Then he told us that the guy that did those things had Kate, and was going to do them to her. It was more powerful than any Silicon Valley pitch I've ever heard."

So far what I've told Dana is all public record, typed up in an FBI report on file in LA. To tell the rest, I have to go off the record. Way,

way off the record. This is my last chance to bail. To stand up, walk away, and go back to the way things have been ever since. So what if Dana doesn't trust me? Does it really matter? Jack's face comes to me again, and I remember.

What will she do when I tell her? Worst case? She reports what I did to Burke, who walks me from the FBI, the last paragraph in my Wikipedia entry changing to "Controversy and Death." Best case? I don't have a best case.

This is the closest I've been to the Unicorn since the tsunami. Back then, I told myself the enormous good of bringing the quantum computer to market would make Kate's death in some way okay. That if I could do something big enough, something worthwhile, it would make up for the mistake I made. Then it disappeared. In my heart, I know that if I don't do everything in my power to get it, no matter how difficult, there will be no coming back from a very dark path. The chances of finding the Unicorn are better with Dana on my side, and for that I need her to trust me. For her to trust me, I need to trust her first.

I tell her everything.

From the app I used to keep an eye on staff to how Jack and I used it to find Sterling, I hold nothing back. When I get to my mistake, and how it gave Sterling enough warning to kill Kate before the help could arrive, shame burns hotly on my face. I'm glad for the dim light.

When I finish, a silence stretches out between us like a chasm.

"And that's why you left for Japan and didn't come back?"

There's one more piece to the puzzle. The capstone on the bridge of my despair.

"At the same moment Sterling was killing Kate, news broke that a tsunami had hit Fukushima and the reactor at the power plant was in meltdown. We'd breached our own encryption, gotten a young woman killed, and the Fukushima deal was in flames. It was too much to process. Everything Jack and I had worked so hard to build was teetering like a house of cards in the wind. So, I made a decision. I convinced Jack not to mention the mistake to the FBI. He went along with it. He never said a word, because he trusted me. I was his friend."

I gaze down at my feet. The black and white contrast of my Converse seemingly glowing in the dark. When I continue, I don't look up.

"Jack was a simple, honest guy. He wasn't cut out to carry that burden. While I was in Japan chasing the Unicorn, he randomly blew up one day, yelling at people. No one knew what set him off, but it ended with him going home to shoot himself in the head in his backyard. No note. No explanation."

Closing my eyes, I press my hands into my temples to fend off the headache that has nothing to do with caffeine this time.

"When I got the news, I disappeared. I shut off my phone and drifted around the Japanese islands until one day, on a dock in Okinawa, I met a fisherman who needed help with his nets. That wise old fisherman had a wise old brother with a dojo on the mountain. Which brings us full circle back to how I ended up at the FBI. Burke even wrote me a letter of recommendation for my application. Drink in that irony for a minute."

When I finally open my eyes, I don't see the look of disappointment on Dana's face that is so familiar in my own reflection. What I see is sympathy, which somehow feels worse.

"You can't keep punishing yourself for what happened," she says, finally, breaking the silence.

"Is this where you tell me we all make mistakes?"

"We do."

"*I* don't."

"You do. Whether you admit it or not. You did your best, but you failed. Now you're trying to reverse it, but you can't. No amount of good work at the FBI will ever be able to undo what's been done."

Is this supposed to be helping? When I look at Dana's eyes, I still see sympathy, but not pity. And not judgment, which confuses me. I frown.

"It's hard to live up to a legend, Will. Even if it's your own."

My mouth opens, but I don't speak because I don't know what to say.

"Let me ask you this: What was your biggest failure in the Valley before the tsunami?"

Looking up and away I rack my brain, thinking of my early companies that didn't become something big. I think about school papers I cut corners on. After a few seconds, she interrupts my thoughts.

"You're struggling because you don't have one. Not like this, where someone died. Now that's happened, and you don't know how to deal with it. You tried running, but that doesn't work because the voice that won't stop judging you is your own."

How does she know all this? It's like she's plugged into my brain and reading the source code.

"According to your Wikipedia page, you had a lot of success from a very young age. I'll bet you could always pull out a win, depending on your brilliance and relentless hard work to pull you through. The problem with that is, sometimes it's not enough. Sometimes no matter how prepared you are, and well trained you are, shit just goes wrong."

There's something in the way she says it that sounds personal. "Firsthand experience?"

"You could say that." She stands up. "I'm going to go get a drink of water. In the meantime, you don't have the only name that will come up in Google."

With that she walks out the door.

*   *   *

I can't pull out my phone fast enough. I can't believe I haven't searched for her name on the web. She's a prominent detective. She must have worked cases that hit the media. And maybe she has. But when I hit search and see the results that come back, none of the hits on the first page have anything to do with Indiana. They're all from Miami, and they aren't good.

As I read, my heart begins to break for her, because I know the pain she must be feeling. Yeah, she made a mistake all right. Immediately, I can't help but compare her mistake to mine. Neither of us meant to make them. Hers was a judgment call that could have gone either way, where mine was sloppiness. Mine involved a murderous monster who did the killing not me, where hers was the finger on the trigger.

When she comes back in the room, I stand.

"I'm sorry."

She stands toe to toe with me. Her eyes locked on mine. They're red and puffy. Maybe she's just tired. I don't think so.

"Yeah, so am I."

The silence between us isn't a chasm anymore. The distance between us disappeared when I read what she'd done.

"So, you—"

"Killed a kid. Yeah, I did. Like the articles said. The staircase was dark. The bulb was burned out. I couldn't see him clearly. He had a replica gun. He thought I was part of a game. He pointed it at me. I was there on a shots-fired call, so connected the dots. And I was wrong."

"But you couldn't have—"

"Don't do that," she says quickly. "I've already been through every reason, every excuse for what I did and I've defeated them all. It was dark? I could have turned on my flashlight. He pointed a gun? I should have known it was a replica. Around and around it goes. No matter how brilliant you are, Will Parker, there's no 'what if' you can think of that I haven't already. Just like you've thought of all the excuses for not changing that code and all the reasons they're bullshit."

She's right. How many sleepless nights did I ask myself those questions? How many times did I go over that day in my head? How many times did my nightmares serve up Jack on his knees between the BBQ and the kiddie pool in his yard?

"I had no idea," I say lamely. "I didn't search your name, and you just seem so . . ." I struggle for the word. Normal is what leaps to mind, but that's not it. Functional?

"Not like someone who made a mistake she's gotta live with the rest of her life?" she says, exhaling sharply.

"Yeah, that."

"Here's where I bake your noodle, Will. I made a choice. And it's one you're going to have to make, too. Right now, you're torn and that means you're stuck."

My brow furrows, but she continues.

"You can choose to keep your eyes on the past. You'll see the same thing every day. It will never change. Keep doing that and eventually it's all you can see. Or, you choose to keep your eyes on the future. Every day is different. And you *can* do something about it."

"But what about Kate, and Jack?"

"They're dead."

My jaw drops at her harshness.

"Will, they are. And there's no amount of self-flagellation that's going to change that. Trust me, I know." She pauses to take a breath.

"Let me ask you another question," she continues. "You're an FBI Agent—"

Special Agent.

"—what's the largest case you've ever worked?" she asks.

The answer comes quickly. "Human trafficking ring between San Francisco, China, and Vancouver."

"How many victims?"

"Forty-three women," I say without hesitation.

"I think I know what choice *they'd* want you to make. Those lives matter, Will. They *all* matter. Not just Kate's. Or Jack's. But it's your call."

Before I can answer, there's a noise out in the main hall. We hold our breath, waiting to see who comes into view. Is it a witness?

No. It's the security guard. We watch as he slowly saunters by, his head down and gaze buried in his phone. He jerks his hands to the right, then the left. He's playing a game, oblivious to everything around him. If Decker saw this, he'd lose his mind. He passes without noticing us in the room off the hall.

Turning from the door, I find Dana right next to me. I can feel her warmth. The smell of new t-shirt mixes with stale coffee, but it isn't unappealing. I've never talked about the mistake I made the night of the tsunami because I feared the judgment that would surely follow, from someone that couldn't possibly understand the responsibility. But I was wrong. Dana can. What if she's right? Is escaping the past as simple as choosing the future?

Forget about t-shirts and fandoms. There's something much deeper we have in common. I must say something; to acknowledge her openness. Somehow. I have to say something.

Before I can speak, my phone vibrates. Bradley.

CHAPTER NINETEEN

Bradley W: Got a ping on Caplan's phone. At the hotel. Around time of shooting. You see anything?

Me: No. Where now?

Bradley W: Disappeared.

Me: Shut off?

Bradley W: No, just gone.

Bradley W: Possibly Faraday bag. Or a ghost in the machine.

Bradley W: Finished profile on Caplan.

Bradley W: Forty-one. Community college diploma. Con thing for six years.

Bradley W: Recently divorced. Amanda, eighteen, only child.

Bradley W: Social media - promotes business, nothing personal. Some gripes. Nothing unusual.

Bradley W: Finances poor. Lots of travel, all budget. Taxes filed on time. No audits.

Bradley W: Credit card debt. Divorce debt. Child support.

Bradley W: $10K savings. Withdrawn three weeks ago.

Me: Japan travel?

Bradley W: Tokyo. Two weeks ago. DHS confirms same trip, same week, for past five years.

Me: Laptop?

Bradley W: Malware galore. Trojans. Mostly inactive on macOS.

Me: Browsing history? Porn?

Bradley W: Divorced guy. What do you think? All legal.

Me: Messages?

Bradley W: Mainly business and travel. Some from Amanda about trip.

Bradley W: One with a Gordon Webb about a *Star Wars* collectible. Refers to convo a month ago. Code?

Me: No, I saw it. Han Solo in carbonite. You'd like it.

Me: Dark Net? Any luck on IDs?

Bradley W: None.

Me: Gotta go. TTYL

The sound of movement echoes down the hall outside the darkened room where Dana and I wait. The conversation about Sterling and what happened in Miami has taken us past midnight. Someone's coming and it's not likely the guard since he wandered by, not too long ago, nose still in his phone.

"Who are we expecting?" Dana whispers, hand going automatically to her Smith and Wesson. She steps back until her face disappears in the gloom, but I can see the whites of her eyes. She's looking toward the hall, still as a statue.

"First, the collectibles thief. Second, whoever broke into the RV." Third, my watcher.

"What RV?"

"More of a mobile display vehicle, really."

"Couldn't it be the same person?"

"Two different MOs," I say, shaking my head. "Collectibles thief grabs things up off the tables that look like they might be worth a buck. The break-in at the RV was more sophisticated. They picked the lock. Lots of valuable gear inside, but they ignored it. They were looking for something that wasn't there. But it is tonight."

"How do you know this?"

"Knock and talks this afternoon."

"A more skilled thief. Professional?"

"Maybe."

"One that might also be after a Fukushima Unicorn?"

"Here they come," I whisper as the sound of footsteps approach.

Dana sweeps silently over to the doorway for a better angle. I follow, sliding up close behind her.

The hall's cavernous space is broken up by pockets of furniture arranged into seating areas. Small, sleek sofas and chairs. I remember seeing them covered with people earlier today.

Dana's blocking my view; I can't see the source of the footsteps. "Do they look dangerous?" I whisper.

"Not exactly," she whispers back.

Leaning out to look around her, I see a group of young people. Late teens. They're sliding along the wall like mimes, heading directly for the long row of maroon fire doors into the vendor hall. The one at the front, a tall boy, slowly slips open one of the doors with barely a squeak and disappears inside. Two more boys and a girl follow him. The door clicks shut. If they had any idea Dana and I were watching them, they didn't show it.

"Did Caplan have any more kids?" Dana asks.

"No, just the one." I fill her in on the profile Bradley worked up.

"Anyone else?" I ask.

"Nothing," she says, looking both ways. "Looks like the kids are alone."

Clapping my hands together shatters the silence of the room. "All right. Let's go talk to some witnesses."

"What witnesses?"

"They just walked by."

"Those kids?" Dana asks, frowning. "I thought we were looking for professionals."

"That was them," I say, walking out into the main hall. "Don't be ageist."

"What the hell is that?"

"Discrimination against a particular age."

"I'm not being ageist. You said it was sophisticated. They picked a lock."

"It's a standard RV lock. There's a how-to for everything on YouTube. Let's go." I look both ways and set out toward the hall.

"Hold up," she says holding out a hand to block the door. "There's four of them and two of us."

"So? They're just kids. I'm sure we can handle them," I say, reaching for the door.

"They're going to bolt," she says, stepping in front of me. "We can't catch them all."

"Why would they bolt?" I ask. "We're just here to talk. Maybe people run when you try to talk to them, but you have an assertive bearing."

"You don't like my bearing?" she asks.

"No, I love your bearing," I say.

"You do. Good to know," she says, flashing her perfect teeth my way. "But there's still four of them and two of us."

Where will those kids go if they run? Back the way they came? I look around the hall, my eyes settling on the seating areas.

"We use the environment to our advantage. Give me a hand with that sofa over there."

The furniture is small, but large enough for this to work. We don't want to harm the kids, just keep them from getting away. For the next few minutes we drag sofas and chairs around until all the doors to the vendor hall are blocked by furniture. All except one. We're short one piece.

"Now what?" Dana asks.

"We bring in some backup."

"The guard? Are you sure? He looked pretty useless."

"Better," I say, easing open the last door to peek inside.

I don't know if all of these kids were here last night, or if they saw and heard the same things. As the closest things to witnesses we've got, we've got to catch them all. If they do bolt, I can't afford any of them to get away.

What I'm looking for stands right where I remembered it from this afternoon. Slipping inside, I silently make my way over to it. When Dana sees what I'm after, she hisses. I turn around to find her holding her hands in the air, and rolling her eyes in a way that clearly expresses WTF. Pointing at the door, I wave it in an opening gesture. Shaking her head in disbelief, she does it anyway.

Eyes wide open, I approach my backup slowly, until I see how it's disabled with a piece of duct tape. Carefully dragging it behind me, I back out into the hallway.

"Are you serious right now?" Dana asks.

"This will totally work," I insist, pointing. "Once I pull the duct tape off the motion sensor, he goes live. You'd better get inside."

Muttering something that sounds like Spanish, she eases open the door and disappears into the vendor hall. The tape comes off easily. Once the eye is clear, I slip around behind him and through the door after Dana.

Being here now, alone in this enormous hall usually filled with people, is eerie. The dull roar of thousands of voices is replaced by the soft whoosh of air handlers. A dull bang from above signals some shift in the HVAC system. Or was it the sound of movement reflected off the ceiling? Can I be sure that the only other people in here are those kids? Or is my watcher here too?

The sounds of laughter drift our way from the direction of the Wasteout 3 mobile display vehicle. Heading down the aisle, we keep to the side, moving quietly, heads up and alert. If there's a straggler, we don't want to stumble across them and give them a chance to sound the alarm.

"We should come at this from different directions," Dana says as we reach the end of the aisle.

"It's not a bad idea. They'll be easier to corral with us on either side of them," I whisper. But I really don't think they're going to run. All we want to do is talk. "You stay out of sight; I'll strike up the conversation. Then, when we're chatting you can come in."

"Strike up a conversation? How do you think you're going to do that?"

"Just talk to them. You know, hang out. I'm cool like that."

"You don't think going in strong and putting them on the deck would work better?"

"You sound like Decker."

Some situations need finesse. These are my kind of people, young and into tech. I'm famous in their world, so they may even recognize me. A brush with celebrity is a better way to start a conversation than shock and awe.

We split up. Leaving Dana behind, the sense of unease at being alone in here returns. I move as quickly as I can without making any noise, coming back to the mobile display vehicle from behind the Game Planet space.

Peering around a rack of recycled video games, I see the teens. One of the guys stands in a square space under the vehicle's awning, wearing the new VR goggles and waving his black-gloved hands around in front of him. I have to admit I'm impressed. Seeing them on the kid's head, they're amazingly slim, with no wires to get in the way.

The other three lounge around in cushy leather chairs, feet up and over the arms. Cans of energy drinks and a pile of chocolate snacks cover one of the end tables. A monitor mounted in the side of the MDV shows them what their friend is seeing in the goggles, currently the creepy ruins of a shack.

Stepping out and strolling over, I keep my hands in my pockets. Chill. Like a celeb should be. Dana's peeking out from the aisle behind them, hanging back. The three kids lounging around catch sight of me at the same time.

"Hey, guys," I say, "don't get up."

They bolt.

One of the guys, launching over furniture with the speed of a spider monkey, screams, "Nick!" The other two loungers scramble after him.

I barely have time to pull my hands out of my pockets before the kid with the goggles tears them off his face, leaps over the end table, and takes off deeper into the hall.

Dana steps out to head off the loungers, arms wide, badge in one hand.

"Stop, police!" she thunders.

Fine. Now that we're in pursuit, it's a good idea. Chasing after the goggles kid, I shout, "FBI, freeze!"

He doesn't, but it was worth a shot. Looking over his shoulder, he sees me gaining on him. If he keeps going straight, I'll have him in a dozen paces.

"Come on, kid, give it up," I shout.

Ignoring me, he slows to turn down another aisle. I pour on the speed to grab him before he changes direction.

Sensing my reach, he cuts the corner with a grunt. I swing around a booth of fan art made from melted beads. When I finally catch up with him, he's zigzagging through the life-sized Lego character display.

"Dude!" I shout. "I just want to talk to you for a minute."

Somehow this kid finds another gear, accelerating into a straight shot for the exit doors. He'll never make it. I've totally got him.

Until he drops two handfuls of loose Lego pieces onto the floor.

Too close to avoid it, I run into the Lego slick full tilt. The bricks are smooth, hard plastic, and the Convention Center floor is smooth, hard concrete. When my full weight comes down on them, the Lego pieces act like marbles, shooting my feet out from under me. As I go down, I tuck my shoulder into a roll. Hitting the ground, the world spins around me twice before I come out of it, leaping to my feet. It's too late. I can't catch him before he gets to the exit doors, but I run as hard as I can. Sure enough, I'm still twenty feet behind when he aims for the only door that doesn't have a piece of furniture on the other side. Slamming into the crash bar with both hands, he flings the door open so hard it bounces closed behind him.

From the other side comes the characteristic roar of Godzilla, the rubber-suited, Tokyo-smashing star of Japanese monster movies, followed immediately by a scream and a thud.

As I push the crash bar myself, the door swings wide to reveal the kid on the floor, scrambling to get up. Above him is the six-foot-tall statue of Godzilla I dragged out from a vendor's booth. The monster's trademark roar blasts through speakers in its chest, the wide-set eyes in his lizard head glowing with white LEDs.

I drop on the kid, pushing him back down to his stomach, a knee in his back.

"Come on, man, you can't escape the King of the Monsters!"

CHAPTER TWENTY

"What did I tell you, Will?" Dana asks when I arrive back at the RV, goggles kid in tow.

She's got a short blond boy and the girl sitting in leather chairs next to the mobile display vehicle. The display screen is still on, showing a world of ruins, a dry wind kicking up clouds of dust. I'm not sure what looks more miserable: the dystopian world of Wasteout 3, or the faces of these kids.

"We're one short," I point out. "You've only got two of them."

"And you've only got one."

"He was fast," I mutter, "and there was Lego."

Dana shakes her head, pointing to an empty chair. I give the kid called Nick a not too gentle push forward.

It bugs me that we only have three. Thinking back in my mind to the moment they bolted, I concentrate on what each of them did. Nick was in the VR rig. The blond kid shouted out his name. The girl climbed across two chairs to get away. The last kid hit the deck. Closing my eyes, I remember he had on an orange shirt. Messy black hair. Looked well fed. Not the kind of kid that would try to win a footrace. If he didn't go anywhere, he must have hidden.

I look around. Living room furniture. Giant screens. The carpet under the awning with cameras mounted all around it to capture motion for the VR rig. The door to the RV. Closed. Was it closed before?

Placing my ear on the door yields nothing. All I hear is the rush of the air handlers in the massive hall. I tap on the thin metal. Still nothing.

"Forget it, man," says Nick, with a grunt of disgust. "You screwed up. You let one get away. Gonna be in trouble I bet, huh?"

"If I were you," Dana says to him, "I'd be worrying about my own troubles."

I'm just about to lift my ear from the RV door when I hear something. I try the latch on the door, finding it's unlocked. The door opens smoothly; I step inside cautiously, in case this kid's got the wrong idea about fight or flight. The shuffling sound comes again, but not from inside the display vehicle.

Climbing back down to the carpeted floor, I take a knee, one hand on my Glock. The carpet is nice and plush between my fingers as I bend down to look underneath the giant vehicle. Looking back at me is the heavy kid in the orange shirt. He's shuffled back almost out the far side.

"Well, hello there," I say. "Come on out and join the party."

The kid wriggles and jiggles his way back. It wasn't a bad idea. Hiding was probably his best option, but he could have picked a better spot.

"All right, let's get this out of the way," I say when the kids are all seated in front of me. "I really don't care about you sneaking in here to play video games."

While three of their faces slide into shock and confusion, Nick looks suspicious, squinting his eyes at me as if trying to figure out the game. Being the one to play first is a privilege that usually goes to whoever's in charge, so he must be the leader of the group.

Nick's the key to getting this show on the road. Not for what he knows, specifically, but because the quickest way to get the other three talking is to break their leader. If they were here last night, they must know something. Dana and I need to figure out what.

"Where were you last night?" I ask. Keep it simple to start. Sound him out. See how difficult this is going to be.

"At home, asleep," he says with a sneer. He looks around, rolling his eyes, like this is just a big inconvenience to him. Okay, difficult it is, then.

My eyes dash back to Dana. She shrugs her shoulders and waves at me. *Your show.*

"What's your name, big shot?" I ask. Less patience in my tone this time.

"What's yours?" he counters. This kid's clearly used to getting his way.

Time to change up that dynamic.

"Hook him up," I say to Dana. "We haven't got time for this. We'll deal with him tomorrow."

"Got it," she says, coming around, the cuffs already jangling in her hands.

She tells Nick to stand up and turn around with his hands behind his back. When he refuses to move, Dana and I move fast, each seizing and arm and taking him to the carpet, facedown.

"Stop resisting," repeats Dana endlessly.

We're gentle as we manipulate his arms behind his back. He's a young kid and we don't want to hurt him. Despite the loud commands, Dana's face is calm. I suspect she's done this many times before, with much bigger, more unruly suspects.

Nick grunts and yelps from underneath us. I've got one knee digging right into the back of his leg.

"Stop, you're hurting him," exclaims the girl, rising out of her seat.

"Sit down!" I shout, taking one hand off Nick to point at her. She settles back into the chair, but lightly, perched on the edge.

We struggle with Nick for a little while, eventually bringing his wrists together, securing them in Dana's cuffs. The second they click closed, his resistance drops away. His shoulders relax and his arms hang limply.

Lifting him to his feet, I pat him down before seating him in a chair. All he's got on him are a wallet and a phone. While he's no longer physically struggling, the fight isn't out of him yet. His eyes glower at us, full of resentment.

"You can't do this," he says defiantly. "I want a phone call."

"Kid, you don't know what you're talking about," Dana says.

"Yeah I do. You can't question me without a lawyer present. I want to call my dad. He's got the best lawyers. You're going to regret this."

Dana laughs, low and slow, flipping open his wallet. She takes her time, looking through all the cards until she finds his driver's license.

"Nick Reynolds, age nineteen." She reads off his address.

"Nice neighborhood?" I ask Dana. Then to Nick, "I'm not from around here. FBI." I show him my badge, holding it up so the others can see.

"It's all right, if you're into that sort of thing," Dana says. Meeting my eyes with a wink signals she's down with the plan. Dad's a big shot, so junior is too. Nick's used to people being impressed. Take that away and he's got nothing. "Big houses on tiny lots out in the 'burbs. Not my cup of tea."

"Well, he wants his phone call, and his lawyer, which is his right," I say clearly, looking at the other three kids. "But you don't get one *here*. You'll get one after you've been booked and processed. What's the wait time on processing in this town, Detective?"

"Busy Friday night?" she says, looking up in the air like she's calculating something. "You've got the usual bar drunk and disorderly traffic, and nice weather like this there'll be a lineup of streetwalkers down there. The heat gets people fighting, too, so add in some brawlers. They're usually covered in blood—cleaning that up takes time. I'd say probably mid-morning before he's assigned to his cell and it's his turn for a phone call."

"Cell?" Nick says, his voice faltering slightly.

Dana snaps her fingers, making Nick twitch. "Oh, you know what? I forgot to tell him, I work Homicide."

Nick's eyes widen slightly, but his jaw is still set in defiance.

"I didn't kill anybody."

"I didn't say you did," says Dana with a shrug, looking at the time on her Fitbit. "But what it means to you, is that I'm busy right now, so the paperwork on your little break and enter can wait. I have twenty-four long hours to file charges, before the slow wheels of justice even start turning. Assuming this is your first offense, I'd say you should be home by lunch time on Monday."

"Right now, you're detained, not under arrest," I explain. "Once she reads you your rights, it's a done deal. A weekend behind bars instead of a weekend here at the Con. Are you ready for that? It's all up to you."

Nick doesn't answer, so I nod to Dana who takes over. It's so smooth, how we're handing off to one another. We're in tune, like we've done this before.

"Let's see if we can save some time," she says. "Can I just have a show of hands? Who else is going along with Nick here to jail for the weekend? Just so I know how big a vehicle to request."

My gaze scans over the other three. The blond kid started out pale, but now he's downright spectral. The girl is biting her lower lip, thinking.

The kid in the pylon-orange shirt is a mess. He's sweating up a storm, pockets of damp forming under his armpits. He rubs his palms together repeatedly like he's washing them.

None of them raise their hands, clinging to solidarity.

"Here's the deal," Dana says, addressing the group. "You're in trouble, but you can still walk away from it. We need information, that's it. Refuse to cooperate, and it's a trip to the cells. Talk to me, and you'll be home snug in your beds in no time. Last chance."

Nick's staring sullenly at the floor in front of him. The kid looks anxiously over at the girl, who's still biting her lip. As the kid in orange stares at his hands, a tear drops off his cheek to the carpet below. The girl looks up at Dana. Bingo. We have a winner.

"Promise? Detective . . ."

"Lopez. Dana Lopez. And you are?"

"Ashley Brewster."

"Nice to meet you Ashley, and yes, I promise. So does Agent Parker," she says, pointing at me.

"Okay, sure, we can talk," she says. "Was someone really murdered?"

Not only has Ashley distinguished herself as the smartest of the bunch, cooperating with us, she also seems compassionate. I don't know what she's doing hanging around these other turkeys. She casts a glance over at Nick who refuses to look at her. Then again, maybe I do. The oldest story.

"I'm afraid so," Dana says. "I can't tell you more than that, okay? But I have a few questions."

"Sure," Ashley replies, folding her hands in her lap. She's sitting up, back straight like Decker. Her parents must be drill sergeants.

"Were you here last night?" Dana asks gently.

"Yeah, we were here. We came to play the new VR game, but we couldn't find it. Just the goggles and gloves. We figured it hadn't been loaded yet."

"Did you leave right away?"

"No, we stayed and played some other games for a while." She looks down at her hands, knotted in her lap.

"That's okay," Dana says. "I would have too, if I were you."

"You play video games?"

"Agent Parker does."

"What do you play?" says Ashley looking at me. "First person shooters?"

"No, I'm lousy at those," I answer wryly. "I prefer MMORPGs. And I have a pretty healthy Pokémon Go collection."

She smiles timidly. "That's cool. What team are you on?"

Do I tell her the truth, or do I guess her team and say that? She seems quiet, thoughtful, smart. Definitely team Instinct. She'll know I'm not. If I say I am, I'll lose credibility.

"Valor," I answer.

"That makes sense," she says, nodding. "I'm Instinct."

Called it.

"What time did you get here last night?" Dana asks.

"Around midnight. Gavin said that was the best time to come."

The kid in orange squeaks, an expression of stark terror splashes across his face.

"You're Gavin, I take it?" I walk over to stand in front of him.

He nods, lips pressed together in a thin line.

"Why come at midnight?"

I'm a little concerned that when he opens his mouth, he's going to barf. Conscious of the fact I didn't bring a spare pair of shoes, I take a step back.

"Gavin's the one who knew how to get in," Ashley explains. "His brother used to work here. He knew about the door and the cameras."

"What about the door and the cameras?" I ask, attempting to loom while staying out of vomit range.

"There's this special door," Gavin says, eyes on the carpet. "In the alley, down from the loading dock. People here at night, including the security guards, use it to go outside and smoke. The guards leave it unlocked to make it easier. That's where we came in."

"And the cameras? Tell me about the cameras," I say.

"You pass three of them to get into the vendor hall from the service hallways, but when they installed new directions signs, they ended up partially blocking the cameras."

"There's a blind spot?" I ask.

Gavin shrugs, tapped out. Ashley steps in, nodding.

"If you stay right close to the wall, and then take a certain angle out to the pillar by the ladies room, and around the corner, hugging the wall, you can get into the vendor hall without being on camera."

"Slick," I say. "You did that last night?"

"Yeah."

"You did the same thing tonight?"

"Yeah."

"What about in here?" I point to the little black globes on the ceiling above us.

"Gavin's brother said they don't have enough TV screens to watch all the cameras at once. During the day, they rotate through all of them. But at night, they replace the main room with the outside cameras because they're more . . . interesting."

She flushes, her cheeks turning red.

"More interesting how?" I ask.

After a moment of silence, Gavin blurts out, "They watch girls."

"I'm sorry, what?" asks Dana. But it's too late, Gavin's clammed up again. Ashley looks down at her hands, her face still flush.

"They watch girls," says the blond kid. The first time he's spoken. He casts a worried glance in Ashley's direction.

"And you are?"

"Trey," he says quickly. "There's a nightclub around the corner. Fancy place. People line up to get in. When the line gets long and wraps around the corner, one of the cameras looks down on it. The guards like to watch the girls in line."

"Charming," says Dana, rolling her eyes. "Decker didn't say anything about that."

"Decker wouldn't have thought to ask," I say. "He's way too uptight for that."

"Can we go now?" asks Trey.

"Not quite yet," I say, frowning at him. "While you were here, did you see anyone else, or hear anything?"

Trey's silent, but his eyes dart to Ashley who meets his gaze. There's a connection between these two. Trey likes her. He's trying to make this easier for her, but he's also letting her call the shots. She nods slightly.

"Yeah, we heard something." His voice cracks and he clears his throat. "Are you sure we're not in trouble?"

"For hearing something? How could you be in trouble for that?" Dana asks.

"We thought maybe we should tell someone," says Ashley, "but then we'd get in trouble for messing with the games. So, we didn't."

She unfolds her hands and braces them on her thighs.

"Then, when we came in to the Con today," she continues, "everything seemed normal. We thought whatever it was, it couldn't have been a big deal. Were we wrong?"

Dana comes around the chair to kneel beside her so they're eye-to-eye. She reaches out to put a reassuring hand on Ashley's knee.

"Why don't you tell us what happened," she says.

"She didn't see anything," says Trey quickly, drawing our attention back to him. "But I did. This short, hairy guy was sneaking around, going from booth to booth. We heard him coming, so we all hid. The others went under the RV, but I went inside. Nick said it was stupid because I'd be trapped. But I don't like small spaces."

He hangs his head, clearly ashamed. Before he couldn't take his eyes off Ashley, now he doesn't look in her direction, likely afraid she'll think less of him.

"Everybody's got something they don't like," Dana says. "That's okay. It's good, in fact, because it helps us. Did you look out the windows?"

"Yeah. It was a little blurry, through the wrap, you know. But I saw him. He went from booth to booth, checking stuff out. He touched a bunch of stuff. Kept going. After a while, we heard a door clank and figured he left."

"But then we weren't so sure," says Ashley. "Because after a bit, we heard something else."

"What did you hear?" asks Dana. She's leaning in now. Like a greyhound straining to be released. We're getting close. These kids know something.

"Yelling. Like people fighting."

"How do you know they were fighting?"

"It sounded just like my parents," says Nick suddenly. "Trust me, I know what fighting sounds like."

"You heard it too?" I ask, looking at him.

"We all did," says Trey.

Even Gavin is nodding slowly.

"Was it muffled? Clear? Could you make out what they were saying?" I ask rapidly.

"No words," says Trey, "but it sounded like they were at the end of a long hall, you know, that echoes."

The tile walls of the large bathroom would give it that "at the end of a hallway" sound. These kids heard the murder.

"What happened next?" asks Dana, looking at Ashley. She's been the most reliable.

"We left," she says.

"We got the hell out of here," adds Nick.

"But before we could get out of the hall, we saw the guy again," says Trey.

"Which guy?" I ask.

"The hairy guy who was checking out the tables," Trey answers. "He came running back. I don't think he'd left after all. Or maybe he came back in again. I dunno. We thought he must have got caught digging around in the booths."

"That fucker was hustling," says Nick. "Looked like the devil himself was on his tail."

"Where did he go?" Dana asks.

"Out the emergency exit," says Trey.

"And where did you go?" I ask.

"We went out the way we came in," says Ashley, "through the blind spot."

Dana spends the next few minutes asking them to repeat their story. Nick eases up, becoming more involved this time. The story's consistent the second time through. Looks like they're telling the truth.

While Dana's talking to them, I do a series of web searches on my phone until I have what I want. I've pulled together a collage of photos. All similar-looking men. One of which is a face we know. I show it to the kids one at a time. Each time they point to the same face. Even Gavin, who is so terrified, I'm not sure he'd recognize his own mother.

The same face. Every time.

I show the phone to Dana. A grid of nine pictures. Her eyes go straight to the left side of the middle row.

Farber.

"One more thing before you go," I say, standing up. "Does anyone here play Big Fish Pyramid?"

CHAPTER TWENTY-ONE

For such a late hour, the police station is a hive of activity. All the lights are on, making the place feel disconnected from time. Tense voices leak out of the conference room where Chief Wilmont is being briefed on the investigation and Farber's role as, at best a witness, and at worst a suspect. Dana and Decker are in there, making the case to bring Farber in now, in the middle of the night. Given we're on a countdown to the end of the Con, I agree with them that we have no time to waste.

Once again, I'm low on caffeine. It's also going on twenty-four hours that I've been up, so even coffee is a stopgap. I need sleep. But I can't do that until I know what's happening with Farber. I need to be here when they bring him in. While I'm not convinced that he's an actual bidder for the Unicorn, he was closer to the scene of Caplan's demise than the video game kids. Based on how he fled the building, he may have witnessed the murder.

I've found a little break area with mismatched plastic chairs and cheap laminate tables. All of which wobble. I checked. The air is filled with the sour stench of abandoned lunches. I hate the smell of cold leftovers. But it's slowly being replaced by the aroma of fresh coffee coming from the well-worn little machine dripping behind me.

No one else is here so I make myself at home, facing two chairs together and putting my feet up. I can see the conference on the far side of the large squad room, but can't quite make out what anyone's saying. Resting my head on the back of the chair, the voices blur and blend together into one.

Decker thinks Farber could have Amanda Caplan, but I'm not convinced. Whoever has Amanda is a bidder on the Unicorn, with access to millions, and has been negotiating with Caplan for weeks.

As a wealthy businessman, Farber could have the funds, but he's not a technical guy, not connected to the industry in any way. It's unlikely he has any use for it, or the resources to make it work, even if he did. Even less likely is the coincidence of Farber finding Caplan's auction on the Dark Web when they just happen to both be connected to this Comic Con. No, whoever's after the Unicorn isn't local.

Griffon and Nassar have arrived. They're in the conference room listening in and getting up to speed. I've met Nassar before. Her appearance is always impeccable, no matter the time of day. Tonight, her watchful, intelligent eyes peer out from behind stylishly wide, black, glasses. I happen to know the tidy outward appearance hides a ribald sense of humor. Most unexpected for a daughter of Muslim immigrants from Lebanon.

Peter Griffon isn't what I expected, based on his reputation at the Bureau as a smooth operator in the field and in internal politics. On the phone, he had the easy confidence of someone used to things working out his way. I imagined tall. In person, Griffon is short. Really short. Despite the stature, he's a handsome fellow with a trim goatee and an easy, disarming smile.

Something struggles to fit together in my fatigue-addled mind. Unable to wait any longer for caffeine, I pull the coffeepot to pour a cup, the slowing stream of drips sizzling on the hot plate under the carafe.

When the hot liquid crosses my lips, it's like a magic potion of intelligence. The elements lurking around in my mind slide together and connect. The RV. I was so focused on who had broken in, and what they'd seen, I missed something else. Wasteout 3 is a big deal for Pyntel, but nothing compared to the Unicorn. If Pyntel sent Hicks here for the quantum computer, handing out t-shirts and showing the executive flag to the front lines is more than enough cover story. Actually getting involved in the launch risks an unnecessary distraction.

What if Pyntel doesn't know about the Unicorn, and Hicks is working the launch to justify why he's here? Why wouldn't he have told them?

Looking up at the clock on the wall, an old-school analog job with a red second hand, and a metal cage on the front, I subtract three hours. Late in California too, but not too late. After a quick glance at the conference room, I pull out my phone.

Me: Need info.

Keira S: Shoot.

Me: Martin Hicks. Buzz?

Keira S: You wouldn't think much but . . .

Me: But . . .

Keira S: What do you have for me?

Keira Solomon is a journalist. Most agents don't like journalists. They fear the almost inevitable hand-biting that follows working with one. Doesn't bother me. Back in the Valley I learned how to handle them. Part of the job. Journalists live out their entire careers

BROKEN GENIUS / 179

reporting on the business of Silicon Valley, interviewing CEOs, and getting the scoop on anticipated mergers and acquisitions.

Keira's different. She focuses on the people of Silicon Valley. She tells their stories. Some call her a gossip writer. I don't mind that. In addition to selling ad space on her blog, gossip solves cases. As a result, I maintain a relationship with Keira the same way you have a relationship with a wolf you've raised from a pup. You have a good time, and lots of adventures together, but you never forget you're one hunger pang away from having your arm ripped off.

Me: A favor.

Keira S: Really? A Will Parker IOU?

Me: Personal.

Keira S: A personal favor as in you'll walk my dogs when I'm away?

Me: Reason I'm asking is personal.

Keira S: Is there a story here?

Me: Not yet.

Keira S: But might be?

Me: Maybe.

Keira S: I keep my message histories you know. One Will Parker favor?

Me: That's the deal.

Keira S: Hicks in trouble. Diddling staffer. Consensual.

Keira S: Gave her promotion. Word got out. Sharks circling.

Me: Got it. Thx.

Keira S: I'll be in touch about that favor. :-)

The phone clatters on the table when I set it down. My eyes are dry, and the world is a little blurry around the edges. Blinking them a bunch of times, I take a long drink of the stuff that came out of the coffee machine.

Hicks was sleeping with a staffer? Hardly the first to do that in corporate America, let alone Silicon Valley. But he promoted her? Stupid. When word of the relationship gets out, which it always does, everyone else who thinks they were entitled to that job files a complaint. Maybe even sues.

Hicks isn't gifted with the vision of an entrepreneur. He's the kind of corporate drone that ends up at the top of the hive through sheer staying power. Rewarded for tenure, not ability. That's a fine strategy as long as you keep your nose clean like a good little worker bee.

Hicks didn't. He dipped into the corporate honey pot.

"Sharks circling" means they're looking for ways to axe him. He made it high enough to expect a golden handshake. Maybe not the kind of payout package that causes Wall Street to scream about the poor shareholders, but enough that he'd be comfortable.

The thing with a guy like Hicks though, is that the pain of separation would outweigh any amount of money. Those long-tenure guys have drunk the Kool-Aid. They define themselves by the narrow confines of their job description and the name of the company they work for. Take that away and you're not just taking a job, you're taking an identity.

Which makes for a pretty powerful motive.

They're wrapping up in the conference room now. Through the glass wall, I can see people standing up. Tonight or tomorrow, we're going to have Farber in an interview room. I'm going to need information.

Checking the time again, I pick up my phone.

Me: Got a lead. Need research.

Me: You there?

Bradley W: At Chronos.

Me: The Klingon home world?

Bradley W: New night club. In the Hills.

Me: Guest list?

Bradley W: Possible Kardashian. Hoping Kim.

Me: Time to work. Anything on photo?

Bradley W: No. Waiting. They text me; I text you. ASAP.

Me: Bringing in a suspect. Need background on a local named Farber.

Bradley W: Wait, something happening. Entourage at the door.

Me: Bradley!

Bradley W: Never mind. Just Kanye. At desk in 15. Send me details.

They're coming out now, and Decker looks pissed. Chief Wilmont and some of his top brass vanish deeper into the station. Griffon and Nassar, roller bags in tow, follow Decker and Dana to my wobbly table. Handshakes all around as Decker introduces the new agents.

"I've heard a lot about you," says Griffon.

"All of it good, I know," I reply, pumping his hand with as much energy as I can muster.

"Yeah, sure," says Griffon with a broad smile.

"Will, good to see you again," says Nassar, wrapping her arms around me in a friendly embrace. "How's Bradley?"

"Working late, like the rest of us," I answer, before turning to Decker. "What's the status?"

Decker raps his knuckles on the laminate and leans over, looking ready to launch an invasion.

"No go," he says through clenched teeth. "We wait until morning."

"Wilmont's going to put surveillance on Farber's house to make sure he doesn't go anywhere," Dana adds hastily.

"Fat lot of good that does if he has the girl," says Decker with a snort.

Dana sinks into the chair next to me, yawning. She scrunches her eyes closed, holding her fist in front of her mouth. Her nose wiggles at the end.

"I think we should look at Hicks."

"The corporate guy?" Dana asks. "Why would we look at him?"

"I think he might be rogue. He's looking for a Hail Mary."

Without using Keira's name, I fill them in on what she told me about Hicks dipping his pen in the company inkwell.

"To save his job, he's got to come up with something so valuable it makes the inevitable lawsuit worth spending a lot of cheddar to defend," I say, swirling the coffee around in the cup. "What could possibly be that valuable?"

"The Fukushima Unicorn," says Dana, clapping her hands and looking me in the eye.

"Bingo. When I visited Hicks and Morley at the RV earlier today, Hicks was a wreck. Far from the schmoozy guy he was first thing in

the morning. The first time, approaching me, he had time to prepare, to put on his game face. But the second time, I caught him off
guard. Then there's Morley. She said his mood shifted to the dark
side overnight. The night of the murder."

"So, he's in a bad mood," says Decker. "That doesn't make him a
kidnapper."

"What if Hicks was after the Unicorn, confronted Caplan for it,
failed to get it, and killed him?" Dana asks. "Caplan said he had an
assistant. We know that he was referring to Amanda, but no one else
would, so Hicks would think the auction was still on. He takes
Amanda figuring she would still be leverage against whoever
Caplan's assistant is."

"Are you sure this isn't a holdover from the Valley? Some beef you
had with him back in the day?" asks Decker.

"Absolutely not," I say, then I think about it. No, still probably not.

"We haven't identified all the bidders," says Dana. "Who else
could be one?"

"All right, all right! You want to take a look at Hicks, be my
guest," says Decker abruptly. "But we're still bringing in Farber in
the morning. He's our best lead."

"Will, what do we know about how they grabbed Amanda?" asks
Nassar, changing the topic and breaking the tension.

"So far Bradley confirmed that she landed in town, and checked
into her hotel. After that nothing. We've been working it back from
the ransom note."

She looks over at Griffon by the coffee machine, pouring himself
a cup. "Why don't Peter and I start working it from the other end?"
she says. "See if we can figure out how they grabbed her."

"Sounds like a good idea. Go ahead," says Decker, glaring at me.

"Ping Bradley, he'll fill you in on the hotel details. Do you still
have his coordinates?" I ask, ignoring Decker. I'm not telling Nassar
what to do. I can't help it if she's looking to me as a thought leader.

"Right here," she says, waving her phone. "We're on it. Let's go, Pete."

The two agents take off down the hall, a spring in their step I'm envious of.

"I'm calling it," I say, stretching my arms above my head. "I'm going back to the hotel to get some sleep."

"Before you go, Decker says you guys found a video loop at the Convention Center," says Dana.

My arms flop back to my sides, a frown creasing my brow. Finishing off the last of the coffee in the paper cup, I crush it in my fist before tossing it in the garbage.

"Decker caught the loop in the video by spotting a bus where it shouldn't be. Which was great, by the way. Amazing that you caught that." Might as well toss him a bone. He'll still be here tomorrow.

Dana nods. "We reviewed that with the chief. He asked if that's why we don't have footage of Farber there last night."

"The video is useless," I say. "They could have recorded the loop days ago and used it to overwrite the entire evening's footage."

"Except they didn't," says Dana. "The bus number Decker gave is a special route that runs Thursday to Saturday for the college kids hitting the patio scene. It only runs during late summer and fall. This year, it started this week. That footage has to be from last night."

My hands rise up to perch on my hips as I consider the implications.

"So?" asks Decker. "Why does it matter when the video came from?"

"If you're planning a hack like this," I say slowly as I gather my thoughts, "you want the most boring footage possible. Nothing unusual in it to draw attention or highlight a date, like a car accident, or a storm. The best thing to do is to get it in advance, so it's clean. You take your time to access and review previous footage to find the best clip before laying it down. Whoever hacked it last night didn't do that. They grabbed the most recent video and replicated it. Copying over all the evening's files. They rushed it."

Decker's eyes widen. "You think they left traces?"

"Good news and bad news," I say with a deep sigh. "Bad news is the hack was clean. Super clean. No way we can track it."

"Well then, what's the good news?" asks Decker clenching his fists.

"Same thing. The hack was super clean. Too clean for teenage kids. Way too clean for a luddite like Farber. Who do we know that could execute a flawless hack, on the fly, that fast?"

Decker thinks for a second. Working it out. Opening his mouth in a silent gasp, he's like a kid at Christmas opening the last present and hoping like hell it's the thing he's been bugging his mother about for weeks.

"Dragoniis?" Decker whispers.

I nod.

"Boo-yeah!" he shouts, pounding on the table.

Dana and I both jump, our backs as straight as Decker's, eyes popping wide open.

"Whoa, easy, big guy," I croak, catching my breath. "Save it for the morning."

CHAPTER TWENTY-TWO

Back at the hotel, I stand looking at the double doors to the Presidential Suite, and inside, its giant, king-sized bed. My eyes are dry and drooping, my breathing is labored, my feet ache, and I'm thinking slowly.

But I can't stop. Not yet. Something nags away at the edges of my mind, not quite coherent enough to form a thought. There's something I'm missing about Caplan the night of his murder. Something at the hotel.

Holding the room's key card in my hand, I review what we know. Caplan came back to the hotel, in shirtsleeves due to the hot night. When he leaves for the Convention Center, he's wearing a jacket, in theory to conceal the Fukushima Unicorn. Leaving the protective Pelican case behind, he carries the Unicorn on him. Why not take the case?

He couldn't conceal it. Why does he need to conceal it? Because one or more bidders found out who he is, and they'll do anything for it. It almost cost Miller his life. Somehow, Caplan figured out they were on to him.

But if he carries the Unicorn without the case, it's giving off radiation. In small doses it's harmless, but prolonged exposure would be dangerous. Not just for him, but for anyone in the same room with it. Miller didn't pick up any radiation at the Convention Center, so either it's not there, or it's shielded.

Why move it in the first place?

When Caplan arrived at the hotel, one of Golovchenko's men was waiting for him. When they got off the elevator, they left video coverage. Did Caplan notice he was being followed sometime after that? We noticed because we were looking for something suspicious. What if Caplan didn't?

My hand hovers over the key card reader. I need sleep. I know my body and I know that if I don't get rest, I won't be thinking clearly. I'll be struggling to keep up with Decker mentally, which is not a good state of affairs. At the same time, I know I won't be able to rest right now. Not with this thing gnawing at me. I need an answer.

I pull my hand back. The thing nagging at me coalesces into a thought. More of a what-if question, really, but I know where I can go to get the answer.

Too tired to text on my way down to the hotel security office, I call Bradley.

"We need to look into Hicks," I say when he answers. "I need to know where he's staying, his travel plans, everything."

"Martin Hicks? The Pyntel guy? He's pretty savvy, he could know we're looking around."

"Then do it on the sly."

"That's harder, Will."

"If he finds out we're looking at him, he'll lawyer up with an army of suits and we won't get anywhere near him. And if he's got the Caplan girl . . ."

"He'll dispose of the evidence. Right, got it, Boss. I'm on it. I'll have something by morning," Bradley says, hanging up.

Dwayne answers right away when I knock on the security office door.

"Agent Parker! I just started. I'm on the night shift this week. Is Agent Decker with you?" he asks, looking over my shoulder.

"No. Do you mind if I take another look at the system?"

His face falls in disappointment, but he lets me in.

The key card data is stored in a relational database. It's structured in a set of tables, each with raw data linked together through a key. One of the tables is called "Guest Room Doors" that logs each time a door opens and closes. To keep the table organized, each time a door opens, the occurrence is assigned a unique number.

Those unique numbers aren't accessible through the key card software system itself. I need software that can read straight from the database. I could upload the entire database to Bradley in LA, but it's large and that would take some time. Besides, he's working on Hicks. It'll be faster if I do this myself.

While the database software I need is downloading from the FBI's servers, Dwayne tells me a story about his dog. At least, I think it was about his dog. It could have been his Mom. I'm not entirely sure, as I struggle to stay awake.

Once the database software is installed, I get to work. I go to the entry where Caplan opened his door at 10:59 p.m. Looking at the raw data, I go backwards, one by one, through the records. I'm in luck, the keys are in sequence.

Caplan's entry was record number 1957862. The entry before, also at 10:59 p.m., was a door on the third floor. At 10:58 p.m., a door on the ninth floor. There are several entries for 10:58 p.m. and 10:57 p.m. It's a big hotel so, in any given minute, several doors are being opened.

I work backwards this way for a while, hunched over the screen and mumbling to myself until even Dwayne loses interest and wanders back to his desk. One at a time, row by row, I go back. My finger leaves a greasy streak on the monitor as I drag it upwards.

Finally, I find what I'm looking for. 10:50 p.m. Two records, right next to each other. 1957791 and 1957789. But there's no 1957790. The record is missing. I go back another ten minutes to be sure, but there are no other gaps in the database. Whatever happened in between has been erased.

Digging deep in the last of my energy reserves, I text Bradley to get a copy of the database.

Momentarily, I consider calling Dana or Decker, but my need for sleep wins out, and I make my way back to my room instead. Leaning against the wall in the elevator, I remember watching Caplan stand right here in the video. Someone went into his room nine minutes earlier.

What did Caplan find when he got there? Was someone still in the room? Or was something out of place, tipping him off? If the intruder had left, wouldn't there be another missing entry?

Pressing my palm to my forehead, I struggle to concentrate as the elevator door opens and I stagger down the hall.

No. Once they were in, they could have propped the door open like cleaning staff do, using the manual flip-lock. Then they could leave without creating another record.

Whatever Caplan found spooked him. The Unicorn was still there, but now he knows his room isn't secure. Minutes later, he leaves with it under his coat, soaking up rads.

Later, someone hacks the hotel security system and erases a single database entry. I'm certain the entry was a record of the door to Caplan's room being opened. Finding and deleting that one entry with such precision, all without leaving a trace, took serious skills. It had to be Dragoniis.

Finally swiping my key card in the reader, I stumble into my suite. The last thing I remember is managing to kick off my Converse before collapsing on top of the bed.

CHAPTER TWENTY-THREE

I wake to the gray light of morning coming in through sheer curtains. In my haste for sleep last night, I didn't close the blackout blinds. Another thing I didn't do was set an alarm, so I have this strange sensation of being disconnected from time and space. Floating that way for a moment, I indulge in the isolation from everything, including my thoughts.

Until memories of my nightmares hit me like a hurricane.

They're the same images that have been haunting me for years. Jack's office. The computer monitor. The speakers. Bruce Sterling. Only this time with a new twist: it isn't Kate Mason's throat he's holding the shining knife to. It's Amanda Caplan's.

Calling out groggily to my phone for the time, it answers with its customary "good morning" at the end. I curse at it, in reply. It's been nearly five hours. At ninety minutes each, that's three complete sleep-state cycles. I can live with that. Throw some caffeine on top, and I'll be good.

Picking up my phone reveals messages from Bradley. I slept right through the alert tones. He has a background on Farber, a location on Hicks, and just an hour ago, a final message that the image analysis is done.

To speed my waking, I shower quickly in cool water. Sleep deprivation isn't as easy to shake off in my thirties as it was in my twenties. Clean and dressed, I check the mini-bar to see what I've got to work with, without going anywhere. Room service crosses my mind, but then I'd have to talk to someone. Inefficient. I need fuel on the run today.

The large fridge is stocked with cold beverages. Skipping past the beer and liquor, I find soda, but that doesn't pack the punch I'm looking for. Thankfully, on the bottom row I find the familiar tall cans of energy drinks. I pick a sugar-free one. Breakfast of champions.

After a long drink from the frosty, cold can, I finally feel like I'm up to full speed. Checking my inbox, I find an email from Bradley with the enhanced image. This is our best clue to where Amanda is being held, and I eagerly tap the icon.

The tech team at the field office has applied their algorithmic wizardry to the original file to get the clearest picture possible. It's ten times the size, but the detail is impressive. Tapping to enlarge it, Amanda Caplan's face fills the screen, eyes wide and glistening behind chunky, teardrop frames. I scroll down to see her nostrils are flared. The orange ball of the gag presses into her open mouth. She's not wearing any lipstick. Makeup overall is minimal.

Bradley said her parents were divorced. How much did she see Roger? Why did she come here? Simply to spend time with her father? Or is she in on the Fukushima Unicorn sale? Would Roger put his daughter in that kind of danger? But then, I'm not sure he knew how much danger he was in until it was too late.

Sliding further down, the laptop's screen comes into view. Before the enhancements, I could clearly see the Google doodle for the day, but not much else. Now I can make out the menu bar at the top of the Mac's screen. It isn't tack-sharp, there's only so much the techs can do, but it's enough to see the browser type and the time.

I'm lucky. They aren't using Apple's Safari, or Google's Chrome. It's Firefox, a browser that used to be popular, but now only has a single-digit percentage of Mac users.

Zooming in on the Google doodle yields even more info. The doodle that day was a long animation after which a button to enter a mini-game appeared. Since the doodle is in mid-animation, with no button visible, I know that the screen had been refreshed just moments before the picture was taken. Certainly, within the minute displayed on the system clock in the upper right corner of the screen.

Zooming back out a bit, I scan the rest of the image. Amanda's arms are tied to the chair. With the enhancements you still can't see much of the chair itself, but you can see that what's holding her are leather cuffs.

Blood rushes to my fingers, a thousand tiny pinpricks announcing the new flow. Real, tangible clues I can work with. I've got a precise moment in time and I know what they were doing in that precise moment. Plus, Amanda's bonds are unusual. Unusual is good. It's too early to put a checkmark in the win column, but I can see the path to get me there.

My heart pounds with excitement. That or the energy drink breakfast. Time will tell.

Next, I have to do something I've been dreading would be necessary since I saw the ransom photo: eat crow.

Opening the curtains reveals the city below, The Convention Center reflecting the early morning sun from its curved white roof. It's even earlier in California. Waking up the person I need to call isn't going to win me points, but somewhere out there in the city before me is a terrified young woman being held against her will. They have what I need to find her. No getting around it. I dial.

When they don't answer on the first attempt, I hang up, close my eyes, and try again. The second time, the call is answered on the third ring.

"What?" says a male voice in irritation.

Not a great start. This is going to be a tall mountain to climb.

"Rick, it's Will."

"You know every phone in the world has call display, right?"

"It's early. I wasn't sure if you'd looked."

"Damn right it's early, nice of you to notice. What do you want, Will?"

"A favor." There's no sense in beating around the bush.

"Are you kidding right now?"

It's not like I don't understand. I do. Rick Downie's a solid guy. And the outfit he ran was decent. But mine was better, and faster. When we put him out of business, he sold what was left to Google. It wasn't a total disaster; he and his team were given jobs in the behemoth. Which is why I'm talking to him now.

"It's not for me," I say. My mouth is dry. I pick up the can of energy drink, only to find it empty.

"Oh, of course not. It never is, is it? Like, breaking up with someone. It's for their benefit, not yours."

Okay, I also went out with his sister. It didn't work out.

"It's for work," I say.

A pause. He knows where I work now.

"Someone's in danger," I add, echoing the words Burke once spoke to me on the night of the tsunami. "A young woman. She's been kidnapped. I can't say more."

"Is this official?"

This is tricky. He's more likely to agree to an official request than a personal one, but it would still put him, and his employer, in a difficult position, compromising the privacy of their users.

"Yes," I reply, "and we're on the clock."

Rick sighs. We were all young when I dated Trish. I'm counting on him to remember those times, and make a connection in his heart between his sister and a kidnapped girl he's never met.

"What do you need?" he says, finally.

Closing my eyes, I silently fist pump the air.

I waste no time laying it out for him. He listens while I fill him in on the picture, the Google doodle, the browser, the time, and where I am. Then I tell him what I need him to do with that information. It's possible I spent more time than necessary describing Amanda's terrified expression and restraints, but I want to make sure he's committed.

"Okay," he says finally. "That's all the info I would need for what you want. There's just one more thing."

Oh no. Not one more thing. I thought we were going to make this work. This can't fail because of something I did in the past. Amanda's life depends on it.

"I need something from you first—"

"I know," I blurt before he can finish. "It's a lot for me to ask. I'm really sorry about what happened with Trish. She's terrific, I swear. I didn't appreciate that and I should have. She can take comfort from the fact that she's not missing out on anything, though. The last few years haven't been great."

There's an awkward silence. Then Rick does something I'm not expecting. He laughs.

"Oh, believe me, she's not missing out," he says, taking a breath. "She married a colleague at SpaceX. They went to Musk's birthday party."

I close my eyes and rub my face. This isn't happening. This is torture. Did I just do that for nothing?

"Listen," says Rick, when his laughter fades. "What I need from you is an Electronic Communications Privacy Act warrant. You're asking for a list of potentially user-identifying information. With how hot privacy and government is right now, my hands are tied. That said, I *do* appreciate the apology. And I know you've had a rough go of it."

There's another pause. Getting a warrant is going to take time, which is in short supply. If Rick won't move until we have a warrant, the answer may come too late to get Amanda back safely. I pinch my eyes shut and shake my head. I don't know what else to do.

When Rick speaks again, there's a kindness there I'm not sure I deserve. "What you're doing now, Will. Helping people. It's a good thing. I'm glad you're doing it. So, I'll tell you what, while you're getting a warrant, I'll get started on the data pull. You're talking about moving a mountain of data in search of a pebble. It's going to take a while anyway. I'll ping you when it's ready. And, Will? Thanks."

He hangs up. I gasp a deep breath, letting it out slowly through pursed lips. My face is hot and my ears are ringing. I look out the window at the Convention Center again. The tall hotels. The office buildings. And beyond the downtown core, miles and miles of suburbia. Amanda Caplan could be anywhere, but now we're on the way.

CHAPTER TWENTY-FOUR

Decker's already there when I get to the station, having set up shop in a conference room. A pad and paper with scribbled notes sit next to a Bureau-issued laptop on the table in front of him. The rest of the floor is unusually quiet. Just a couple of detectives at their desks, slogging away on their computers. No sign of Dana.

"Nice of you to join us," says Decker without looking up when I walk in.

"Had a late night. Where's Dana?"

"*Detective Lopez* is bringing in Farber," Decker says with a smirk. "Should be here any minute."

Griffon and Nassar arrive next, looking spectacularly well rested, paper coffee cups in hand, a familiar green logo peeking out around their fingers.

"Whoa," I say, holding up a hand as they enter the room. "There's a Starbucks?"

Nassar chuckles. "Amanda Caplan's hotel is way out by the airport. By the time we were finished talking to the front desk staff, we decided to just stay out there. Don't worry, Will, you're not missing anything. This—" she holds up the paper cup—"was courtesy of a machine in the lobby."

"Forget the damn coffee. What did you find out?" Decker asks. He's jumpy today. Irritable. More so than normal.

"We were lucky," says Griffon. "We got there just as the shift was changing over. The morning guy remembered Amanda. Early check-in request. Said she'd come straight from the airport."

"Why didn't she stay in the same hotel as her father?" Decker asks, scratching his chin. "It's downtown, closer to the Convention Center."

Nassar shrugs. "Maybe she didn't want to stay too close to her father's hotel, if the divorce was ugly. Strained relations?"

"Or maybe he was protecting her," says Griffon. "He was here to sell this Fukushima Unicorn after all. He had to have some awareness it was risky."

"Or she just booked too late and it was sold out," I say.

"Fine, that's her into the hotel. Then what?" asks Decker, bringing us back to the timeline.

"All we've got is what the front desk clerk told us," Nassar says, putting her hands on her hips. "There's no surveillance at all. Like I said, budget. And being out by the airport, this isn't the kind of place where people hang around in the lobby. So, no other witnesses."

"He said she dropped her bags and left pretty much right away," says Griffon.

"How? Did she have a rental?" Decker asks.

"Nope. A car picked her up," he answers. "The clerk thought it was a ride share. It wasn't in taxi livery, but Amanda got into the back seat. Nondescript vehicle. Sedan. Light color. Possibly gray, possibly silver, possibly beige. The guy wasn't real specific. Didn't see the plates."

I pull out my phone. "There can't be a lot of the ride sharing apps operating in this town."

"That's what we thought, too," says Griffon, "so we already looked into it."

Nassar catches my eye and casts a sideways glance at Griffon. The nod that follows is her way of telling me Griffon's a solid agent.

"There's one," he continues. "I called them last night and tech support got back to me this morning. They had a no-show at Amanda's hotel, five minutes after she left. When the driver went to contact the fare, the request was gone. He figured it was a glitch in the system and opened a trouble ticket. If the clerk saw her get into a car, and it wasn't the ride share, then it had to be the kidnappers."

"What about other businesses in the area? Maybe we can get some video footage?" Decker suggests.

"We looked around. There was a gas station with a camera but it doesn't have a view of the road," says Nassar tilting her head at the door. "You may have noticed, this isn't exactly Midtown Manhattan."

Decker continues asking Griffon and Nassar questions about the clerk's story, but it's pointless. There's nothing more to be learned there. Whoever scooped Amanda did it in broad daylight by pretending to be her ride share. Bold. Slick, even. No violence. No resistance. Just took her. Hacking the ride sharing seems too sophisticated for Golovchenko.

My phone buzzes. It's Bradley with more info on Hicks. Flew in two days ago. Checked into a hotel. That's it. That's all he could pull together without a warrant and without alerting Hicks that he was digging.

It's not enough. I need more.

"Griffon, I'm going to need a couple of warrants."

Decker shoots me a dark glare. Apparently, he wasn't finished asking his repetitive questions.

"What do you need?" asks Griffon, taking out his phone to take notes.

I lead off with the Google request. It's the most important, and may take a little time to secure the warrant under the Electronic Communication Privacy Act. Rick was right, user privacy's a hot topic. For some reason it's okay for advertisers to know everything about you: from your sexual preferences to where you order your takeout. But as soon as the government makes a request, such as a list of who's using a service like Search, people lose their minds.

"And the other?" asks Griffon as he finishes making notes on his phone.

"Let's get a sneak and peek warrant for Martin Hicks' hotel room." I don't want Hicks to know we're looking, and that type of warrant will let us search the room when he isn't there.

Decker huffs at the front of the room, but doesn't say anything. He said I could look into Hicks and that's what I'm doing. But I can tell by the way he's biting his lip that he wants me to drop it, and get back to hunting Dragoniis.

"I'm on it," says Griffon. "It may take a bit to get a sneak and peek. But don't worry, I'll get it done." He takes down the details and leaves to find a quiet place to call and set the legal wheels in motion.

"In the meantime, we need to know where Hicks was last night. We should ask around at his hotel," I say. Decker's already vexed, might as well get it all out of the way.

There's a commotion at the doors to the squad room. A small crowd of people bursts out of the elevators. Dana's in the lead with Farber, hands cuffed behind his back. Two uniformed officers follow behind, faces set in grim expressions.

"I can check on that while you two handle the interview with this Farber guy," says Nassar.

I catch up with Dana as she guides Farber into one of the interview rooms, closing the door behind him.

"Good morning, Agent Parker," she says.

Agent Parker? What happened to Will? She reaches out and grabs my arm. To anyone watching, it's a gesture of camaraderie, but the slow squeeze she puts on it seems like more to me. Last night, when I told her about Bruce Sterling and Kate Mason, it felt like we had a connection. Something deeper than a couple of cops working the same case. Or maybe that's wishful thinking.

Before I can speak, Decker pushes between us to get to the observation room. "Don't worry, Parker, I'm sure we'll find Amanda today and get back to why we're here."

"I'm not sure it was Farber," I say.

"What the fuck, Parker?" Decker blurts out, pulling at the fuzz of shorn hair on his head.

"Come again, Will?" Dana says, shaking her head and holding her hand up in front of her. "You're the one that proved he was there."

"I did. He was there all right. But he definitely doesn't have the Fukushima Unicorn, and almost certainly didn't kidnap Amanda."

"Bullshit he doesn't," says Decker, rubbing his eyes.

Dana's a bit more patient. "Why not?" she asks.

"Farber knows Caplan. This isn't their first convention together."

There's a long, pregnant pause while they digest what I've just said.

"Shit," says Dana putting her hand to her forehead and gazing up at the ceiling.

"He knows Caplan is a lone wolf. No assistant. Even if he was a bidder, he'd know kidnapping Amanda isn't going to get him anything," says Decker smacking a fist into his open palm.

"He could still be a murderer, Agent Decker," says Dana. "I know you're all about catching your hacker-spy, and Parker's after his Unicorn, but I still have a homicide to close."

It takes some time before Farber's lawyer, a guy with whitened teeth, fake tan, and a ten-thousand-dollar suit, can be found on the golf course. Dana tells me he's some big, local hotshot, exactly who you would expect for a guy like Farber.

When it's time to begin, Dana takes the lead. Decker and I watch through the one-way glass of the old-fashioned observation room. There's no sign of Chief Wilmont today, and I'm not surprised. Farber's a political hot potato the chief isn't going to touch.

"Mr. Farber, where were you on Thursday night?" Dana asks, putting down her pen. She's got her notebook in front of her, but she isn't looking at it. She's looking straight at him. Sweating him out.

"At my office, working late. Where I should be now, taking care of my event, not sitting here talking to some police*woman*."

Out of the gate hostility, mixed with sexism. Not how I would have started the interview. The lawyer obviously thinks so, too, reaching out to place a hand on his client's elbow. Dana takes it in stride without flinching. This isn't her first rodeo.

"About what time did you leave your office?" she asks.

"Midnight."

"Where did you go then?"

"Home."

"Straight home?"

"Yes."

"You're sure you didn't go anywhere else? Make any stops?"

"My client answered the question," says the lawyer. "Asking him to repeat the answer is harassment."

Dana laughs. "Actually, it's being thorough."

"Unless he exercises his right to not answer during questioning."

"We can skip questioning and go right to charges."

"Such as?" asks the lawyer.

"Bear with me," says Dana. "Now, Mr. Farber, answer the question." This time the lawyer nods.

"No, I went straight home," Farber says, still clearly annoyed.

Dana slides a picture of Caplan out from underneath her notepad.

"Tell me, Mr. Farber, do you recognize this man?"

"Should I?"

"You tell me," says Dana, holding it up at eye height for him. "Take a good look."

"I think he's one of the vendors. At the Comic Con. He sells the junk that these people buy. He's a Bedouin."

"A what now?" asks Dana.

"A Bedouin. A nomadic people in the Middle East," explains the lawyer.

"A gypsy," says Farber, spitting out the word in disgust.

"Right," says Dana looking down at the picture. "So, tell me, Mr. Farber. Did you have any problems with Mr. Caplan?"

"I don't see what this has to do with my client," says the lawyer.

Dana pulls out another picture of Caplan. This one from the postmortem, his cranial ridge crushed, a long red gash indelicately sewn shut.

"Because this is what he looks like now," says Dana.

"This is the guy? From the bathroom, at the Convention Center?" blurts Farber. "You're asking me about him? Why me? I don't talk to these people; I just cash their checks."

Farber stops when the lawyer once again touches his hand.

"This lawyer keeps breaking the momentum," I say to Decker. "It's letting the pressure off Farber, giving him a chance to cool down."

"We need something to really rattle his chain," he says. "Get him to shed the act and lose control. What do we have on him?"

Distracted by the image analysis on the ransom photo, I never read the background Bradley worked up on Farber. I check it now.

"Charles Farber. Fifty-two years old. Born and raised in St. Petersburg, Florida. University graduate. Moved up here after. Owned and operated various businesses over the years, most recently a dry cleaner, before moving into property in '09. Good timing. Snapped up properties all around the city, mostly commercial, and turned them into rentals. Steady revenue stream. Taxes paid. Model citizen."

"I don't buy it," says Decker. "He's unclean."

"Give me a minute."

As I look over the details, the pace of property buying seems high, even for 2009. At the height of the financial crisis, banks took dramatic steps to reduce their exposure to risk. For a time, they stopped lending money, especially for real estate. They were too busy bracing for Armageddon.

Me: Farber. Pre-09 tax income?

Bradley W: Businesses all in the black. Netted around $100K.

Me: Value of current properties?

Bradley W: Owned by Farber, $10 million. Owned by his REIT, $200 million.

A Real-Estate Investment Trust is a fund that uses money from investors to buy properties. Which explains how he was able to snap up so much in '09. No banks involved. The Trust maintains and manages the properties. The investors each own a percentage of the total value, based on their initial investment. Where did they get that kind of capital in the middle of the financial crisis? Who were Farber's initial investors?

Me: Investors? Nothing in report.

Bradley W: Just came in from IRS. Foreign. Israelis.

Me: Legit?

Bradley W: Yup. Techies sheltering.

Makes sense. There's a booming tech sector in Israel, especially around industrial and security software. Lots of guys in Tel Aviv running big shops, making good money. But Israel is still Israel, surrounded by enemies that want to push them back into the sea and all that. So wealthy Israelis, like the wealthy people of any country with instability, want to shelter their money somewhere safe. Offshore.

I fill in Decker.

"Farber set up that kind of operation *here*? For Israelis? That's how he went from dry cleaners to senators?" Decker shakes his head. "Millions of dollars of other people's money."

He walks over to the window and stares through it like he's got laser vision that would melt through the glass. "People that far away only care about the stability of their investment. Russians shelter billions in New York real estate, and they do it without drawing attention to themselves. But Farber's flashy. He enjoys being a big shot. Something doesn't fit."

Me: Why is Farber running a Comic Con? Clearly not a fan.

Bradley W: Cash flow? Media reports say he had a deal to buy the old courthouse from the county, fix it up, then lease it back to them. Construction took too long. County backed out. Went and built something cheap and cheerful, leaving Farber high and dry.

Me: In REIT?

Bradley W: No. His own deal.

In the interview room, Dana's leaning forward.

"Here's the thing," she says. "We know that you're lying about where you were the night that Roger Caplan had his head bashed in at *your* event. So why not come clean and just tell me where you were?"

"This again? You people are wasting my time, and unlike you, my time is worth something. I'm out of here." Farber makes a show of standing up.

"Sit down," says Dana. "We're not done."

"Unless you have something new to say, Detective, I think we are," says the lawyer.

There's a knock at the door behind Decker, and a uniform walks in carrying large, clear plastic evidence bags filled with small shiny objects. When he plops them down on a table by the wall, they make a metallic clinking noise.

"What's that?" asks Decker.

"Found all this stuff in the trunk of his car," says the uniform. "Thought you might know what it is."

Peering through the plastic, I know what I'm looking at right away. There's a *Deathly Hallows* pin. A time-turner necklace. Jewelry made from chain mail. Some brassy steampunk-looking stuff. All the sorts of things commonly found on sale at Comic Cons.

Showing Decker the last texts from Bradley, I explain what's in the bag.

"Finally," says Decker. "I've had enough of this shit."

He grabs a bag from the table and stomps out the door. A moment later, through the one-way glass, I see him enter the interview room, throwing the bag of merchandise down in front of Farber, who recoils.

"What's this crap?" he says, sinking down into his seat.

"You tell me," says Decker. "We found it in the trunk of your car."

"Who are you?" asks the lawyer.

While Decker gleefully identifies himself as a Special Agent for the Federal Bureau of Investigation, Dana sits stock still, staring down Farber. Eventually, he shifts around in his seat. Dana keeps staring, making sure he knows his bravado isn't working. His face stays locked in a scowl, but the fidgeting suggests he's feeling the pressure.

"So, Mr. Farber, where'd you get this 'crap'?" demands Decker.

"I don't know, my wife maybe," he says, shrugging and holding up his hands. "I don't know what that is."

"Well, I believe that," says Decker. "Because I don't get this stuff either. But I know where it came from, and so do you."

Farber stays silent this time.

"Let me paint a picture," says Decker, holding his hands up like a Hollywood director framing a shot. "It's late at night. The first day of the Comic Con is in the books. The vendors have all set up their wares. Enter Charles Farber. After everyone goes home, you wander up and down the aisles, doing a little shopping. It's discount day. Five-finger discount, that is. You lift anything you think is high-buck. Am I close?"

"You better have something to back up these accusations," says the lawyer defiantly. But he doesn't stop the interview.

"I have witnesses," says Decker.

"You're lying," says Farber.

"I have this," says Decker, pointing at the bag.

"It's not mine."

"Come on, what year is this? Fingerprints," says Decker.

"What would I want with this junk?" Farber asks, changing angles.

"You're broke," says Decker.

"Fucking lies," says Farber. "You only wish that were true. You're jealous. Policeman's salary doesn't go very far, does it?"

Storm Decker suddenly falls forward, leaning on the table, his face a foot from Farber's.

"We *do* have an eyewitness that was there that night. They heard shouting, like an argument, from the bathroom where Roger Caplan was murdered. And not a minute later, you know what they saw?"

"No idea."

"They saw you, running away like you're on fire. You killed Caplan and then you ran!"

"It wasn't me, you lying *peasant*," says Farber.

Still trying to bluster his way out of this. If in doubt, say something shocking to distract from the answer. Unfortunately, what might work for a politician doesn't work when you're staring down one of the hardest asses in the FBI. Especially when you're guilty. I choke back a laugh at what's coming.

Decker smiles, cool as a cucumber. The eye of the storm. I swear he enjoys this.

"The old courthouse," he says quietly. "You bought it. Not your investors. You wanted this one all to yourself. But you blew it. Spent too much, and now the county doesn't want it." He takes his time, never breaking eye contact. Farber's forced to look up at him. "That's what my momma used to call a 'white elephant.' Something you put a lot of money into and you're stuck with. So, you did what any sleazy businessman would do. You skimmed from your investors. You robbed Peter to pay Paul."

Decker wraps his speech by pointing a finger at Farber's chest. I hold my breath. It's a solid guess. If he took on debt for the renovations on a building he can't rent, he has to cover it somehow. A few collectibles alone won't cut it. So, he borrows from the REIT, intending to pay it back with proceeds from the Con, before his overseas investors notice what he's done. Which explains why he's so desperate for the show to go on. The only problem is, we don't have direct evidence of Farber stealing from the REIT investors.

"You've been paying it back ever since," Decker continues, circling the table. "Running this convention. Stealing things you think you can sell for quick cash to keep the flashy lifestyle going. How deep are you? A million? Two? Then Caplan walks in on you. If word gets out you're the thief, the other vendors all pull out. No vendors means fewer fans, which means less money. Before you know it, the whole thing implodes, leaving you with your hand in the Tel Aviv cookie jar."

"No," says Farber, quietly.

"Caplan caught you red-handed. Nothing more than a petty thief!" Decker raises his voice to a resonant booming.

"No."

"You argued. You fought," accuses Decker, standing beside Farber now. "You pushed him down into the counter, cracking his skull open."

"No."

"You left him bleeding. You left him there to die!" Decker slams his open hands down on the table. "Tell me the truth! That's what happened. You killed him!"

"No!" Farber bellows.

"Bahhhh," says Decker, heading for the door. "Doesn't matter. We've got the evidence we need. Book him through for murder, Detective. He can sit in a cell until Monday."

Farber turns to his lawyer, who shrugs. I get it. This guy's no criminal attorney. He's a white-collar corporate lawyer. I'll bet he's never defended a shoplifting case in his entire career, let alone murder.

"Wait." Farber's shoulders slump, his hands falling to his lap. "What do you want?"

Decker stops at the door and turns around. "I want to know what happened."

"I didn't kill that guy," says Farber.

"Okay, then tell us what did happen," says Dana.

"Hold on," says the lawyer, finally catching his breath. "If Mr. Farber cooperates, what assurance do we have that he'll be released?"

"Assuming he's not a murderer? I think if he hands over the stolen property, we can let it go with a warning," says Dana.

"Fine," says Farber. "I don't know who killed that guy, but I can tell you what I saw."

CHAPTER TWENTY-FIVE

Farber might be slimy and obnoxious, but he's not stupid. With Dana staring him down across the table in the interview room, and Decker looming over his shoulder, he takes a minute to gather his thoughts. Dana's given him an out, and he'll take it. Guys like him always do.

While Farber contemplates his immediate future, I check the time on my phone and perform a mental calculation I've done a million times before, adding the hours to Tokyo. Night. A good time to catch Han when he's ready to do some gaming.

Turns out Ashley Brewster, the teenage girl we caught sneaking in for Wasteout 3, is addicted to Big Fish Pyramid. According to her, not many people make it past level 42 because there's a glitch in the game, but she's figured out how to work around it. Clever girl.

Quickly, I fire off a message to Han on how to beat level 42. There's no better way to learn if and how Caplan got the Fukushima Unicorn into America. Han will be faster than formal requests through State or Interpol, and have access to what I need without red tape on the Japanese side. He'll take the time to beat the level, then pull together the information. Even as specific as I made my request, it may take digging.

Han does things on his own schedule. There's nothing I can do to rush him. But that doesn't mean there's nothing to do.

Farber looks like he's ready to continue, though with his hands in front of him and shoulders rounded, he looks nervous in a way he didn't before. Perhaps he's now fully processed the situation he's in. His Israeli investors are going to hear about trouble with the police relating to a murder. When they start pulling out their money, I wonder how long it will take for them to expose his embezzlement. Once they do, he'll be in real trouble. Just because his investors are legit, doesn't mean they're passive.

"What do you want to know?" he asks, glowering at Dana. He won't make eye contact with Decker who is standing against the side wall with his arms crossed.

Decker's bulk is intimidating enough, but having him hovering at the edge of your peripheral vision would even stress me out.

"Everything," says Dana. "Tell me how you got in there in the first place."

"I gave a guard a tip years ago, and he told me about a way in through a blind spot."

"What about the victim, Roger Caplan? Where did you see him?"

"At the end of Row K."

"What's Row K?"

"One row over from where Caplan had his booth," he says, with a frustrated sigh. "He was coming out of that row, and heading to the back wall, where the washrooms are."

"Was he carrying anything?"

"He had a black fabric bag, you know, like at the grocery store. But it had that geek stuff on the side. Some kind of advertising."

"What did he do with the bag?"

"He took it with him to the bathroom."

"What was in it?"

"How should I know?"

"You didn't see where he came from?" Dana asks.

"No, I told you, I only saw him at the end of the row. I don't go down that row."

"Why not that one?"

Farber hangs his head and looks at his hands, which he's wringing in front of himself on the table. "There's a security camera."

"But you already worked all that out, with the guard," Decker says.

"Not the Convention Center cameras," says Farber with a tone that says he thinks Decker's an idiot. "There was one at the top of one of the junk booths."

Dana perks up, obviously remembering the dummy camera Webb uses to scare people off. The one he said he never plugged in, just put up there as a deterrent, like an owl statue.

"On the wall behind Caplan's booth?" she asks. Her tone is light, but I see her shoulders tense. "Are you sure it was on?"

"Isn't that what I just said?"

"How do you know?"

"There was a light on it. On the back where the power cord plugs in."

"And the light was on?"

"How would I see it, if the light was off?" Farber throws his hands up in front of himself.

"Just answer the questions," says Decker.

"Then don't ask stupid ones," says Farber. His lawyer reaches out and puts a hand on his elbow, but he shakes it off. "Who cares about this light, that light? That's not important."

"Then tell me what *is* important," says Dana.

"After I saw Caplan disappear into to the bathroom with the bag, I kept walking the floor."

"Stealing," says Decker.

"Let's call it collecting," says Farber with a squint of his eyes. "Then I heard the doors open again, and someone came in, heading right for Caplan's booth."

"How do you know where they were headed?" Dana asks.

"Because they were making a lot of noise. Big loud footsteps. Huffing and puffing."

"What do you mean huffing and puffing?" Dana asks.

"Like they're carrying something big and heavy. They make this racket all the way to Caplan's booth."

"What happened next?" Dana asks when it's clear Farber isn't continuing.

"Isn't that enough? Can't you figure it out from here? That's a good clue, yes?" Farber smacks his hands on the table.

"I'll tell you when it's enough," says Dana, putting down her notebook. "Once again, what happened next?"

"Yelling. A fight."

"Could you hear what they were saying?"

Farber's quiet, but it's not sullen this time. He's thinking, remembering back. He rubs his chin and closes his eyes.

"If I had to say . . . someone was upset at being cheated. Something about a deal, but that's all I could make out. It was too much noise, too much drama, so I left as fast as I could. I really couldn't tell you any more about what happened back there."

"Then where did you go?" asks Dana.

"You wanted to hear about this Caplan guy. I told you."

"And I told *you*, you're done when I say you're done." Dana leans back and crosses her arms. "I've got all day. And all night. And all day after that. Do you?"

A long, tense silence fills the room. Dana sits still with that amazing patience. Decker picks at his fingernails. Farber looks back and forth between them.

"Fine," he says finally. "I backtracked through the blind spot and out to my car in the alley."

"What kind of car?" asks Decker.

"Why?"

"Paint a picture for me."

"Cadillac. Black. Tinted windows."

"And what did you do when you got to your car?" Dana asks, picking up her notebook and pen.

"I was getting organized."

"You were looking through what you stole," she says flatly.

"Yes, whatever," says Farber with another one of his irritated sighs. "That's when the guy on the motorcycle showed up."

"What guy on a motorcycle?"

"I don't know, the guy. The guy! He rides up to the building. By the door."

"Okay, hold on," says Dana. "You were parked by the alley door. Which alley?"

"By the loading dock. Where they leave a door open."

"So, who's this guy on the motorcycle?"

"How the fuck should I know? Some guy on a bike."

"What did he look like?"

"Red bike. Red and white leather jacket and pants, like racers wear. White helmet with red stripes on it. Don't ask me about his face, he never took his helmet off."

"That's a good description," says Decker. "You seem pretty confident."

"I am." Farber grabs the top of his head in frustration. "I had to sit there for a while. He didn't notice me when he rode up, and I didn't want him to see me, so I waited while he did whatever he was doing."

"What was he doing?"

"I don't know. Where's that nerdy one of you guys—it's more up his alley."

In the observation room, I perk up, moving closer to the window.

"What do you mean by that?" Decker asks.

"This guy, on the bike. He was some tech nerd. He takes out this thing, this white plastic thing, looked like a megaphone or something. He clips it on the front of his bike and points it at the building. Then he takes out this keyboard and starts typing on it."

"Sorry, a keyboard? You mean a laptop?" asks Decker.

"If I meant a laptop, I would have said a laptop," says Farber, rolling his eyes. "I mean a keyboard, just a keyboard. He takes it out from somewhere inside his jacket, puts it on the gas tank, types on it for a bit, waves his hand around, and then packs it all up."

I quickly do another image search on my phone. What I'm looking for doesn't come up right away. It's rare. If it's what I think it is, then another piece of the puzzle just clicked into place. Growling in frustration, I try a few variations on the search terms while I listen.

"How long did he do all that for?"

"Eleven minutes."

"Pretty precise," says Dana, eyebrows raised in surprise.

"I wanted to get out of there. I watched the clock in my car. Eleven minutes."

"Then he leaves, this motorcycle guy?"

"Yeah, and then I left."

"Which way did he go?"

"Who?"

"The motorcycle guy," says Dana. "Which way did he ride off?"

Bingo. Found what I'm looking for. Zooming in on the image, I head for the door. It takes me a few seconds to get to the interview room and I miss Farber's answer.

"Sorry, which way did he go?" I ask, standing in the doorway. "FBI, Special Agent Will Parker," I add hastily as the lawyer opens his mouth.

"I just told her, he went inside," says Farber.

"Inside the door that's always open. By the loading dock?" I ask, closing the door behind me.

"That's the one."

"Okay, just one more question," I say. Dana glares at me. "Was this what he had on his motorcycle? The plastic thing?"

I show Farber the picture on my phone.

"Yeah, that's it. Exactly. He had one of those and he clipped it to the handlebars."

"Pointed at the building?"

"Yeah."

My hands are shaking so badly as I go back through the door, I almost drop my phone.

CHAPTER TWENTY-SIX

Me: Need you.

Ace P: Call you in 5? In a meeting.

Me: No, need you to fly out here.

Ace P: When?

Me: Now.

Ace P: Busy this weekend. Staff event. Monday?

Me: Now. And bring $1 million cash.

Ace P: WTF? Seriously?

Me: Found the Unicorn.

Ace P: On my way.

Wallace "Ace" Prior has been the CEO of CastorNet since I left. It hasn't been more than a handful of times that I've spoken to him since I handed over the reins.

Jack was my partner, but Ace was my chief lieutenant, running things day to day. He's an operational genius, but I still left him holding the bag when I walked away with no transition plan. He's a good man, and a friend. At least he used to be. He deserved better than what he got.

Back in the day, he used to invite me over for BBQs with his wife, Laureen, and their kids. Three of them. Blond. Running around and squealing. Not my thing, but a kindness all the same.

Ever since Burke called me in the middle of the night, it's been one bad memory after another. Kate Mason. Bruce Sterling. Jack. The tsunami. But now, something comfortable stirs inside me, along with the adrenaline rush of gaining traction on the Unicorn. I'm looking forward to seeing Ace again. He pre-dates my life going off the rails. Maybe that's why I haven't talked to him since. I wanted to keep him a part of that *before*.

Now that I believe the Unicorn's actually here, there's another dimension: Who will keep it? Assuming we stay ahead of the auction and get our hands on it first, the government won't let it go. It'll be evidence. Best-case scenario, I'm directed by Burke to take it back to our labs in California. Worst-case scenario, another agent takes it away, never to be seen again. Who am I kidding? I know where it will end up. Vanishing into the NSA, it'll be put to work surveilling . . . well, everyone on earth.

Running on the Unicorn, CastorNet's software would start a technology revolution. From autonomous vehicles to virtual physicians, the Unicorn and its descendants would improve the lives of billions.

If the government is able to take the Unicorn in secret, they'd be able to weaponize it. With access to any surveillance device and every piece of data ever collected about a person, the Unicorn could predict a person's thoughts and actions before they happen. What could any government do with that power, including our own? The Unicorn was intended to be a tool of empowerment, not oppression. For that to happen, it needs to stay out of government hands.

Which brings me to my current problem. I kind of *am* the government right now.

The safest place to put it is with Ace. CastorNet bought the remains of Fukushima Semiconductor including all intellectual property rights. Ace is now the CEO of that company. Once it's in his possession, armies of lawyers in a very public fight would make it impossible for the government to take it in secret.

The trick is getting to Ace before the government can take it.

*   *   *

The interview over, Decker's holding court in the conference room, pacing back and forth like a dog before a thunderstorm.

"What the hell is going on?" he demands as I walk in. "Who's this guy on the bike? And what's this plastic megaphone thing you're all fired up about?"

Nassar's still off chasing down where Hicks was the night of the murder. Griffon's finished his phone calls and, along with Dana, is sitting at the table with his arms crossed. I drop into a seat with a sigh.

"The guy on the bike is Dragoniis."

"Is that a guess?" Decker says, drilling me with his most intense glare.

"Since he's not here to ask, of course it's a guess," I say. "But it's a really good one."

After all the standing around watching Farber's interrogation I'm stiff, but also full of nervous energy. It's impossible to sit still right now, so I stand and grasp the back of a chair. Leaning over, I stretch my legs out behind me, alternating between left and right.

"How do you know it's not some guy on a bike messing with his GPS? Farber's not exactly tech savvy. What makes you think it's a Chinese government hacker?" Dana asks.

"It isn't," I say and Decker looks like he's going to explode, so I continue quickly. "Hackers aren't the most orderly bunch. They shift allegiances. They do *jobs* for governments; they don't *work* for them. Not hackers of this caliber. This one has worked for China, but only when it suits him. What's important is that he's definitely here, and he's here for the Unicorn."

For the next few minutes, I explain the missing data entry in the hotel security database. Someone went into Caplan's room, and then covered their tracks with such skill and precision, no one would ever find it. Except me, of course. That someone had to be Dragoniis. Beyond me, he's the only player at the table with the skills to pull off that hack; and if he'd had more time, maybe even I wouldn't have found it.

"But that could have been done from anywhere," says Decker. "How do you know he's actually here?"

"Because someone actually went in the room, and someone actually went to the Convention Center. It could have been Dragoniis hacking remotely with another agent on the ground. After hearing Farber now, I'm sure it wasn't. It's him," I say.

"Because of the thing on his bike? The white megaphone thing?" asks Dana.

"It's an antenna," I say, nodding. "Dragoniis goes to Caplan's room and is interrupted before he can find the Unicorn. But Caplan's spooked. Now he needs to move the Unicorn. So, he takes off, and heads for the Convention Center. Dragoniis is watching and follows. But this guy has a real aversion to being on surveillance video."

"No one's ever captured an image of him," explains Decker.

"And he's not about to let that happen now," I continue. "Not even for the Unicorn. He doesn't have time to work a hack coming in from the web, so he's got to go with a different play. The security office is deep inside the building. Using the antenna to boost his signal, Dragoniis can connect directly to the Wi-Fi chips in the security office computers, find an exploit in the firmware, and he's in."

"But why?" asks Griffon. "Everyone seems to be in and out of that place like a McDonald's, all without being on camera. Why go to the effort?"

"He doesn't know that," says Dana. "The blind spot path is local knowledge. It's one of those things that's only ever passed on by word of mouth. He wouldn't be able to find that online."

"Once he's in, he creates the loop I saw. That's why the loop is flawed, he was in a rush," says Decker.

"He thought the Fukushima Unicorn was just inside those walls, and couldn't take the time for a perfect hack. Though for a rush job, it was *almost* perfect."

Dragoniis has incredible technical knowledge, but the thing I admire the most is how he's prepared to improvise. We called it "planned spontaneity" in the Valley. You provide the tools to be creative and then you just let things happen. He went to Caplan's hotel to search it, and when things went sideways, he adapted and went with the flow.

"Did he kill Caplan?" Griffon asks.

Decker makes an expression like a kid at Christmas. If Dragoniis killed an American on U.S. soil, Decker will own him. He either works for the U.S., or he goes to prison for the rest of his life. I almost hate bursting his bubble.

"He couldn't have," I say. Decker casts me a dark glare. "Farber admits he heard the fight and ran out after. The gamers corroborate his story, because they heard it, too. That's when Farber saw Dragoniis arrive, well after the fight and the murder."

"Okay, if Farber's out, and Dragoniis is out, then who's left?" Dana asks, counting them off on her fingers.

"Golovchenko?" asks Griffon. "What if the newspaper guy followed them?"

"If his guys had the Unicorn, they wouldn't have gone after the case," I say.

"And shot two people," adds Dana, rubbing her rib cage. "No, he definitely thought the Unicorn was in that case."

"So maybe this Hicks guy then?" Griffon offers.

"I don't think so."

"Why not?" barks Decker. "Isn't that why you've got Nassar out there looking at him?"

"Same as Golovchenko. He's still here, and the only reason he'd still be here is because he's still looking for the Unicorn."

According to Bradley, there are four bidders and we've only figured out three possibilities: the Russians, Hicks, and Dragoniis. That leaves the fourth bidder a complete mystery. Before I can remind Decker of that, he hits me with more questions.

"So, it was Dragoniis," says Decker. "Where did he go? And where is he now?"

"After the hack, he went inside to find Caplan dead and the Unicorn gone. I don't know where he is now, but he took one important thing with him."

"What's that?" Decker asks.

"Caplan's phone," Dana answers, snapping her fingers. "It was never recovered at the crime scene, but Caplan's index finger was wiped clean."

"We know he had one, because that's how we tracked him out of the hotel." I nod. "Either his killer took it, or Dragoniis did. My money's on Dragoniis. The phone doesn't have much value to the killer, but it does to him."

"It does?" asks Griffon.

"He'd hack it, and maybe find a clue to where the Unicorn could be," says Decker, running a hand over his head.

"And use it to get my attention," I say, settling back into the chair.

"Come again?" says Decker.

It takes only a couple of minutes to fill everyone in on the message I got right before the shooting.

"He turned it on, used it to send a message, and then shut it down again?" asks Griffon. "If he's spoofing, why not use his own phone, or a burner phone? Why Caplan's?"

"Because he knew we'd be watching that number at the network level, and we'd know it was Caplan's," I say. "He wanted us to know the Russians weren't running the table."

"Why?" asks Dana.

"He's a hacker, he's got an ego," I answer with a frown.

"You're just telling me about this now?" Decker says with a hand on his forehead.

"It wouldn't have changed anything, and I didn't know who had it. Now I do."

"And now it's gone," says Decker.

"It's not transmitting."

"You mean it's off?" asks Griffon.

"Could be," I answer. "Or Dragoniis has it in a Faraday bag."

"A what?" asks Dana.

"Faraday bag," says Decker, stopping his pacing to run a hand over his head. "A clear bag with fine threads of metal woven into the plastic. We used them in Afghanistan. Whenever we caught a possible terrorist actor, we put their phone into the bag right away to preserve usable intelligence. If a signal couldn't get through, their command structure couldn't wipe it remotely, or track our unit's position. But we could still access the touch screen through the plastic."

"How did he get your number?" asks Griffon. "You said he texted you. How did he get your contact info?"

"It's on his business cards," says Decker with a shrug. "It's out there, and Dragoniis found it."

"But he texted your personal phone," says Dana, "not your Bureau phone. I noticed you have two."

Decker's eyebrows rise. He hadn't noticed. If that's bothering him, this next part is really going to bake his noodle.

"He grabbed it from close contact with me."

"Say what?" asks Decker. His tone low and threatening. "You've been in contact?"

"Almost, but not quite." I wobble my hand in front of me. "Your phone sends out signals to the carrier all the time. Walk by someone, or ride by someone, and you can pick it up."

"Holy shit, the motorcycle," says Dana.

"Mother fucker!" shouts Decker, jumping to his feet.

Griffon, looking alarmed, says, "Can someone fill me in?"

"When we walked to the Convention Center from the hotel yesterday, I almost got run down by a guy on a motorcycle," I explain. "Red and white bike, just like Farber described. He definitely passed close enough to scan my phones."

Decker kicks the trash can at the front of the room so hard, detectives outside the glass walls stand up and look over at the conference room.

"I've been after this guy for years," moans Decker, putting both hands on top of his head. "And he was *right there*."

"It's not all bad news, Decker," I say reassuringly. It's not hard to feel sorry for him, being close to something that means so much to you. "He's still here bidding, and he doesn't have the Unicorn."

My phone rings the distinctive pattern for Bradley. A voice call? There's only one reason for voice. Something's gone wrong.

CHAPTER TWENTY-SEVEN

"Bradley, you're on speaker," I warn him. I've done enough repeating today.

"Will, something just came in to Caplan's Dark Net account," he says. His voice is wavering. He's upset. Even though he's not here in the field, I know he's feeling the pressure too. "It's instructions on the ransom drop. They want the Fukushima Unicorn in a radioactive safe container, delivered to the main hall of the Comic Con at two o'clock *today*."

"What about Amanda?" I ask.

"It says they'll release her once they have the Unicorn. They say she's perfectly fine but she's scared and wants to go home."

"Do you think they're onto us?" asks Decker, a hand under his chin.

"No. They think they're still talking to Caplan," says Griffon. "It's in the tone. They said she's scared and wants to go home. Those words are meant for a dad. I know I'd lose my mind if that was my daughter. I'd do whatever they said. Well, until I had her back safe and sound, then I'd go after the bastards."

"How are we going to do a drop at two o'clock?" asks Dana. "We've got nothing to trade."

"Can we trace them back through the Dark Net?" Decker asks.

"Definitely not in a few hours," I reply.

"But they figured out who Caplan is," says Dana. "They must have. If they didn't know who he was, how would they know to grab his daughter? Can't we just do what they did?"

"Caplan made mistakes that allowed them to find him. He was an amateur," I say, waving my hand back and forth, "but the people bidding on the Fukushima Unicorn won't be."

"What if we round up the Russians?" Decker asks. "Put the heat on all of them. At least we'd rule them out."

"Forget the Russians," says Griffon with a sigh. "I'm telling you it's a dead end. Whether they took her or not, they'd never talk."

"Who else has the muscle to do this, if not the Russians?" Decker asks.

"I can answer that," says Bradley over the phone. "But you're not going to like it."

"What else is new?" Decker mutters, pushing his knuckles down on the table in frustration. That must be uncomfortable.

"I found more activity for DarkRiderX on the Dark Net. They were on a message board looking to hire freelance PMCs."

"Oh fuck," says Decker.

"What's a PMC?" asks Dana.

"Private Military Contractors," I say flopping back in my seat. "Mercenaries."

"Who would be hiring mercenaries?" she asks.

"Not Golovchenko," says Griffon. "He'd only trust his own men. What about Dragoniis?"

"Possibly," says Decker. "But if he's here for the Chinese, I would think they'd have people for him to use."

"So, we know this bidder hired professional kidnappers, and we still don't know who they are?" says Dana.

"Basically, yes," says Bradley with a gulp.

"That's just awesome." Dana puts her head in one hand and pulls at her hair with the other.

"Then, we fake it. Take the empty case, and draw them out," says Decker.

Totally a good idea. It didn't work out well the first time. But it could, with a few tweaks. Ideas start to cycle through my head.

"Leaving aside, for a second, the fact that Miller and I got shot last time," says Dana, "what happens when they open the case? You don't think they'll want to check what they're getting?"

"We fab up a convincing-looking fake. Will knows what it looks like," says Decker.

"It's supposed to be radioactive," she says.

"We'll get something radioactive from the hospital," says Decker. "There's got to be something we can use to set off a detector."

"If they came into this thing prepared to drop $10 million on this deal, they've done their homework." Feeling stiff again, I stand up for more stretching. "They'll know exactly how hot a legitimate Fukushima artifact should be. We can't fake that. Not with the time we have. If we try and we blow it, Amanda dies."

"Stop that," says Decker, glaring at me.

"Stop what?"

"You're doing yoga or something."

"It's stretching." I shift into a deep lunge.

"We stall," says Griffon. "We respond and tell them we need more time."

"For what?" asks Decker. "I say we go now. Full tactical. Take them down. Then we can have a dialogue about where they're keeping Amanda."

"Hold on, in a crowded convention center?" Dana asks loudly, leaning forward and putting her arms on the table. "No way. Chief Wilmont will never allow it. *I* won't allow it. You're talking about fucking mercenaries. We go tactical and fuck it up, she dies. Not to mention the risk to thousands of civilians. We don't have any control over the circumstances."

Despite the ruckus between Decker and Dana, details of a workable plan are coalescing in my head. But I'm missing something. I need more. "Bradley, the auction end date was supposed to be Sunday, right?"

"Yeah, Boss, according to Caplan's private messages, Sunday at noon."

"Who's got a panel on Sunday?"

"You mean guests?" asks Bradley. The sound of typing comes from the phone as he pulls up the website. "Well, for one, your friend Jerry Oldham."

"I'm a fan. I wouldn't say he's my friend."

"Haven't checked your Twitter feed lately, have you, Boss?"

"Been busy, Bradley."

Jerry Oldham is an actor on *The Double Limit*, my favorite show about a time-traveling detective. Pulling out my phone now, I open Twitter.

"It seems Jerry's a fan of you too, Boss," continues Bradley. "He tagged you in a picture at the Comic Con."

I see it now on my feed.

Just rolled into #ComicCFRS and saw @Truewillparker! #awesome #techceo

The image shows me walking through the Con. He caught me just as I was going back into the vendor hall. Dana's behind me, but blurry. It must have been last night when we went back for the Wasteout 3 kids.

The vague idea rolling around in my head snaps into sharp focus. So far, the kidnappers are calling the shots, tilting the field in their favor. If my idea works out, it would make us even again.

"What time's his panel on Sunday?" I ask.

"One o'clock," says Bradley.

"Like Griffon said, we delay. We tell the kidnappers the Unicorn is out of town and our associate is bringing it in on Sunday. The earliest we can do is tomorrow morning, right at the opening of the Con. Then we set a trap."

"At the Con? I'm telling you, Wilmont will never go for that," says Dana.

"Once he hears my plan, he will."

CHAPTER TWENTY-EIGHT

A couple of hours later, the conference room is devoid of sound and full of tension. The initial thrill of having a plan is gone. We're in the midst of the repetitive planning process, Decker walking us through it over and over until we've memorized every detail. Feeling like we're starting to drive events, rather than just react to them, makes it bearable. The plan doesn't solve everything, but buys us time.

The response is almost ready to go back. The kidnappers need to believe their best chance of getting the Unicorn is following through with Caplan and making the meet first thing in the morning. We've carefully crafted every word to sound as much like Caplan as we can, based on his previous messages. Desperate, but not so much so that he's unstable. They need to believe "Caplan" can deliver.

"It's done," says Bradley, coming back on the line. "We've got all the pieces. The Unicorn will be here Sunday morning as scheduled. Meeting at the Comic Con is fine. Please don't hurt Amanda. Details of the exchange when the show opens at eight. Once more, please don't hurt Amanda."

Seeing nods from everyone around the table, I tell Bradley to hit SEND.

"Done, Boss."

There's no turning back now. Whichever bidder kidnapped Amanda Caplan is going to arrive at the Comic Con tomorrow at eight in the morning, whether we're ready or not.

I'm spared yet another walkthrough with Decker when Nassar returns with information on Hicks.

"He was highly visible at the hotel. All night," she says, opening the notes on her phone. "He had a team-builder with Pyntel staff in the hotel restaurant, then turned to the bar to keep the party going on his own, when the rest of the team left. Darryl Parr, the bartender, remembers him clearly."

"He just sat there? Alone?" asks Decker.

"Oh no. Not at all," snickers Nassar. "Which is why Darryl remembered him. He had female company. Took some persuading, but eventually Darryl admitted that he knew her. Top-dollar escort. Frequently seen in the hotels. Anyway, he says they were there until closing."

"Then what?" asks Decker.

"What do you think?" I ask Decker, making a gesture with my fingers. "On to the main event."

It takes Decker a second but his eyes widen and he shakes his head. "We'll need to confirm when she left."

"Already did," says Nassar. "I got her on the phone."

"Awesome," Griffon chuckles.

"How did you manage that?" I ask. "Normally escorts don't answer anonymous numbers, and all Bureau phones are blocked."

"Simple," says Nassar. "I borrowed Darryl's phone, and she answered right away."

"Well played," says Dana. "If she's working the hotels, she's got to have the bartenders onboard. They probably get referral fees. Either way, it takes this Hicks out of the equation."

"Did you keep her number? Can I have it?" I ask.

Decker rolls his eyes at me.

"For the investigation," I add, rolling my eyes in return as Nassar sends the number.

Nassar goes on to tell us by the time she finished interviewing Darryl, Griffon had the sneak and peak warrant back. Hotel security let her into Hicks' room, but there was nothing out of the ordinary. All she found was a normal hotel suite filled with the normal stuff of a business traveler. Definitely no Fukushima Unicorn, and no young woman bound to a chair.

We'll never find Amanda this way. If DarkRiderX managed to contract a private military company, they're already at arm's length from people that know how to cover their tracks. The only hard clue to work with is the ransom picture. I've cashed in two mighty big chips with Rick and Kumar chasing down that lead, but if it leads us to Amanda Caplan in time, it'll be worth it. Once we've saved her life, we can focus on the rest.

Like the guy who bludgeoned Roger Caplan to death, currently still on the loose. Or capturing Dragoniis, so Decker can turn him. And last, but not least, there's finding the Fukushima Unicorn while not letting it fall into government hands.

When we break to eat, I feel an overwhelming desire to get out of the room. I keep going right out of the building to the hot, but fresh, air outside. Grudgingly admitting to myself that I'm hungry, I stop at a convenience store down the street. There, I find another energy drink and a pair of Clif Bars to solve the problem. I'm just tapping my watch to the pay terminal when Dana walks in the door.

"I had a hunch I'd find you here," she says.

"I can't drink another cup of what you guys call coffee," I say, attempting a smile.

"So instead of our watered-down java you come here for a tall boy of heart-attack-in-a-can? Sounds reasonable," she says dryly. "I'll join you."

She picks out a can of energy drink and a Clif Bar. With no hesitation picking her flavors, she's clearly no stranger to either product.

Leaving the store, she leads me down the street to a small plaza with a fountain. It's a quiet, pleasant place between office buildings. Benches sheltered from the glare of the sun underneath the trees planted throughout the space. Dana picks an empty one.

"I'm a little concerned," she says, peeling the wrapper of her Clif Bar. Chocolate Chip. "The plan seems to have some holes in it."

"Such as?"

"What if we don't find Amanda first?"

"We will," I say, tearing open my own bar. Peanut Butter.

"Assume we don't. What happens then?"

Hidden behind her reflective aviators, her expression is hard to read. I hold my gaze level with my reflection in her lenses. "Then we have to make the trade."

"For the Fukushima Unicorn."

"Right."

"Which we don't have. You see where I'm going here."

"I do," I say before taking a bite of the bar and looking away at the fountain. It seems to be nothing but offices around here, but there's a long parade of children being led through the plaza and around the water. They're tethered together with a bright green, curly plastic cord. Protected.

"This doesn't concern you?"

"Of course it concerns me."

"Then what do we do about it?"

"Before the exchange goes down, we find Amanda or we find the Fukushima Unicorn."

"Right," she says, tucking a strand of hair that's come loose from her ponytail behind her ear. "And if it's the Unicorn we find, you'd be willing to turn it over?"

When I don't answer, she continues. "If we can't produce the Unicorn, they're not going to just let her go. She's the only person who can identify them."

"I know."

"Will, they're going to kill her."

My phone buzzes. Standard message pattern.

Rick W: Data ready.

Me: Super. Can you send?

Rick W: I can send a link.

Rick W: Warrant?

Me: Just a sec.

My fingers tremble as I dial Griffon's mobile. There's no time to wait for him to read a text and peck out a response. Talking will be faster. It can't happen soon enough.

"Need that warrant," I say when Griffon answers.

"It just came through," he says. "I'll send you the electronic copy."

Dana sits silently watching me and finishing her Clif Bar, exercising that miraculous patience. I have none. Every nerve is raw. One of the children tethered to the green cord squeals in delight. I jump, my hand shakes, and I almost drop my phone.

When Griffon's message comes in, the phone's barely stopped vibrating when I copy the attachment and send it to Rick.

Me: Warrant attached.

Me: *attached file*

I start counting seconds. I get to a hundred. Is he actually reading it? What's taking so long? When I can't stand it anymore, I text him again.

Me: We good? I can send someone to serve in person if you need it.

Rick W: What, paper? No. Just looking it over.

Me: You don't trust me?

Rick W: Really?

Me: Fine. Never mind.

Me: Done reading yet?

Rick W: *link attached*

Jabbing my finger at the link opens a spreadsheet with the data I requested. A list of IP addresses in the city that hit Google's main search page, using a Firefox browser, on a Mac, during the minute the ransom photo was taken. It's exactly what I asked for. But that's where the good news ends.

"We get anything?" asks Dana.

"A lot," I say, forwarding the link to Bradley. "Too much."

"How much is too much?" Dana asks, crumpling the empty energy drink can in her hand.

Looking up to see her staring at me, the excitement I felt moments ago when I heard from Rick is already souring into bitter disappointment. I'd hoped the list would be short enough to work without cross-referencing against Kumar's data.

"About a hundred possible locations." My stomach clenches around that Clif Bar.

"There's no way we can hit that many by morning. Not safely," Dana says. "We could canvass that many addresses, but if someone just shows up at the door with a badge, she's as good as dead. We don't have the resources to even watch that many locations."

"That's why we have to narrow the list."

"And how do we do that?"

Already, I've wrestled my initial disappointment into submission. Did I really think we'd land it on the first data set? If we had, I could have kept Kumar out of it, but Rick's list is just too long. When Dana crosses her arms, I sense her commitment to my plan slipping away. She needs to know the rest.

Finishing the last of my energy drink, I crush the can just as she did.

"Simple," I say. "Porn."

CHAPTER TWENTY-NINE

Me: Need a favor.

Kumar P: What's up?

Me: Looking for someone.

Kumar P: Try Tinder?

Me: Kink.

Kumar P: Ah, gotcha! You've come to the right place. :-) :-) :-)

Me: Got time, location, IPs. Cross-reference?

Kumar P: We don't sell user info. :-(

Me: You collect it though.

My phone rings in my hand. It's Kumar.

"I'm not putting that in writing. Are you crazy, bro?"

Kumar Patel is a pornographer. He's got the number one fetish site in the U.S., producing their own content as well as collecting it from around the web. A few years back, he landed in the news for the URL of one of his websites. It was "kpop-" something or other, similar to a site for Korean Pop music and videos, popular with teenagers. Though Kumar insisted the "k" stood for kink, and agreed to change the name of the site, it wasn't until after he'd made news around the world, getting the kind of advertising that money can't buy.

I first met him years ago at this outrageous party in the Valley. The hosts had assembled giant tents next to their mansion, all lined with rich carpets and fabrics like the sultans of old. They'd hired gorgeous young models, male and female, to walk around in genie costumes serving food. Kumar supplied the models.

"Crazy?" I laugh. "For thinking you track your clients' online behavior? Everybody tracks everybody online. That's why the internet is free, Kumar. If you don't pay for the product, you *are* the product."

"Yeah, but people don't think about that. You got to keep the illusion alive, man. People like to think they're private in their pastime." Sarcasm seeps into his words like rain through an open sunroof.

"Sure, especially your clients."

"Not everyone is ready to come clean about their kink, and I don't judge," says Kumar. "I mean, you should see some of the shit going on these days."

"Still a lot of bondage traffic?"

"The classics," Kumar says, "they never go out of style."

"I've got a ball-gag—"

"Good for you, you little subbie," Kumar interrupts. "Black and chrome, or did you go with a splash of color?"

"Not me."

"Oh right, for a friend, I get you," says Kumar. "I'm winking right now."

"It's for a case. Someone's in danger."

"Sorry, Will, tell me what you need." Kumar's demeanor changes immediately. He's a businessman at heart, not a pervert, and if the FBI's calling about someone in danger with a connection to kink, then it could be bad for business. Plus, he's not a bad guy. He's diligent about weeding out anything on his site that may be the product of human trafficking or exploitation. He's cleanly dirty.

Running down the situation with Amanda Caplan, I leave out anything to do with the Fukushima Unicorn, or my conversation with Rick Downie at Google. I describe the enhanced image in detail, including the ball-gag and bondage cuffs used to restrain Amanda. The photos are clear enough to tell they're quality items, not novelties. Which means they belong to someone. Someone with a fetish. Someone who's likely visited Kumar's site.

"Jesus, man, that's awful," says Kumar. "You know that's not what BDSM play is about, right? It's consensual. Kidnapping, coercion, that's not part of it. When this goes public, there'll be a backlash against the industry."

"Help me out, and I'll do what I can to leave those details out of the public eye," I assure him.

It only takes me a couple of minutes to explain what I need. Being able to cross-reference what I get from Kumar with what Rick provided me should tell me where Amanda Caplan is being held, or at least narrow it down.

"Sure, of course, Will, you got it."

"Thanks, Kumar. If this works, you'll literally be a lifesaver."

"My momma would be so proud," he says with a melodramatic sniff. "Just one more thing."

Dammit. Not this again.

"Yeah?" I ask.

"We should think about how you come by this information."

"What do you mean?"

"I wasn't kidding about our clients. They don't want to think that Papa FBI's looking through our records. People should be able to engage in their fantasies without worrying that the Feds are watching. It's healthy."

Healthy for Kumar's bottom line anyway. But he does have a point.

"I take it you have a suggestion?"

"I've got a guy who's leaving the team. He's a good guy, but he's moving across the country with his fiancée. Anyone asks, we say a former employee released it by accident. And we don't say what kind of data."

"Until it goes to court. This is evidence. Someone may have to testify."

"By the time that happens, we can say we've 'changed our practices' around data collection."

"I see where you're going." I nod. "We can do that."

The sound of a woman moaning in the background reaches the phone.

"A little early, isn't it?" I ask, looking at the time on my watch.

"This is Vegas, baby. Never too early in Vegas," says Kumar.

CHAPTER THIRTY

"What are you smiling about?" Decker demands when we walk back into the conference room.

Griffon and Nassar are still huddled with him around the conference table. The remains of cafeteria sandwiches and salads are scattered among the laptops and papers. A map of the Convention Center hangs from the whiteboard. Griffon's tie is loosened and Nassar's blazer is tossed over the back of her chair, but Decker's still as buttoned up as ever, jacket and tie firmly in place.

"He's got a porn plan," says Dana. "It's actually pretty good."

Griffon coughs on part of a mouthful of sandwich. Nassar puts down a plastic fork, her eyes wide with the ghost of a smile at the corners of her mouth.

"Not you too," Decker says to Dana, frowning and shaking his head in dismay. "You're starting to sound like him. You don't make any sense. What the fuck is a porn plan?"

"He told me about it on the way back," she says. "It's all about the ransom image."

"The ball-gag?" asks Griffon.

"The ball what?" says Decker, dropping his fists on the table. "Would someone around here please start speaking English?"

"In the photo, Amanda has a ball-gag in her mouth to keep her from making any noise," says Dana. "Clean, safe, and effective. No chemicals or fibers to cause coughing or choking."

"How do you know that?" says Decker.

"That's what they're designed for," says Nassar, as if explaining why water is wet. "A common item for sexual domination sessions. But why is it important, Will? You think we'll be able to track the purchase?"

Decker looks at Nassar with wide eyes, and before he can put his foot in his mouth, I answer. "No. The kidnapper's a Unicorn bidder, which means they came from out of town. A ball-gag is common for BDSM, but generally speaking, a pretty specialized piece of kit. You have to get it from a sex shop. Which isn't something you do if you're planning a kidnapping. Too few customers and too easy to be remembered. There are plenty of more ordinary items that could do the job. All easier to come by."

"They brought it with them," says Griffon.

"Give the man a star," I say, pointing at him.

"They planned the kidnapping?" Decker asks.

"I don't think so," I say, sitting down at the table. "Working human trafficking cases, I've seen a lot of restraints. They never use a ball-gag, even when it's sexual slavery. It's almost always what they have easiest access to. Then there are her wrists."

"Leather cuffs," says Griffon.

"Good memory. Well done, Peter."

Griffon seems really familiar with this stuff.

"Will said people use whatever they have easiest access to, suggesting the kidnapper had it with them anyway," says Dana. "And if the kidnapper is into BDSM so much that they travel with their gear, then chances are . . ."

"They're visiting kink porn sites," finishes Nassar. "Genius."

"Thank you," I say, sending her a nod and a smile.

"So, they're going to kinky porn sites, so what? A lot of people go to them," says Decker, adding under his breath, "including everyone in this room but me."

"You're right," I say, watching him look like he smelled something sour. "We needed to narrow it down. Fortunately, we've got four factors to cross-reference."

Pulling the map of the Convention Center off the whiteboard, I pick up a marker and draw a large circle. Somewhere behind me Decker says something about using the map.

"These are the people that use Google," I say, pointing to the circle.

"So pretty much everyone," says Griffon with no small amount of sarcasm.

"And Firefox," I add, drawing a smaller circle inside the first.

Griffon leans forward.

"Who were using computers within a hundred miles of here." I draw an even smaller circle inside the second one.

"That are Macs," I say, drawing a fourth circle inside the third.

Decker cocks his head as understanding dawns on him.

"And who visit bondage porn sites," I add, scribbling a tiny speck at the center.

Nassar claps her hands. "Nice."

"Now we have a very short list," I finish, laying down the marker.

"How short?" asks Decker. Typical. Never takes the time to admire the brilliance.

"I don't know," I say with a shrug.

"I sent you the Google ECPA warrant," says Griffon. "Didn't you get anything back?"

"From Google, yes, but they can only give us the first four circles."

"How do we trace this back to a physical location?" Decker asks.

"Google sent us a list of IP addresses. Bradley can translate them into physical addresses. That info's easy to come by," I say.

"What if this person was surfing anonymously?" Nassar asks. "What if they had the privacy mode on?"

"We would have seen that in the image. But even if we did, that just hides the browsing history on the computer. Google still needs to know where to send the packets."

"They track every single IP that hits their page?" asks Griffon. "That has to be billions of times a day."

"At least. And, of course, they do, that's why it took hours for them to parse it down." I hold up my phone. "Here it is. Just over a hundred people in the local area that used Firefox for Mac to hit Google search in that minute."

"There has to be millions of porn sites," says Griffon. "How do we cross-reference?"

"Just like the gear, this is specialized porn," says Nassar. "The majority of the individual kink sites are owned or hosted by only a few people."

"Mostly one," I correct her. "A company run by a guy named Kumar Patel."

"Who just happens to be a friend of our own Will Parker," finishes Dana holding her hands up in the air.

"Of course, he is," says Decker.

"The thing is, we don't know *when* they would have hit the site. It certainly wasn't when they were taking ransom photos. If we assume they're here for the Comic Con, that gives us a window of the last forty-eight hours."

"That's also going to be a big list," says Griffon.

"When do we get the data from this Kumar guy?" Decker asks.

"Whenever he sends it to us."

"Let's speed that up," Decker says, smacking his fist into his open palm. "Griffon, can we get another warrant? If we turn up the pressure—"

"Hold on," I interrupt, waving my hand in warning. "Kumar's doing this as a favor. An underling who's already leaving the company is going to send it, as soon as it's ready."

"All right," says Decker after a long pause. "Then we're going to have to add to the plan. I have some ideas."

*　　*　　*

With all the cards now on the table, the planning process continues into the night. Along the way there are several reviews and go/no-go decisions with Burke and Chief Wilmont. We go over the meet at the Comic Con. We connect with the local SWAT team and review tactical entry procedures. We go over the security plans for the Convention Center. And then we do it again. And again.

The good news, coming late in the day, is that Miller is out of the ICU. There's a long road of recovery ahead, but he's going to make it. Everyone's relieved to hear it and, on the heels of a workable plan to get Amanda Caplan back safely, everyone seems just a little more optimistic.

Repetition isn't my thing. It's unnecessary for my retention of information. As the day goes on, it wears on me, to the point I'm just about to start banging my head on the table or walk out the door when I'm saved by a familiar vibration from my phone.

Ace P: At the hotel.

Me: Good.

Ace P: Next?

Me: Wait for my signal.

Ace P: What, are you Batman now? Reclusive almost billionaire . . .

Me: Did you bring security?

Ace P: Of course.

Like most Silicon Valley CEOs, Ace has around-the-clock armed bodyguards. When you become a public figure, an alarming number of angry, dangerous whack-jobs come out of the woodwork. I had more than my fair share, before I dropped out of the public eye.

The others have momentarily left the room, leaving me alone with Dana. She's looking over the blueprints for the Convention Center. While she may not celebrate it like Decker, she also seems to appreciate repetition. This must be the tenth time she's reviewed them. I sit down next to her.

"I'm impressed that you managed to convince Chief Wilmont," I say, cracking open a bottle of water left over from lunch. "For a while there, I didn't think we'd be able to persuade him to take the risk on a public venue."

"He has a daughter," she tells me. "She's a little older than Amanda, around twenty, I think? But close enough I knew there'd be an emotional connection."

"You didn't mention that when we were talking to him."

"Some things are best left unsaid." She picks up her own bottle of warm grocery water and licks her lips. Locking her eyes on mine, she says, "Sometimes you just have to trust that the connection is there."

Wait. Is she still talking about the Chief of Police? Before I can come up with an answer, she turns away and changes the topic, asking me if I really think we can keep people from getting hurt.

"We should be able to," I tell her, thinking it over yet again. "The biggest danger comes from stray bullets. But, if the uniforms do their screening properly, including staff, the chance of a gun making it in is low."

We're using Jerry Oldham. Reaching out on a Twitter direct message, I told him we may need his help and to be ready in the morning. His response was immediate and enthusiastic. I saved the details of what we need him to do for tomorrow, because actors love to talk about their upcoming roles. Not knowing who the bidders are, we can't risk word of our operation getting out.

"What if the kidnapper takes another hostage?" Dana asks.

This worries me, too. If we don't do this right, we may end up trading Amanda Caplan for another victim. There'll be no shortage of innocent people to grab.

"Separating the bidder from the crowds reduces the chance of that happening. There's not much more we can do."

In the ransom response, I said our assistant would be wearing a red fez. Decker immediately lost his mind, demanding to know where we'd possibly find something so unique. He worried for nothing, of course. We're at a fan convention. *Doctor Who*, one of the biggest sci-fi shows on British television, made that style of hat iconic. Easy enough to find at one of the vendors. But it's also been years since Matt Smith was on the show, so the chance of a fan cosplaying him is low.

Jerry's scheduled to sign autographs first thing in the morning. Fans pay $20 to $100 per signature, but it isn't just the scribbled note on the photo that makes it worth it. They crave the precious time they get to spend one-on-one with their favorite celebrity. For a few seconds or even minutes, it's just them and the star, separated from the crowds. Exactly what we need the bidder to be. Thus, while Jerry signs autograph after autograph, perched on his head will be a brand-new, bright red fez. When the bidder approaches for the Unicorn, the closest people, aside from Jerry and his handler, will be Dana and I, behind the curtain, ready for the takedown.

"Are you sure this Oldham guy is okay with this?"

"Why wouldn't he be?" I answer.

The fact that he'll be facing off with a dangerous kidnapper, possibly also a killer, is something else I saved for tomorrow. No sense in him getting worked up about it. Before I can explain that to Dana, my phone vibrates again. A distinctive pattern. One I've been waiting for. My heart leaps so hard it feels like I'm going to choke on it.

(In Japanese)

Han: Level 42 complete!

Han: Thank you, Parker-san.

Han: Here's what you are looking for.

Han: *images attached*

Me: Many thanks.

Han: Good luck!

Without delay, I flip through the pictures Han attached. A member of Japanese intelligence, he's a pro, and knew exactly what I needed. Excitement of the kind I haven't felt since the Fukushima deal was about to close, awakens inside me. I'm on the edge of something huge. A turning point in history. I force myself to look again, to be absolutely sure. There's still no doubt in my mind.

The first photo confirms that the Fukushima Unicorn passed through Narita International Airport in Tokyo. The second photo confirms that it was Roger Caplan who had it with him. The third photo tells me exactly where it is now.

It also tells me someone has been lying.

CHAPTER THIRTY-ONE

Me: Convention Center.

Me: Comic Con. Door 4.

Me: Tell them you're with me.

Me: Bring $ and security.

Me: Go now.

Ace P: OK.

I'm halfway out the door, slipping my phone back in my pocket when Dana stops me.

"Where are you going?" she asks.

To get the Unicorn. Which is in the hands of a killer. I look back over my shoulder at where she's sitting at the conference table, blazer over a chair, hair pulled back out of the way for a clear view of her suspicious frown.

Dana's not a federal agent. She can't make the Unicorn disappear into a government cyber arsenal. But she *is* a homicide detective, with experience arresting murderers.

"Give me a lift and I'll tell you," I offer.

Her eyes narrow even further. After a moment, she shrugs, releasing the frown and grabbing the blazer from the chair. "Let's go."

We arrive at the Convention Center with only a few minutes until closing. People stream out of the brightly lit building, hundreds more still visible inside. But there's only one that matters to me right now, and I spot him standing by the escalators.

Ace Prior cuts a tall, slim figure in a crisp, white oxford, tucked into a pair of well-worn Levi's. The first impression that leaps to mind is "unobtrusive." Even his glasses are rimless so that nothing stands out about him. But imagining he's unremarkable is a mistake. Beneath the bland outward appearance, Ace has one of the sharpest minds I know. Which he needed, to take over from me. Three big, squat guys in jeans with rumpled navy-blue blazers surround him. His security detail.

While Dana stops to talk to the uniformed officers at the doors, I seize the opportunity for a moment alone with Ace. Ignoring my outstretched hand, he pulls me into a warm hug. On some level this is worse. That he's still my friend, despite leaving him in the lurch, salts me with guilt. And yet, mostly, I'm just happy to see my friend again.

It doesn't take long for me to lay out what I need him to do. Ace listens alertly, nodding his understanding at each key point. For a moment it feels like old times, back in the Valley, making magic happen.

But there's no time for nostalgia, and Ace disappears quickly into the vendor hall along with his guards while I wait for Dana.

"All right, what are we here for?" she asks, catching up with me at the escalators.

I hand her my phone, open to the first photo from Han.

"What am I looking at?"

"Still frames from security footage at Narita International Airport. Two weeks ago."

She zooms in on the image. "That's Roger Caplan," she says.

"It is. The others? What do you see?"

She swipes to the next photo. "This looks like an X-ray scan of luggage, but what's that big black square in the center? Is it redacted? Where did you get this?" She turns the phone sideways and back again, trying to orient herself to the image.

"Big Fish Pyramid."

"The video game? The one you talked to Ashley Brewster about?"

"The very same." I nod, leading the way to the vendor hall. "I have a contact in Japan with access to video footage from Narita. But he's a quirky guy. To get these shots, I had to tell him how to beat Big Fish Pyramid."

"Which Ashley showed you last night."

"Right."

"Why look at Narita?"

"Caplan drained his account two weeks ago, before getting on a plane for Tokyo and coming back a week later. The timing coincides with his annual collectibles buying trip, but he never took that kind of cash before."

"You think he took it to Japan to buy the Fukushima Unicorn?" she says, raising an eyebrow.

"I don't think, I know. Once he had it, he needed to bring it back."

"You think he took it in carry-on?" She taps the phone screen. "Here, behind the redacting?"

"It's not redacted. The X-rays are blocked."

"By what?"

"The kind of material you need to surround something radioactive, like a quantum computer from Fukushima."

"There's no way they'd let this through screening without looking in it. They would have found the Unicorn."

Silently, I swipe the phone to the final picture.

Dana gasps softly. "No shit," she says. "But that's not Caplan's."

"It was, then he sold it."

"Oh my God, that means—" I cut her off with a hand on her arm as we turn onto Row K.

Halfway down the long aisle is Spider Webb's booth, surrounded by a dozen other vendors of collectibles, comics, and fan art. Pulling Dana into a booth filled with playful water colors of well-known genre characters, I lean over to tell her we need to blend in.

"Fine, we're just another couple browsing for art," she says, taking my arm. "But do you mind telling me why?"

Peering through the racks of paintings, I can make out Webb waddling around his booth, getting ready to close for the night.

"Any second now, a guy with a red nylon bag is going to come up and offer cash for the Han Solo statue," I say, pointing.

"I thought he didn't want to sell it," she says, leaning in close to get a look.

"That's what he said. But being an almost-billionaire has taught me an unpretty truth: everything has its price."

"How do you know what that is?"

"I don't. But I'm betting a million should cover it."

"Did you say a million? As in dollars?" Dana whispers in surprise, turning toward me.

A shiver slides slowly down my spine, goose bumps rising on my arms as her breath hits my neck. The scent of soap and lilac fills my nose again.

"I did," I answer, breathing in deeply. "After they make a deal, and the man walks away with the statue, we move in and arrest Webb."

"For murder?"

"Terrorism."

She squints sideways at me, but before she can say anything, Ace arrives with the red bag slung over his shoulder. His security detail lurks a couple of booths back, keeping an eye on him in rotation.

Beyond his unassuming appearance and natural easygoing nature, Ace has a gift for communication. Which makes him one of the best salesmen I've ever seen. Not only could he convince you to sell the shirt off your back, you'd also gladly throw in your pants for free. Watching Ace negotiate is like watching Picasso paint.

After a brief conversation, Webb laughs. It's a deep and rolling sound that fills the aisle. Shortly after, Ace scratches his head, signaling he's cracked Webb's complete refusal. Now it's a matter of price.

I want to walk over, shove the bag with the million into Webb's hands, and call it done. But if we're too aggressive, he might refuse to sell it at all, until he knows why we want it. We don't have time for that. It's now or never.

As if reading my mind, Dana looks over at Webb, asking, "What if he doesn't sell?"

"We have enough to bring him in. But questioning takes time. It's better if he sells." Better for me, anyway.

My pulse pounds so hard in my ears, I almost miss the woman behind us ask if we want a painting before she closes.

"It's too hard to decide," Dana says apologetically, laying a hand on my arm. "Will just loves your work. We'll be back tomorrow for sure."

"Yes, we will, I promise," I say, putting my hand on top of hers to maintain the illusion. She doesn't move or pull away.

"All right then," says the young tattooed woman, closing up the arms of the display. "I also do commissions, so if there's something you want that you don't see, let me know."

Back at Webb's booth, Ace is shaking his head and backing away. I've seen him do the same thing to close a deal in the Valley. Letting Webb think he's lost the deal cements in his mind that he wants it.

Dana tenses up under my hand. Instinctively, I grip tighter with my own.

The young tattooed woman finishes closing the display of water colors, leaving us exposed. Dana leads us to the next booth over, this one filled with overwhelmingly cute stuffed animals from Japanese arcades.

Under Webb's pleading, Ace has returned, and with the crowds gone, we're close enough to hear the final part of the negotiation. In the end, ten thousand dollars is all it took.

Ace removes a bundle of cash from the bag and hands it over, asking Webb if he wants to count it. But he only wants to fan through the money with his thumb, as if he could tell the difference between ninety-nine and a hundred bills by the breeze on his face. Stacks of cash make people behave in strange ways.

Satisfied with the money, Webb lifts down the statue, producing a bag from under the table that catches my breath in my throat. Printed on the side is the same logo for a video game as the bags under Caplan's tables.

In an impressive display of forearm strength, Webb lifts the statue with one hand and slips it inside the bag before handing it to Ace.

"Go. Now." I say to Dana. "Hard."

We break apart, drawing our weapons and holding them safely at our sides as we close the gap to Webb's booth.

"Gordon Webb, FBI, you're under arrest!" I bellow the words, forcing my voice to stay low and intimidating as I raise my gun.

"Hands in the air where we can see them!" Dana commands from beside me, M&P held out in front of her.

"What? Who? Me?" asks Webb, his left hand pointing at his chest. His right drops below the table. *Oh shit.*

Ace bolts out of the booth, with the statue in a bag, his security detail swooping up to surround him.

"Hands! Now!" says Dana, staying cool while leveling the M&P at Webb's chest.

"Okay, okay," says Webb, his voice wobbling on the edge of panic. Being at the business end of two pistols will do that to a person, and it's exactly how I want him. He manages to get both hands up in the air, empty.

"Gordon Webb, you're under arrest on suspicion of terrorism," I say, reciting his Miranda rights as Dana pulls his hands behind his back and into cuffs.

Webb's eyes widen from beneath his unruly brows. Genuine surprise. Not what he was expecting me to say.

"Terrorism? What? No, you've made a mistake," he says. "I'm not a terrorist."

"Then what's this?" I ask, waving Ace back over with the bag.

Taking a pair of nitrile gloves from my pocket, I make a show of putting them on. Dana keeps a grip on Webb's arm, in case he tries to run. He won't. Not understanding what's happening yet, he still believes he can talk his way out of it. Time to crush that belief.

"A statue. Just a statue," Webb says nodding at it in relief. "Take a look. What did you think it was?"

Sliding the sculpture of Solo out of the bag, I carefully set it on the table. With an app on my phone, I zoom in with the camera like a magnifying glass, examining the surface of the statue.

"Where did you get this?" I ask.

"I bought it," says Webb irritably.

"Where?"

"From a guy."

"What guy?"

Webb hesitates.

"What guy?" I repeat, more forcefully.

"Another vendor."

"Does he have a name?"

Webb is silent again. He doesn't want to say. I don't blame him, because I know why. Standing up straight, I make eye contact face-to-face.

"This is going to go a whole lot better for you if you answer the questions. You say this is a mistake? That this is just a statue? Then help me sort it out. Who sold it to you?"

"Roger Caplan," says Webb. His eyes dart ever so briefly to the floor and back to mine. "But what does that have to do with terrorism? It's *just a statue.*"

"You didn't buy a statue. You bought materials for a bomb. A dirty bomb in fact."

"A what? A dirty . . . no! What are you talking about?" Webb shuffles his substantial weight back and forth. His lips are pressed together in a thin line, but his eyes are red and puffy.

Having called the shot, I have to deliver. With the magnifying glass app, I focus in on the small, rectangular representation of a control panel for the carbonite. It's perched on the side in the perfect position. It has to be here somewhere. I turn on the flashlight and move it in an arc, watching how the beam slides around on the metal. The light catches on a fine vertical scratch beneath the miniature control panel.

I've done it.

With my trembling hand, I gently push down on the control panel. At first nothing happens, but gradually I increase the pressure until it snaps open, revealing a button, which I push.

"Everyone, step back."

"Are you sure that's safe?" Dana asks, taking a sharp step backwards, dragging Webb with her.

"Wait a second. Safe? Dirty? Is that thing *radioactive*?" Webb's bravado vanishes with a squeal as he shuffles around, knocking over delicately stacked merchandise on a chair.

"It's safe enough," I answer, ignoring Webb. "Like getting an X-ray. I'm only going to open it for a few seconds."

Ace slips away from his security, coming over to stand next to me. "Is it really there, Will?" he asks.

"Let's find out," I whisper.

Holding my breath, I lift the top edge, splitting the statue in two like a coffin. Inside is a secret compartment, filled with foam, except for a precisely cut-out space, just like the Pelican case. Unlike the Pelican case, the space is filled.

There, nestled into the center, is a long, rectangular object made from metal, glass, and silicon, bristling with plugs and contacts plated in gold.

The Fukushima Unicorn.

CHAPTER THIRTY-TWO

A relief so deep it reaches my soul washes over me. After eluding me for months in Japan, followed by years of being God only knows where, the Fukushima Unicorn has found its way back to me.

If I can fix this, there's hope the rest isn't out of reach either. Maybe the life I left behind isn't gone forever after all. While nothing can bring Kate Mason back, there's still time to save Amanda Caplan, and maybe that's enough.

Ace claps a hand on my back, but doesn't say anything. He doesn't have to. Looking over at Dana, a frown still creases her brow, but the traces of a smile flicker at the edges of her mouth. Her nod is almost imperceptible, but I read it loud and clear. *Congratulations.*

Conscious of the invisible radiation coming off the Unicorn, I close the statue's lid. Pressing down firmly, I'm rewarded when the button pops out, sealing the lead-lined sarcophagus.

Now, there's only one thing left to do. This one's for Dana.

"Mr. Webb," I say, meeting the roly-poly man's gaze. "This is radioactive material suitable for use in a weapon of mass destruction, namely a dirty bomb."

"What? That? I don't know anything about that. I didn't even know it opened. I thought it was just a statue, I swear!"

He pulls suddenly away from Dana, lurching to break free, but her grip stays firm. Like a trapped animal he's searching frantically for any chance of escape. I'm going to give him one.

"If that's true, then why did you sell a bronze and lead statue for ten thousand dollars? A little high for a statue, don't you think, Detective Lopez?"

"Just about right for bomb materials though, Agent Parker," she says.

"No, no, no!" howls Webb. "It's supposed to be just a statue. That was the deal! That's what I told him I wanted!"

"Told who?"

"Roger Caplan!" says Webb, leaning forward. "There's this sculptor in Japan. Every year he does a new design, and every year Roger brings them back. This year, it's the Solo in carbonite freezing. I told Roger to get me one. I'm a huge fan of the original trilogy."

"How much did you pay for it?"

"Five hundred dollars."

Rolling my eyes and shaking my head, I let him know I don't buy any of it. "You expect me to believe that this thing's worth ten grand, and Caplan just walks away for five hundred?"

"Wait! He didn't just walk away," says Webb.

Got him.

"He didn't?"

"No. He tried to steal it back. *He* tried to screw *me*!"

"I don't buy it," says Dana.

"I can prove it," says Webb. "I have him on camera."

"You said that camera wasn't even connected," Dana says. Of course, she knows that it was, because Farber saw it powered on.

"That was just a misunderstanding. I got the motion alert on my phone, while I was at Karaoke," he says, hanging his head. "That's when I saw Roger stealing the statue. He must have been after what was inside it! He's the terrorist!"

"What did you do about it when you saw him stealing it?" I ask.

Webb doesn't answer. He's confused. Not sure which way is out.

"Is that why you left this Klingon Karaoke thing? To confront him?" Dana asks.

"Yeah. Besides," Webb snorts in disgust, "there was another guy there with the same uniform. I hate that."

That explains the sketchy alibi when Dana asked around. People only remembered seeing that type of Starfleet uniform there all night, but because no one actually talks to each other at these things, they assumed it was one person. I shake my head.

"When you found Caplan, what did he say?" I ask.

"He said he needed to hold onto it a little longer."

"Did you believe him?" Dana asks.

"In the middle of the night? No! He was stealing it. I told him if he wanted to *hold onto* it, then I wanted to *hold onto* my money. But he wouldn't give that back, either. He gave me some story about needing it for his daughter and he'd give it to me later. But I'm no sucker. I'm not going to fall for it. Roger was always looking for an angle. If he got a better offer, he'd take that deal, but hold on to my cash in case it fell through. I told him a deal was a deal and he had to stick to it!"

"And that's when you killed him," says Dana, plainly.

"What? He's dead?" Webb's mouth hangs open, but he's lying, and not very well. Time to wrap this up.

"Let me explain something to you. Just now, you put the statue in a bag that matches the type used by Roger Caplan and handed the whole thing over to my associate."

"So what? Those bags were giveaways a couple of years ago at Super-Con. Anybody could have the same one."

"Anybody could have one that looks like this one, it's true. But it wouldn't be the same." I pick it up with two gloved fingers, looking closely at the logo and pointing. "See the smear right there? That's blood. I'm willing to bet my beach house that when the lab lifts it off, they'll match it to Roger Caplan.

"You fought with Caplan over the statue," I continue, watching Webb turn an alarming shade of deep red. "Not only did he take it back, he found another buyer. One that could have been yours. Leaving you a chump, with no statue, and no cash. So, you killed him."

"It was an accident," says Webb hoarsely. "I just wanted what's mine."

"Accident? It was no accident," Dana says. "You smashed his head in."

"That's not what happened!"

"Then tell me what *did* happen," I say.

"I found him in the bathroom with the statue," says Webb, letting a little whimper slip out, shoulders rolling forward. "We fought about it. He shoved me, I shoved him. Back and forth. He slipped and fell. Cracked his head on the sink. I grabbed the bag and left."

"You left him dead on the floor?"

"No, I swear." Webb looks up, terror in his eyes. "He was up and staggering around when I left. I thought he'd shake it off and I didn't want to be there when he did. I took the statue, and I went home."

"You didn't tell anyone? You didn't say anything?" Dana asks.

Webb drops his eyes to the floor, slumping forward. "No. I figured if it was really bad, the place would be closed down. When everything was open, I thought he must be off getting stitches. Or nursing a bad headache."

Dana and I exchange a look. It never ceases to amaze me the stories people tell themselves. Based on the spatter in the bathroom, Caplan would have been gushing blood like a hose.

And if Farber hadn't been in debt up to his eyeballs with his Israeli investors, maybe the Con would have been shut down, giving Webb time to flee, taking the Unicorn with him.

"Gordon Webb, you're under arrest on suspicion of murder in the death of Roger Caplan," she says.

Though the Convention Center is almost empty when we walk him through, we leave the cuffs off to minimize the scene. He clams up on the way, refusing to say another word. But it's too late, he's said enough. He'll go down for Caplan's death. And even though a lawyer with a mail-order degree should be able to get it reduced to manslaughter, it's still a case closed for Dana and someone brought to justice for Roger Caplan.

Outside, Dana hustles Webb quickly and efficiently into the back of her car. Ace hovers a discreet distance away on the sidewalk, surrounded by his detail, the red bag still over his shoulder.

Popping the trunk, Dana takes out a large plastic evidence pouch and hands it to me.

"Put it in there," she says, waving at the video game bag in my hand.

When I don't move, she glares at me warningly.

"It's evidence, Will."

"It's the rightful property of my old company."

"Don't say 'old,'" she says, tilting her head. "You still own a big piece of it. Big enough to get the CEO to fly out here with a million dollars in a backpack."

"Doesn't change that it belongs to CastorNet."

"Doesn't change that it's evidence."

"Not the Unicorn."

She hesitates.

"The statue and the bag it was bundled in are evidence," I agree. "But not the Unicorn. Webb didn't even know it was there."

Dana looks down at the bag, her brow creased in a frown as she thinks it over.

"You know how dangerous it is," I add.

"Which is why it should be in custody, where no one can get it," she says, latching her eyes onto mine.

"Only that's not true and you know it," I reply. "Someone shows up with a national security warrant, you hand it over, it disappears forever."

"Will, that's a little paranoid."

"Is it? You've seen what people are willing do to for it." Reaching out, I softly put a finger on her torso where the bullet hole was yesterday. "Ace will keep it in a sealed container. That way we know it won't disappear before we need it for the ransom drop tomorrow. Think of Amanda."

"Are you?" she asks, putting her hands on her hips.

Fair question. Finding the Unicorn wasn't about Amanda Caplan. I could walk away right now with the Unicorn, and go back to the life I had before. Only, it wouldn't be. Bruce Sterling, Kate Mason, and Jack are all dead. Amanda's not—she still has a chance.

"Yes, I am," I answer, letting out a deep breath. "This is the best way."

Dana bites her lip, deep in thought for what seems like an eternity.

"All right," she says. "But just the Unicorn. The statue goes in for evidence."

Without taking my eyes off Dana, I wave over Ace. He opens another pocket in the red bag to pull out a thin, sleek carbon fiber case. The weight of the lead inside is unmistakable. He opens an app on his phone, and a small touch screen on the case lights up red. I put my hand on it for a second until it turns green. The lock is now coded to my handprint.

The case opens with a quiet *snick* to reveal a padded compartment, filled with foam, already cut out in the exact shape of the Unicorn, based on CastorNet's schematics. Setting the statue on the trunk of Dana's car, I quickly transfer the Unicorn to the carbon fiber case. When I close the lid, it *snicks* again as the lock engages, the screen flashing red for a moment before going dark.

"There you go," I say to Dana. "Secure. Only I can open it. Ace's security will keep it safe until tomorrow's drop."

"I hope you're right about this," she says, watching Ace walk away, surrounded by his security.

"Trust me, no one will get their hands on it."

CHAPTER THIRTY-THREE

When Dana pulls up to the hotel a few hours later, it's deserted. Through the window we see the lobby is empty, save a single employee at the front desk. A lone valet outside. Even the Hawaiian coffee shop is closed for the night.

"Let me see that picture again," says Dana, turning off the car.

I hand over my phone, open to the third and final photo from Han. An overhead shot from a camera in the ceiling, set up to peer straight down into the inspection area. Nestled in the center of an open carry-on bag between Caplan and a guard is the sculpture of Han Solo in carbonite.

"Why didn't they make him open it?" she asks.

"Because they didn't know it was hollow. It looks like a solid statue made of heavy metal, perfectly matching the image from the X-ray machine. So, they let him through."

I shift around to face Dana, who is leaning sideways in the driver's seat. It's late, but I don't think either of us is tired. I have the Unicorn back, and Dana's put another killer behind bars. There have been worse days.

"What made you go to this contact in Tokyo?" she asks.

"From his booth, Caplan's connection to Japan was obvious. All those authentic Japanese market items. Especially the statues. That level of craftsmanship isn't the kind of thing you see for sale online. So he had to go to Japan himself to get them, giving him an opportunity to buy the Unicorn while he was there. There's no way he'd ship the Unicorn, so he must have brought it back himself. The Pelican case would have been good protection, but never would have made it past security or customs."

"So why switch it to the Pelican case here?" Dana asks.

"The Pelican case is lighter and stronger." I run a hand through my hair. "But if I were to bet, I'd say it was because he needed to sell the statue to Webb, to avoid a confrontation."

"Well that didn't work well, did it?" she says.

"It could have, until something spooked Caplan into moving the Unicorn in the middle of the night. He needed to hide it. The only other radiation-safe container available would have been the one he used to get it out of Japan. Figure out how he did that, and we'd know what we were looking for."

The valet makes a half-hearted attempt to open Dana's door before she waves him off. I watch him cross back in front of the car, hands in his pockets.

"So then Han," she says, nodding. "You knew that whatever he carried it in would block the X-rays and they'd have to open his bag."

"So then Han," I agree with a smile. "Webb didn't even know what he had. He thought it was just a statue of Han Solo he really wanted, and Caplan was trying to renege on their deal."

"People have been killed for less," says Dana shaking her head. She pauses, looking out the windshield. "Now that you have the Unicorn, are you going to go back to Silicon Valley?"

The sudden topic change takes me by surprise. It's a question I haven't confronted, too focused on finding the Unicorn to consider what comes next.

"Do you think I would?" I ask.

"Maybe." She shrugs, nodding her head. "You're a hell of an investigator, but the Unicorn was everything to you. Now that it's back, how far do you follow it? What about the plans you had for it in 2011? Do you take back the reins or let it go?"

"I don't know," I reply finally as the silence stretches into awkward. Try as I might, it's too hard to see beyond the image of Amanda bound to a chair.

"Well, that's definitely new," says Dana, lifting one eyebrow.

"What is?"

"You look confused," she says with a laugh. It isn't the sharp, sarcastic laugh I'm used to. It's something different, something free, something fun.

Shaking my head to clear it, I look her in the eyes, saying, "I guess I'm just too wound up still."

While her eyes stay locked on mine, she squeezes my hand, sliding a finger across my palm. "I think I can help with that."

Yes. Yes. So much, yes.

Without another word, we get out of the car. Dana tosses the keys to the valet, barely slowing down to take a ticket. Crossing the lobby at a near run, we wait what seems like an eternity for the elevator. When it finally opens, Dana and I dart inside, jabbing at the buttons and clenching our hands, willing the doors to close quickly.

They slide shut and we turn to face each other in unison. I lean forward, she lifts her chin, and our mouths meet. We aren't gentle. There's a nervous, hungry energy in our kiss. Tongues cross and my arms slip around her waist. Her hands on my shoulders, pull me closer. I feel every inch of her body from head to toe.

Embracing someone wearing body armor is weird. I feel her hips, her waist, and her arms, but in between is a big solid block of nothing, so I reach for what I can. Sliding one hand up, I grab the back of her head, right below her ponytail. She tilts her head further and probes deeper with her tongue. The smell of her hair, the taste of her mouth, and the heat of her body swirl together in a kaleidoscope.

She pulls away as the elevator doors open, dragging me into the hall.

"Which way?" she asks, her voice low and urgent.

Leading her by the hand to my door, I fumble for the access card. She teases the back of my neck, with a touch as light as air, giving me goose bumps. Slamming the card to the reader, the door unlocks and I pull her inside. When I lean forward again, she turns away looking at the room.

"Holy shit," she says, her gaze sweeping the suite. "This is a big fucking room."

"The bedroom's over there." I point a finger, shaking with anticipation.

"The sofa's closer," she says, unbuttoning her shirt.

*   *   *

An hour later I'm downstairs in the hot, humid parking garage breathing in an odor of oil and garbage. Wearing hastily pulled on jeans, a t-shirt, and my Converse over bare feet, I twirl the key to Dana's unmarked car in my hand.

The valet told me where to look for the car, but there's a lot of them. He offered to bring it up for me, but there's no way I'm waiting that long. A beautiful woman is lying nude in my bed. One I'm looking forward to still being there in the morning. I can't remember the last time that happened.

Where the hell is her car?

After a few more minutes of impatient searching, I find it parked next to a gray Charger with a license plate dented in the bottom-right corner. Decker's rental.

We haven't told him about the Unicorn. That's probably what he meant by staying in touch, but whatever. Caplan's killer is Dana's win, and the Unicorn is mine. We'll all share in the victory of finding Amanda Caplan tomorrow.

Popping the trunk, I find a black gym bag with the Police Department logo and "Lopez" embroidered on it, just as Dana described. Unsurprisingly for someone wearing a Fitbit, she carries workout clothes in her car all the time in case she hits the gym. That's a lot of fitness, but hey, Kumar will tell you, everyone's got their obsessions. And if they keep Dana in my bed for the night because they're comfortable enough to sleep in, who am I to judge?

You can tell a lot about a person by the contents of their car. In Dana's trunk, there's a roadside emergency kit with the department logo on it, a soccer ball, and peeking out from under her gym bag, a menu for a Cuban restaurant. The place must be pretty good to measure up to the home cooking served from her mother's food truck in Miami. Where we grew up was a topic during the post-coital cuddling I'm eager to get back to.

After closing the trunk with a thud, Decker's car in the next row catches my eye again. Shouldering Dana's gym bag, I hesitate. Something's bothering me about the rental car, now that I see it again.

I left LA in the middle of the night. Even with the time difference, it was early morning when I got here. How did Decker beat me here and get a rental car so quickly?

You can tell a lot about a person by the contents of their car.

Dana's waiting for me upstairs.

This won't take long.

As I walk over to Decker's car, I pull up another handy app on my phone. The lights of the rental flash and the doors unlock. Working as quickly as I can, I search the car starting with the driver's seat. I cover all the map pockets, the center console, cup holders, and the glove box. The trunk is empty except for a snow brush the rental company must leave there year round.

All I find are coffee stains around the cup holder, and the rental company contract. I don't know what I expected. The car is as buttoned up and squared away as Decker himself.

Flipping open the paperwork, I skim through it, not sure why I'm even doing this. Dana is upstairs. The flawless, smooth skin of her thigh leaps to mind, muscles rippling under my hand as I slide it up—wait a minute.

My brows crash together in a deep frown. Double-checking the time and date on my smartwatch, I work backwards in my head to the date on the contract.

Son of a bitch.

Decker picked the car up on Thursday afternoon. Caplan wasn't murdered until late Thursday night. He told me the FBI got called in by Farber's connections *after* Caplan's body was discovered.

What the fuck was Decker doing here the day before?

My thoughts are interrupted by a text message from Kumar's soon-to-be ex-employee.

Unknown #: Hey. Got the info you were looking for.
  Hope this helps.

Unknown #: *file attached*

Me: Thanks. Good luck at the new job.

Unknown #: :-)

The attached file is a simple Excel spreadsheet, but it's bigger than I'd hoped. I expected a smaller number of kinky people in the Midwest. Swiping my thumb, I forward the data off to Bradley. If he gets started now, we could have Amanda's location by dawn.

Me: Here's the data from Kumar.

Me: *file attached*

Me: Do I need to say this is a rush?

Bradley W: Nope. I'm good to go. How many records?

Me: A lot.

Bradley W: OK. I'm on it. Burning the midnight oil.
Text you right away. Get some rest.

My finger hovers over the keyboard. There's nothing more to say. Bradley knows what to do. All I can do is wait. The larger list is a setback, but it doesn't mean the plan won't still work. Even so, my shoulders tighten as uncertainty seeps back in.

Inside the suite, Dana's already asleep. I want to let her know the Kumar data came in, but when I see her face calm and relaxed, I can't bring myself to do it. She needs sleep. So do I. Amanda's life could depend on me being at my best.

Assuming Bradley has a location by sunup, we'll have a couple of hours before the Con opens and the meet is scheduled to take place. Despite my earlier confidence with Burke and Chief Wilmont, I'm not at all convinced that the uniformed officers at the doors will be able to keep the bidders unarmed. There are too many alternate entrances, and not enough time to secure them. The Russians, particularly, are skilled at getting their gunmen where they need to be. Better to find Amanda first and avoid the meet all together.

Dragoniis is still nearby, watching me. Decker never said how he knew Dragoniis was here, and I never asked, my attention focused on the Unicorn.

Lying down next to Dana, feeling her nakedness next to mine, it's easier than I thought it would be to let it all go. The unresolved issues that would normally gnaw at me, keeping me awake, fade into the darkness. Dana shifts in her slumber, burrowing deeper into my embrace with a satisfied sigh. She's warm. I'm spent. Sleep takes me.

CHAPTER THIRTY-FOUR

The sound of a *Star Trek* transporter energizing cuts through the darkness, and my sleep. Lying there for a moment in that gray area before fully waking, I'm not sure I actually heard it. Rolling over on my back, away from Dana, the fog of sleep dissipates slowly. When the familiar sound of materialization comes again, I throw back the covers, and reach for my phone.

Bradley W: It's done. Analysis complete. There's a problem.

Me: We didn't get a location?

Bradley W: That's the problem. We got two.

Me: Two? What do you mean two?

Bradley W: Two separate locations. Both hitting Google on Firefox for Mac in that minute, and both also on Kumar's list of bondage porno clients.

Me: What can we do? We need to know which one.

Bradley W: Close as I can get you. All the data we have. Sorry, Will.

Running my hands through my hair, I check the glowing clock next to Dana. There are only a few hours left until the Con opens, and we're supposed to deliver the Fukushima Unicorn to whatever bidder is holding Amanda hostage. With so many variables—the operating system, browser, time of day, and narrow focus of kink—I was hoping for a single location to come out of Rick's and Kumar's lists. Two means we're not finished, yet.

"What is it?" asks Dana, sitting up on the bed and rubbing her eyes. She nods at the phone in my hand. "Is that Bradley?"

"Yeah."

"Did he get the location?"

"Not exactly," I answer, taking a deep breath. "He got two."

"We can work with that," she says with a yawn, turning on a bed-side light. "It'll be tight, but we can do it."

While she hammers out a text message, I admire her silhouette: fit and strong, yet soft and feminine. Her dark, shiny hair spreads out behind her, reaching just past her shoulders.

Money draws people. It's something I've had to deal with since my first company crossed the million-mark, and continued even after I left the Valley. Men and women both offer their companionship, sexual or otherwise, in exchange for a piece of the lucre. By now I can sniff those people out a mile away.

That's not Dana.

She's earned every inch of where she's gotten, and reaped the re-wards. In fact, I suspect that I'm one of those rewards, coming on the heels of solving the Caplan murder.

"How long was I out?" she asks, finishing with the message.

"Four hours."

"Yuck. Well, that'll have to do."

"Yuck?" I ask in concern, earning me a laugh.

"I mean four hours isn't a lot. It was nice having you here, though," she says, leaning over to kiss my cheek.

"Having *me* here? This is my room."

"You know the customary response is, 'I liked it too,'" she says, rolling her eyes.

"Ahh, right. Sorry. Lack of sleep. Foggy. It's been a while . . ."

"Don't worry, you were great," she says, magnificently stretching her arms overhead.

"You were more than great," I say.

"I know."

Pushing the blankets out of the way, she walks naked over to the mini-bar fridge. My admiration of her form as she bends to look inside is interrupted by a loud ping from her phone.

"Pre-action briefing in thirty minutes," she says, glancing at the screen. Producing a tall can of energy drink, she tosses it to me on the bed. "We'll take one of these and a cold shower. We'll be alert in no time."

I'm already halfway to the bathroom by the time I crack the tab on the can.

* * *

In the still and stifling stairwell, the air is heavy with the scent of gun oil, leather, and sweat. Looking up, a long line of SWAT officers disappears above me.

Decker's with Griffon and Nassar in a command vehicle around the corner, shielded from view of the building. They're wired into the cameras and mics on the SWAT team, seeing what we see, which means they probably see better than I do.

Nobody says a word, tensely waiting for the go command.

During the painfully long briefing, the two locations were revealed to be a condo apartment in an affluent part of town and another hotel. In the night a domestic dispute turned into a hostage situation, consuming one of the city's two SWAT teams. With a single team remaining until the standoff is resolved, we can't hit two locations simultaneously. A choice had to be made on the most likely of the two. If we have to go to the second, time will be tight.

The plain white walls in the photo and the absence of visible furniture doesn't reveal enough about the location to tell us which it could be. The hotel room is registered to a common name on a common credit card. It could be a false identity setup by a PMC, or it could be a guy with a common name. It'll be hours before the bank gets back to us with more information on the cardholder. Too long. Ultimately, Director Burke let Chief Wilmont make the call, and he chose the hotel, based on the assumption that the kidnappers are from out of town.

Thanks to Dana, I get to ride along with the entry team. The SWAT team commander is a surly dude with a shaved head and no discernible neck, who didn't want any "civilians" tagging along. But Dana's SWAT certified, and managed to pull some strings to get me as far as the stairwell. They threw body armor over my t-shirt, slapped a helmet on my head, and told me to wait down here at the tail end of the line.

It feels to me like we've been sitting in this sweltering stairwell for two or three weeks while they try to get eyes inside the room. I would have just gone up and knocked on the door, so it's probably a good thing I'm not on the FBI's Hostage Rescue Team.

The layout of the suite is preventing them from seeing enough of the room using the fiber optic camera inserted under the door. With sunrise breaking across the windows, they can't see anything from across the street, even using thermal scanners. They've got good tech, but the bad circumstances win out.

The guy in front of me says this happens sometimes, and not to worry. Easy for him to say. He doesn't see Amanda Caplan, terrified and bound to a chair, every time he closes his eyes. Or Kate Mason, throat slashed open and bleeding out. I do.

The SWAT commander's voice comes through the tiny wireless monitor in my ear. "If we wait any longer, people are going to start waking up. We've gotta go with the intel we've got. Set condition blue."

The team in the stairwell rises as one, assuming the hunched-over tactical position, each man with a hand on the shoulder of the man in front of them. Following suit, I reach out and put mine on the shoulder of the guy in front of me, shuffling along behind him. With more than enough guns in the hands of the other twenty cops in front of me, I leave mine holstered. It's safer for everyone that way.

Reaching the hall, we crouch-walk, fast and silent, until we're outside the room in question. A suite. While that's more than enough space to hold Amanda, all we know for sure is somewhere inside is a Mac that's been surfing bondage kink. It could be anyone. A kid that clicked on the wrong link on YouTube. A business traveler looking to pass the time. What if Amanda isn't in there? Worse, what if they kill her before we can get to her?

"Breech team: green light," says the SWAT commander.

The beep of the master key opening the door lock down the hall cuts off my thoughts. Flash-bang grenades go inside, and all hell breaks loose.

The SWAT team moves in single file, hard and fast, shouting commands about hands and getting down on the ground. That means someone's there. Is it Amanda? I got us here, to this location. But was it soon enough? Or is a dead, young woman inside, my fault again?

Leaning back on the wall in the hallway, I sink to the ground, face in hand. Deploying every mental technique and trick I learned in Okinawa, I try to slow my heart, but I can't shake the image of Kate

Mason, the knife, and Sterling's sickening grin from my head. Nothing can separate me from this moment, where Amanda Caplan lives or dies.

Shouts of "clear" ring out. The room is secure. I can go in.

Forcing my rubbery legs to respond, I climb to my feet. My stomach churning like an angry badger running laps, I take a step toward the door, then another. Using every ounce of willpower I can muster, I turn the corner and walk into the room.

Right away, I have a sinking feeling. The colors are wrong. The furniture's wrong. The photos posted online by the hotel are different, showing newer, fresher rooms than this, with neutral-colored walls. Here, there's wallpaper. The doorframes are nicked, exposing wood underneath. The carpet is a faded but rich pattern, and the curtains, sun bleached. The photos we looked at online, that matched the ransom note, must be newly renovated. This is an old room.

Dana comes out of the bedroom.

"Agent Parker, I know," she says, holding up her hands.

"This isn't it," I say in a rush. "The room's all wrong. They didn't say anything about renovations online. We didn't ask about renovations?"

"Take it easy," she says poking a warning finger into my chest.

"Who's in there?" I push forward around her to take a look at the bedroom.

Perched on the edge of a messy bed is a pudgy white guy wearing boxers with pale blue stripes and nothing else. He's got short-cropped hair that doesn't quite hide that he's mostly bald. Sitting next to him is a middle-aged woman with obviously colored, jet-black hair. Her entire face is made up like she works at a makeup counter at Macy's. She's wearing a black leather corset over a matching black leather thong. Her pale cleavage overflows the top. Her hands are empty now, but judging by the redness of the pudgy guy's back, when

SWAT came in, she was holding the cat-of-nine-tails now sitting on the dresser.

"Robert Johnson and Kaitlyn Morris, both of Toledo, Ohio," says a SWAT officer holding two driver's licenses in front of him. "Separate addresses, though."

"You're not going to tell my wife, are you?" The pudgy guy leans forward putting his head in his hands with a mewing sound like a distressed cat.

"Fuck. It's just some guy cheating on his wife," I exclaim in disgust. Not at the couple's infidelity, but at the fact that we chose the wrong location. Pivoting on the ball of my foot, I go back out to the living room with Dana hot on my heels.

"We have to get to the other place," I tell her. "The condo. How long until they can set up?"

"There's no time, Will," she says, looking at her watch. "We lost too much getting set up here. The other location is way out in the suburbs. Whoever the bidder is sending is already on the way. There's no way we can get out there, hit it, then get back down to the Convention Center in time to meet them."

"Fine, we'll have Decker handle the meet, while we hit the second location," I say. I'm agitated. Jumpy. "It can be done, but we have to be fast."

"I know you want to be there, Will, but that's not the best place for you," she says, her tone low and strong. "They're going to need you at the Convention Center. It's *your* CEO that has the Fukushima Unicorn. It's *you* that knows the technology. *You* know the Convention Center inside and out. And the whole connection with that actor is *you*. What if he won't follow through for Decker?"

Good point. I wouldn't.

"But that's not where I want to be." I want to be there because I'm responsible for Amanda, just like I was responsible for Kate Mason.

"You don't trust the SWAT team?"

"They're fine," I say, looking around the room. "I still think I should be there."

"Of course, you do. And we both know why that is," she says. "But the question I have for you is this: Do you trust *me*?"

In any other situation, hearing that question from a woman I just spent the night with, after knowing her less than forty-eight hours, would be terrifyingly psychotic. But in this situation, it's exactly the right question.

"Yes."

"Then go," she says. "I got this."

CHAPTER THIRTY-FIVE

I don't do well with waiting.

Stuck behind a curtain at the Convention Center while Dana sets up at the second location, I peek through a seam at the crowd on the far side. And wait. Of the thousands of people pouring into the building, one of them is the bidder holding Amanda Caplan's life in their hands. In a matter of minutes, they'll be expecting us to hand over the Fukushima Unicorn. I'm under no illusions about what will happen to her if they don't get it.

In the wrong hands, the Unicorn could hurt millions. But if I don't give the bidder the Unicorn, Amanda's going to die. Right now. Today. I don't know what I'll do if I have to decide between the Unicorn and Amanda. If Dana succeeds, I won't have to confront that choice so, for now, I put my hope there.

I found the address of the condo on a home sharing website. The owners may actually live there and travel a lot. Or they may be operating an unlicensed B&B. I don't know, and I don't care. What's important is that it's available and out of sight. Just the kind of thing mercenaries look for. I feel good about our chances of finding Amanda, but Dana getting there in time is another issue.

Decker wanted to find out who's renting the place right now, but even I can't pull a string to answer that question in the next few minutes. We're just out of time.

On the other side of the curtain, Jerry Oldham sits at a table, signing autographs for his legion of adoring fans, a red fez perched on his head at a jaunty angle. Beyond the table is a red carpet serving as a buffer between the crowds and the celebrities. I'm as close as I can be while remaining hidden, only a few feet away.

Next to Jerry is a handler whose job it is to take the fans' money and let them pick out a glossy 8x10 photo to be signed. The whole thing works like a well-oiled machine. Fans get their celebrity experience and the celebs get cash. Dance monkey, dance.

Beyond the carpet, Farber's assistant, Sally Park, controls Jerry's line of fans. Decker wouldn't let us tell them who was coming and why, just that it was important to the investigation of a murder. Sally's relieved to have Farber off her back. Jerry's excited to be working on a "real case." And his assistant loves her job, happily doing whatever he asks.

The Unicorn is hidden at the handler's feet, locked in its carbon fiber case. She'll protect it until Oldham says a code phrase. When he says, "Oh, I have that right here," the moment will have arrived to decide between Amanda Caplan's life and letting the most dangerous cyber weapon in history walk off into the wild.

Decker argued with me hard to let it go this far. He didn't want Oldham to touch the case with the Unicorn inside. And that was before I programmed the case to also open for Jerry. Giving the bidder a chance to verify the Unicorn could buy us another minute, possibly two, for Dana to get her back. I'll be fired if Decker finds out what I've done, but if that's the price of getting Amanda Caplan home safely, I'm ready for retirement.

Easily a hundred people have lined up to see Oldham already, and more arrive all the time. With lines beginning to form for the other celebrities, it's becoming difficult to scan the crowd from my spot behind the curtain.

"How are things looking, Bradley?" I ask into my earpiece. Two channels are currently active: one listening in on the SWAT team so we know what's happening at the condo; and the other for us here at the Convention Center. Bradley's tapped in remotely from LA.

"Nothing yet, Boss," he says amid the crumbling of a candy wrapper. "I'm logged into the building's security and automation systems. Everything seems normal."

"Where is he?" Decker's voice grumbles in my ear. "We said the meet would be at opening."

Through the seam, I spot Decker on the mezzanine level above, leaning over the railing. In an effort to blend in, he's wearing a *Battlestar Galactica* t-shirt with "What the Frak?" across the front in bold font.

"The Unicorn's here, he'll be here," I say into the radio, adding, "Looking good up there, Decker."

From a hundred yards away, I clearly see him raise his middle finger.

"There are some huge lines to get in," says Griffon. "It's taking a long time for everybody to get past the screening."

"Any sign of our Russian friends?" I ask.

"Not yet, but there's a lot of people out here."

"Making any money?"

As it turns out, Griffon is a musician. With an old guitar we found kicking around the police station, and some thrift shop clothes, he's outside strumming the occasional few bars while watching for familiar faces.

"Would you believe yes? And one phone number, so far."

"So *far*?" says Nassar. "I told you we shouldn't have let him have the guitar."

She's at the far end of autograph alley, near a broad set of fire doors, in case the bidder makes a break for it. Zipped into a *Ghostbusters* jumpsuit we bought before the doors opened, she fits right in with another lineup of fans.

Like anyone else in the world running out of patience, I pull out my phone. But instead of passing the time with an endless stream of social media, I review the case notes until something catches my eye. The number Nassar gave me for the escort. A smile breaks out on my face as I remember Decker's reaction. But then something else clicks. Opening messages, I paste in the number.

Will P: Got your name from Darryl. Can I make an appointment?

Unknown: When? How long were you thinking?

Will P: Flexible on time. From out of town. Here for the weekend. Thinking an hour?

Unknown: I generally prefer multi-hour appointments.

Unknown: *link*

Of course, you do. You get paid by the hour. Tapping on the link brings up her website. Typical for the industry, there's a bio page, a gallery with tasteful erotic photos, and some tabs for more information. The photos are professionally done and, if accurate, she has an extremely attractive body. None of the pictures show her face. This is a high-end escort. To see how much Hicks paid, I tap on the rates tab. When the page loads, it also lists her services.

I freeze.

"Are we sure they're going to take the bait?" Decker asks over the radio, yanking me back to the moment. "What if they're not looking at this Oldham guy, expecting Caplan's assistant to be walking around?"

"It's getting crowded fast," says Nassar. "Maybe they can't see him."

"Give me a second," I reply, pounding out a quick message. *Time to earn your keep, Jerry.*

Through the curtain, I see Oldham's handler look at her phone. She leans over to Jerry while he finishes dazzling a preteen girl with his heroic hair and brilliant white teeth.

In my pocket, I flip the switch on the radio, adding the SWAT channel. They can't hear us, but we can listen in.

They're live at the Convention Center, people. Backup team, are you in position?

Roger that, in position now.

Sniper one. Any movement?

Negative.

Sniper two.

Negative.

Breach team, sit rep.

In position. Deploying camera.

Hearing Dana's voice shrinks the distance between us. Knowing she's there is the reason I'm not losing my mind.

Jerry listens to the handler for a second, then stands, spreading his arms wide apart in the air.

"How's everybody doing today?" he bellows over the crowd.

As one, a hundred voices rise in a cheer.

"Do we have some Double Limiters here?" He makes a show of putting a hand next to his ear.

The roar from the crowd is twice as loud. This time fans from neighboring lines, and the mobs just passing by, look to see what the excitement is all about.

"There was a TIME!" Jerry shouts his character's catchphrase, looking up at the ceiling as if he's about to disappear, teleporting to another time and place.

The crowd goes nuts. His line of autograph seekers jumps up and down, vibrating the concrete floor underneath my feet. Young female fans let out ear-splitting shrieks of delight.

I'll say this: the man's a performer. A hush falls on the rest of the hall as everyone watches Jerry's antics. Through it all, the red fez never leaves his head. If our bidder is in the building, he's seen it now.

The voice of SWAT at the condo crackles in my ear:

Command, we have movement near the foyer. Partial view in a mirror. One unsub. White male. Mid-twenties. Beard. Large ear spacers. Bluetooth headset.

That doesn't sound like the owner of the suburban luxury condo. Maybe in the Valley, but not here in the Corn Belt. The hope in my heart burns a little brighter.

Glancing down at my phone, I jump, remembering what I was doing before Decker interrupted me. Switching to the phone app, I dial. She answers on the first ring.

"Hello?"

"I was just texting you."

"Right. I don't know if this is your first time or not, but most girls don't answer calls from blocked numbers."

"Then why did you?"

"Because Darryl gave you my number and he does a good job of pre-screening for me."

"Your name is?"

"You can call me Eliza."

"Well, Eliza, please don't hang up the phone. This won't go well for either one of us if you do. You are *not in trouble*. My name is Special Agent Will Parker. I'm with the FBI."

"What? Is this a joke?"

"My colleague interviewed Darryl Parr at work. You can text him right now to confirm that, but don't hang up. We're investigating the kidnapping of an eighteen-year-old girl. Time is of the essence."

"Is she in danger?"

I swallow, hard. "Yes."

"Wait a sec."

Every second she's gone passes so slowly I wonder if time is moving at all.

"Okay, I sent him a message."

"Two nights ago, you had a client."

There's a long pause. Caution is smart in her line of work, but I don't have time for that.

A moment of static in my ear and voices from the SWAT team intrude.

Balcony team, do you have eyes on?

Drone is in position. Curtains closed. Looking for a gap.

The plan called for a second team to gain entry next door, and use the shared balcony to place a small, wheeled drone on the terrace.

"Possibly," Eliza finally answers.

"You did. White male, late forties, from out of town."

"That's ninety percent of my clients."

A low buzzing rumbles across the line. Vibration at her end. Another pause while she reads the text.

"Darryl says you're legit. Are you sure I'm not in trouble?"

"I promise. The Bureau has no interest in your professional activities beyond this particular client."

"Okay, Special Agent Parker. What do you need to know?"

"Heads up," says Decker in my other ear. "Crowds are moving again."

Resisting the urge to poke my head out through the seam, I make do with trying to see through the thin material itself.

"On your website it says you offer dominatrix services. Is that correct?"

"Sure. I see a lot of business travelers. Some are subbies that have a regular Dom at home. Some just want to try it. It's a popular service."

"The client you had two nights ago; did he request Dom services?"

"Let me check my call notes. How much detail do you want?"

"Bondage? Yes or no."

Another pause, this one short, while she looks it up. "Oh yeah, that guy. Yes, to bondage."

"You probably don't have a name, but was there anything unique about him?"

"Oh no, I have a name," she says quickly. "Discretion is important, Special Agent, but my safety is top priority. For Dom services, I always check IDs."

Why didn't you tell me that at the beginning? Clenching my free hand into a fist, I pace away from the curtain.

"What was the name?" I ask as calmly as possible.

"Martin Hicks."

"Decker, we need eyes on Martin Hicks, right now. He's the kidnapper," I say, the words coming out of me in a rush as I hang up the phone.

"Who can get to the Pyntel display?" Decker asks.

"I'm just outside it," answers Griffon.

"Move!" Decker commands.

"Bradley!" I call into the radio, my voice low but urgent.

"I'm on it, Boss. Looking. But there's a lot of people there."

"Facial recognition?"

"No time to load the comparator," he says, "and the camera feeds aren't that good."

"I've got movement!" says Decker. "Headed up the Oldham line. Walking past everyone."

"Is it Hicks?" I push the words out around the thickness in my throat.

"All I see is his back. White male. Phone to his ear. That's all I've got," says Decker. "Stay alert," he adds, unhelpfully.

"I've got him," says Bradley, "but I can't make out the face. The cameras are too far. Sorry, Boss."

The SWAT channel comes to life in my ear. The voices are faster, more urgent.

Command, Balcony Team, hostage confirmed in the bedroom.

Say again, Balcony, can you confirm ID?

Confirmed. It's her. Bound and gagged in a chair.

Hostiles?

Stand by.

"Sir, are you here to see Mr. Oldham?" I hear Sally Park's voice through the curtain. Crisp, professional, but the noise drowns out the response. "The line for Mr. Oldham starts here and ends over there. Oh, you have VIP? No problem, you are next, sir."

The urgent voices continue at a rapid clip on the SWAT radio.

Command, Balcony Team. There are two, count two, hostiles in the bedroom with the hostage. Armed. Semi-auto pistols.

Roger that. Go to Plan C. Backup, send two.

Plan C is for the second team to climb around and make entry through the balcony door. With hostiles guarding her in the bedroom, an entry through the front door would be too slow. But officers climbing around ten stories off the ground takes time. Something we don't have.

In a flurry of giggles, the preteen girl in front of Jerry leaves with her mother, making way for the VIP. Whoever it is must be eager because the girl's giggles are still fading when I hear the handler offer a photo. While I can't make out their response, I know what they must have asked for when I hear what Jerry says next.

"Oh sure, I have that right here."

CHAPTER THIRTY-SIX

"It's him, it's Hicks," I hiss into my radio.

"That was garbled. Say again?" Decker demands.

The shape of the handler, blurry through the curtain, reaches under the table for the sleek carbon fiber case containing the Unicorn. From his vantage point in the mezzanine above, Decker should be able to see it too.

We're out of time. The SWAT team doesn't have Amanda and the bidder; Hicks is here for the Unicorn. If he doesn't get it, Amanda's life is in danger. Do I protect the Unicorn, or do I let Hicks take it? If it makes it out of the building, I'm certain I'll never see it again.

If I'm going to stall, I need to know exactly what Hicks is doing. Decker can only see his back, and Bradley said the cameras are no help. But if Hicks sees me, he'll know we're on to him. Sidling up to the curtain, I open a gap in the curtain just wide enough to put my eye to it. Just as my face reaches the fabric, the curtains fly apart, revealing the girl and her mother. They're not supposed to come this way.

"Come on, Mom, I can see the sign for the bathrooms right there!" shouts the little girl. The crowd was too loud; I didn't hear them double back on the thick red carpet.

Oldham's leaning over to take the case from his handler. Martin Hicks stands in front of him with a phone to his ear. Sally Park is holding back the rest of the fans.

His attention drawn by the motion of the curtains, Hicks looks straight at me.

The SWAT commander's voice, now impatient, rings clear over the radio.

Balcony Team, are you in position?

Two in position. Two on the way. Difficult climb.

The condo. Amanda. Her guard. Wearing a Bluetooth headset. Hicks on the phone.

"Bradley, tell Dana to breach now!"

Hicks frowns at first, processing. Then his eyes and mouth open wide in recognition. If he's talking to the condo, there are only a few seconds left.

Shoving her mother aside, I push past the preteen girl, knocking her to the ground. My legs are agonizingly slow, like they're numb with cold. It will take too long to draw my gun. And with a thousand people behind Hicks, too dangerous. Instead, I lock my eyes onto his chest. That's where I'll hit, with all the force I can muster.

Every muscle strains. No one else is moving. They're all statues. In this instant, it's just me and Hicks. His nostrils are narrowed. He's taking in a breath. I have until his lungs are filled to get to him.

One, two, three steps and I launch myself through the air, over the table, slamming into his chest head-first, like a battering ram. His breath comes out in a grunt, rather than words. We topple over, landing hard on the red carpet that's thinner than it looks.

The phone flies out of his hand, bouncing away but still within reach.

There's a new voice in my ear. Dana.

Command, Breach. We need to go now.

Almost there, Breach.

The message got through to Dana, but now there's hesitation. I hate that. Why can't people just do what I tell them to do, when I tell them to do it?

Hicks tries to fend me off, but I'm trained for this. Sliding my forearm up and onto his throat, I lean down. I don't quite have the leverage to crush it, but I manage to stifle his cries into a sickly choking sound. One I hope isn't heard at the other end of the phone.

Dana's voice is on the radio again, her voice level.

Command, Breach. Code Black.

Dana invokes the code that means a hostage is about to die. It's the best she can do in the shortest amount of time.

Focusing on my offense, I've left myself exposed. That corporate drone Hicks would be an easy, untrained target is a bet I would take over and over again. Unfortunately, I'm wrong.

He rams his knee up, connecting it solidly with my crotch. Dirty fighting, but as Sensei used to say, "When it's for your life, all is forgiven." Hicks believes he's fighting for his life.

Spots flare in my vision as the pain hits. Gasping for a breath to fight through it gives Hicks all the opportunity he needs. His entire body convulses, finding the weak point of my leverage and throwing me off to the side. Instead of pursuing the attack, he rolls over and reaches for the phone.

The SWAT commander's voice rings out loud and clear.

All teams, Command. Green light! Green light! Green light!

My teeth jam together, clenching so hard I feel like they'll crack. While taking another breath in through my nose, I roll over onto all fours to lunge after Hicks. Landing a hand on his foot, I pull on it as hard as I can. He falls face-first to the ground, his hand less than an inch from the phone.

In my ear, there's a jumbled roar of sound. Breaking glass. A crunching thud. Bangs so loud the earpiece speaker is a distorted blur. Shouting.

Hicks yanks his leg, but I hold on, using the momentum to propel myself forward onto his back. In the blink of an eye, I've grabbed his neck. But before I can lock the choke hold, he manages to shout out, "It's a trap!"

The SWAT team is already in the condo and Dana along with them. There's nothing more I can do but have faith that Dana won't make a mistake, like I did with Bruce Sterling.

The years of frustration and pain for my role in what Sterling did pour into the choke hold on Hicks. He falls silent, and as long as I feel him fighting me, I keep the pressure on. His weekends spent at some mixed martial arts gym caught me by surprise, but I've got him now and I'm not letting go. His struggling quickly weakens and fades. A little harder, a little longer, and I can guarantee he'll never hurt anyone again like Bruce Sterling.

But Hicks isn't Bruce Sterling, and that's not my way. My grip eases, allowing him to breathe.

As the roar of the tactical entry at the condo fades away, new and clearer sounds emerge in the earpiece. At first, I have trouble making them out around the shrieking and screaming of the confused crowd around me. Concentration brings out Dana's voice, this time raised, almost shouting.

Command, Breach. Hostage is secure. Repeat: hostage is secure.

Roger that, Breach. Good job.

Whatever relief I have in mind is short lived, because Decker's drill-sergeant-yelling is the next thing I'm able to make out.

". . . Unicorn!!! Will! The Unicorn!"

Looking up, I'm just in time to see someone running away down the red carpet with the carbon fiber case, dressed in an anime-styled costume. Two crossed Samurai sword scabbards adorn their back overtop of motorcycle leathers and a helmet. Red and white leathers.

Dragoniis has the Fukushima Unicorn.

Something lands with a thud on the carpet beside me, smacking me in the face.

"Selfie!" says Oldham, holding up an iPhone. "Fighting crime with the FBI!"

The screen shows a live image of his face next to mine. Emoticons flow across the bottom.

"Hold him down, don't let him get away," I tell Oldham, leaping to my feet.

"Got it, Will, you can count on me, buddy!"

"And stop livestreaming!" I shout back as I take off at a run.

"I'm behind the curtains, heading your way," says Nassar between heavy breaths.

"I'll cut him off at the escalators," says Decker.

"Tell me where he's headed," says Griffon. "I'll circle around."

"Scrap that, Griffon," I shout between breaths. "Tell the uniforms to shut down the building. Close all the exits!"

Dragoniis has a lead of only a few seconds, but it might as well be an hour. He dives into the crowd of thousands in the main hall, just one more cosplayer in a sea of them.

In a blink he's vanished, along with the Fukushima Unicorn.

CHAPTER THIRTY-SEVEN

Dragoniis has just disappeared with the Fukushima Unicorn into a crowd of thousands. People are packed tightly into two streams moving in opposite directions. If I pick the wrong way, I'll never get turned around in time. I only get one chance at this.

"Bradley, have you got eyes on him?"

"Yeah, I've got him, Will. Fifty feet ahead of you. Angling left towards the front entrance," he replies through the earpiece.

Starting into the crowd, I move as quickly as I can. But people keep stopping at random, forcing me to weave and shuffle around them. Decker would be shouting at everyone to move for the FBI, but I think that would only cause more people to stop in curiosity. The silver lining here is that Dragoniis is stuck in the same crowd and can't be going any faster.

"I'm at the escalator," says Decker over the radio. "Coming down now. I should be able to get ahead of him."

A long escalator stretches from the main floor to the mezzanine far above the cavernous hall. I spot Decker at the top, but there are a lot of fans blocking the way in front of him. It's going to take him time to get down.

"I'm out of it," says Nassar. "There are a bunch of Stormtroopers marching in a line with a ton of people taking pictures blocking the way. I can't get back to you."

"Step it up, Decker," says Bradley.

"I'm going, dammit!" Decker says. I see him look around in frustration before shouting at a pair of security guards below. "Stop that guy in red leather!"

"What?" they shout back, looking at the fans on the escalator.

"Wait, he's stopped," says Bradley. "Looking down at something. I can't make it out."

"Ah, forget this," says Decker, pushing his way forward. The fans he plows by grab the railing in alarm, squealing indignantly.

With a wrenching clunk, the escalator stops abruptly. Some riders stumble and fall into those in front of them, creating a heap of bodies. A few scream. Accompanied by a loud buzzing, the escalator starts moving again, this time in the opposite direction, heading back up. Any chance Decker had of getting down to cut off Dragoniis is gone.

"What the hell happened to the escalators, Bradley?" I shout into the radio.

"Someone else is in the system!" Bradley answers amid pounding keystrokes. "It must be Dragoniis."

"Well, get him out!"

"I'm trying, but I don't know how he's done it."

"I'll circle around," says Griffon. "Where's he headed?"

"Looks like he's headed for the vendor hall," says Bradley. "Decker spooked him."

"I'm at a staff access hallway," says Nassar. "I'll use that to get around to the vendor hall and cut back towards him."

Good plan. With five of us against one of him, the numbers are on our side. Continuing to work my way through the crowd, elbows jab me in the side, some of them accidental. But foot by foot I make my way deeper.

"Dammit," Nassar grunts over the radio.

"What's wrong?" I ask.

"Just as I got to the door, the light on the handle turned red. Now I can't open it. Hold on, there's another one down the hall."

"Will, get a move on; he's almost at the vendor room," says Bradley. "The crowd's thin out there. He'll be fast once he makes it through the doors."

A small circle of space appears in front of me, centered around a guy in elaborate space armor. Cutting between him and a row of people snapping photos, I'm a little too close and trip on his boots. Stumbling head-first, my face mashes into a guy wearing gray coveralls, a camera in his hand.

"Hey," he says shoving me back on my feet. "I'm taking a picture here."

The size of Decker, his coveralls provide ample space for an array of patches. One on his shoulder says "Bertane Gas" another on his chest says "Amos."

"Dammit, the second one did the same thing," says Nassar. "It just went red and locked me out."

"It's Dragoniis. He's in there fucking around with us, Bradley. Get him out!"

"Now you're talking to yourself. What the hell's wrong with you, man?" asks Amos.

"Griffon, get to the security office," says Bradley. "I need you there to try something."

"On my way," he answers.

"Sorry in advance," I say with a tilt of my head.

"For wha—" Before Amos can finish, I step in and sweep his leg, dropping him to his back. Leaping over his prone form, I plummet back into the crowd.

The wall of humanity thickens, and I resort to pushing people out of the way, earning me angry comments. But no one else puts up a fuss like Amos, and I make it into the vendor hall.

"Which way do I go?"

"Boss, I don't know," says Bradley.

"What? You were watching him." I start up the middle of the vendor hall while I wait for better direction.

"I was! He was just about at the doors, then he vanished. I'm blind!"

The blind spot.

Somehow Dragoniis found out about the blind spot. Systematically, he's taken away our advantage, cutting our numbers one by one, adapting to keep one step ahead of us. And he's got the Fukushima Unicorn. After being *in my hands*, it's on the verge of slipping away again. Only this time, instead of vanishing into myth, it's into the hands of an enemy. As long as we keep him on the run, he won't have time to get around the handprint. I need to get that case back.

Cursing the waste of time, I work my way back to the doors. Dragoniis never came into the vendor hall. Using the blind spot route to stay off camera, he's widened his lead. Bursting out of the vendor hall doors, I take a hard left past where the Godzilla statue stood.

"Will, I'm in the stairwell," says Griffon. "Heading up to the— Hey, I know you," he shouts, his tone turning dark. "FBI. *Stoi! Stoi!*"

"What's happening?" Decker demands.

"That's Russian," says Nassar.

"Where is he?" Decker shouts.

"Southwest fire stairs," says Bradley. "Not alone. Two guys. Griffon has them at gunpoint. They're drawing!"

Two rapid gunshots ring out over the radio. Running along the blind spot path, my steps falter.

"One down," says Griffon between heavy breaths. "But the other one took off. He's gone up to the mezzanine."

"I'm on him," says Decker. "Headed your way."

"I'll go after him," says Griffon, panting hard. "You keep on the Unicorn. I'm all right."

"I still need someone in the security office," Bradley says.

"Got it," says Nassar. "I'm not getting anywhere on this floor."

Leaning back into it, I move surprisingly fast. The blind spot path hugs the walls, out of the way of the crowds. Later in the day it'll be lined with people sitting on the floor, but this early it's smooth sailing.

"There he is," exclaims Bradley. "Just hit the south lobby, right behind the girl with big fabulous wings."

Rounding the corner into a wide hallway with blue carpet, I see the south entrance in the distance, sunlight pouring through the glass. Rising above the throng of people are an elaborate pair of wings, easily seven feet tall. I pump my arms in an all-out sprint.

Finally, I spot the red and white leathers. As I grow closer, I make out the sword handles crossed on his back, which must be foam props—otherwise security would have taken them away.

Griffon must have gotten word to the uniformed officers because they're not letting anyone in or out. Dragoniis slows, walking toward an exit door while tapping the phone in his hand.

"Bradley, he's up to something—"

A klaxon alarm rings out, accompanied by flashing strobe lights.

Everyone in sight stops what they're doing to look around. Most modern fire alarms have a two-stage rhythm. Slow means prepare to evacuate. Fast means get the fuck out. This klaxon kicks off at a pace faster than my pounding heartbeat.

Two kids holding hands break for the doors first, and like a broken dam, the crowds surge after them. Hundreds of people in the lobby lunge for the same three doors. The uniformed officers can't leave the doors closed in a fire alarm, and when they open, Dragoniis will slip right past them in the press of evacuees.

"Bradley, shut it down!"

"But, Will, what if it's a real fire, oh my God!" Bradley screeches in panic. This is why he never goes into the field.

"If it is, you can turn it back on. But right now, turn it off!"

"Okay, okay!"

Dragoniis is almost at the doors when the alarm stops as abruptly as it started. The crowd immediately loses cohesion. Dragoniis doesn't stop, continuing to the first door he can get to. If he makes it through, he and the Fukushima Unicorn will be gone forever.

"Police! Police! Police!" I shout.

Predictably, no one inside pays any attention, but I'm not yelling at them. I'm yelling at the cops outside, who turn around immediately. Waving my badge in one hand, I point with the other to the door Dragoniis is heading for. Frowning, not entirely sure what I mean, they move anyway to converge on that exit, cutting Dragoniis off.

Finally, he acknowledges me, turning around. The visor is deeply tinted, hiding his face. For a moment, I see my own reflection running at him before he breaks into a sprint for the south escalators.

Now we're getting somewhere. With uniformed officers blocking the entrances and FBI agents tearing around inside, he's not going anywhere. Deeper into the building means he's fresh out of tricks.

"Oh, come on," shouts Bradley. "I'm locked out. I've got nothing! Will, he cut me off."

Okay, he's not out of tricks.

CHAPTER THIRTY-EIGHT

As I power my way up the escalator, two things are on my mind. First, I can't lose sight of Dragoniis. Without Bradley watching on the CCTV, I'll never find him again if I lose visual contact. Second, I need to hit the Stairmaster more often.

By the time I reach the top of the long climb, my knees are a raging hornets' nest and I'm breathing hard and fast. But I never lose Dragoniis, even as he flies with alarming speed down the mezzanine.

On this side of the building, the sprawling second level is filled with a network of wire frames and curtains arranged in a complex system of temporary hallways.

This is Photo Ops where fans spend up to two hundred dollars each for a picture with their favorite celebrity. At the center of the maze, makeshift photo studios allow each fan their precious few seconds with the star.

It's a great place to lose someone, and it's right where Dragoniis is heading.

Pouring on the speed, I keep my eyes locked on the red and white costume. Once in the maze, I'll have to slow down and make decisions about which way he went. All he has to do is run. It's a losing proposition for me.

So, I change the rules.

Reaching the entrance, I ram through the curtains like a bull, following Dragoniis in a straight line instead of trying to follow the defined hallways. Right away, walls start falling over and people in the rabbit warren start screaming. He turns left; I smash through behind him. He turns right; a loud rip announces I'm still right there.

I'm not as fast as I'd like, but it's enough.

A scream from directly ahead tells me I'm still on target. Slamming through a final panel of curtain wall, I find myself in a photo area. A handsome young guy with dark, floppy hair and a white, skintight t-shirt poses for the camera. A fit, forty-year-old woman hangs on to him with both arms, her smile of delight giving way to shock at the unexpected intruders.

Dragoniis dashes into the open space, earning a second high-pitched shriek from the guy in the t-shirt. Caught off-guard by the noise, he stumbles left, slowing him down long enough to give me the opportunity I need. One last adrenaline-fueled push and I'm within arm's reach.

Dragoniis dodges my lunge at the last second, but I manage to get a handful of sword hilt. With the lithe acrobatics of a frightened cat, he twists, trying in vain to throw me off. Pulling him closer with the sword handle, my free hand grabs the edge of his helmet. Sliding easily off of his head, it reveals long, dark, flowing hair underneath. When he turns to face me, the wind is sucked out of my lungs. Satisfaction greets my wide-eyed surprise. The speed. The flexibility. Even the fit of the leather. All of it failed to land, now leaving me frozen as I process.

* * *

Dragoniis is a young Chinese woman, no more than thirty years old.

Before I can recover from the shock, she swings out with her arm, breaking my grip. Leaping up onto the table that holds people's purses and bags while they do their photo, she flashes me a smile and runs to the other end, jumping into another hallway.

There's something glowing in the empty helmet in my hand. Looking inside, I see a transparent LCD screen integrated into the visor. She must have been looking at this hacking the building while in front of Farber's Cadillac. When he saw her typing on "just a keyboard" it was connected to a computer integrated into her suit. Right now, the screen is showing a video feed from the Convention Center's surveillance. But now she doesn't have it. The field is evening out.

Dropping the helmet, I leap up onto the table after her.

"Will, I'm in the security office," says Nassar. "I've got eyes on the cameras."

"Fantastic, I'm right behind Dragoniis."

"I see you, but, where is he?"

"Not *he*. *She*. The woman in front of me. Look for the swords!"

Dragoniis is only a few feet ahead of me when we emerge from the maze of curtains.

To our right is a U-shaped table for photo pickup, covered with glossy printouts and a disorganized crowd browsing through them, looking for their own smiling faces. To our left are the long lines of waiting fans, stretching beyond the velvet ropes, blocking the way out. Dragoniis jumps up on the table, and this time I'm right behind her.

"That's it," I call out. "It's over, Dragoniis. Let's just do this peacefully."

But she has other ideas. Wheeling to face me, she draws two full-length foam Samurai swords over her head.

"Seriously?" I ask, holding my hands out in front of me.

A flick of the handles drops the foam tubes away to reveal ultra-thin blades made of what looks like carbon ceramic material. I don't know what it is, exactly, but it's black and looks damn sharp.

"Seriously," she says with a light accent.

"Whoa, hold on, you don't want to do that," I say. Shrugging off my blazer, one hand reaches for the Glock at my back, the other held out in front of me, palm first. "FBI. I'm armed. I don't want to shoot you."

"I know who you are, Agent Will Parker."

"*Special* Agent, actually."

"Special or not, you'll bleed all the same," she says, swinging the sword in a casual loop in front of her. The speed of her swing is frightening.

"Okay, yeah, close enough, you're right," I say, wiggling my hand back and forth.

Those blades look mean. Lightweight, like a surgical scalpel, I get the impression they'd sever your leg so fast they wouldn't even get bloody.

"You're not going to shoot me," she says. "With this many people to get caught in the cross fire? With your proficiency ratings? Bad idea, *Special* Agent Parker."

My proficiency ratings? It would appear she's been more places than even Decker knows about, like the FBI personnel system. What else does she know about me? She's right though. My proficiency rating sucks, so there's no way I can pull the trigger here.

"I can't let you leave with that," I say, pointing to the carbon fiber case clipped to her waist.

"You can, and you will," she says, backing away. "What other choice do you have?"

"I've already killed one innocent person for it," I say, drawing my Glock to my side. "Do you really think I'll stop now?"

Doubt ripples across her face like a cloud. She doesn't know about Kate Mason, but it's enough to make her hesitate.

"Nassar?" I ask into the radio.

"Decker's on his way, but it's going to take a minute."

"I don't have that."

No backup. I can't shoot. And since I don't want my limbs anywhere near those blades, all the punching and kicking I trained for won't help me.

To beat her, I need to be just as adaptable. Looking around the room for anything that could help me, I spot a line of fans who must be here for an actor from a fantasy series because they've brought props: replica swords. Made from real metal, this is the only place at the Con they are allowed. It's a crazy long shot. But it's all I've got.

My eye settles on a guy wearing a bulky, black, faux-fur pelt over his shoulders. A giant scabbard hangs on his waist, a sword hilt ending in a wolf's head pommel sticking out of it.

"Hey, John Snow, I'll give you a thousand dollars cash for that sword right now," I shout.

"What thousand dollars?" the guy asks. Fair question.

Leaving my Glock at my side, with my other hand I fish out my wallet and chuck it at him.

"Fuck yeah, man," he says, pulling out the stack of bills. "Here you go!"

With a grin, he tosses over the scabbard. Snatching it out of the air, I draw the blade in a smooth, fluid motion. The LED lights overhead reflecting in the solid, highly polished metal. I holster my Glock, swinging the sword in front of me.

"Are you kidding?" says Dragoniis with a mischievous smile. Were she not threatening me with lethal Samurai swords, she'd be devastatingly beautiful. Launching forward in a spinning whirlwind, she comes at me with eight linear feet of what I'm willing to bet is razor sharp blade.

In Okinawa, I trained in sword fighting with the finest steel Japan could offer, honed to an edge sharp enough to slice through bundled bamboo in a single swing. What I have now is five feet of junk Chinese steel about as sharp as the side of a fork. Shuffling back, my feet find the edge of the table. Nowhere else to go. Wobbling for a second, I hold the replica sword in front of me defensively.

She strikes, slashing with the speed of a cobra. I parry. Her sword hits mine with a hideous shriek, but the replica holds. The advanced carbon whatever-it-is of her blade is too light. Hooray for heavy, junk Chinese steel!

With both hands, I push my sword sideways against hers, using my greater weight to push her back. She staggers a few steps, disengages, and springs forward with another attack.

Up and down the table we go. The lines of fans ooh and ahh as we move back and forth, forgetting their places in line and wandering toward us, thinking it's a performance.

With no real ability to attack using the clumsy, dull sword, I focus on blocking hers, one after another, pushing her back whenever I can. Sweat, dripping down my face, soaks my shirt. Dragoniis' hair sticks to her forehead in a matted mess, her cheeks flushed red with the exertion.

"Enough," she finally screams, swinging both blades over her head.

This time, when I lift the replica sword to block, the steel breaks cleanly, the cruel black blades carrying through to slice my left shoulder. Fiery heat burns down my arm followed by wetness. Someone screams as my blood sprays.

Falling to the table, I drop what's left of the replica sword with a clatter. Dragoniis stands over me, pointing a carbon sword at my throat.

"Thanks for the Unicorn," she says with a smile. "I promise I'll put it to good use."

A commotion breaks out at the entrance, a dozen voices raised in frustration at once as someone plows through them. Storm Decker has arrived in full fury, badge out, gun drawn, and looking hungry for a fight.

"FBI! Get out of my goddamn way! Move it," he shouts, his deep voice resonating like a shock wave.

"How are Decker's proficiency ratings?" I ask Dragoniis. "Pretty hot shit, I bet."

With a grimace, she leaps off the table, disappearing back into the rabbit warren of curtains. Scrambling up to follow her, I slip, crashing off the table onto my shoulder, firing off a lightning bolt of pain to the center of my brain.

"Will, you're hurt," says Decker.

"Thanks for the bulletin," I say, pulling myself up with a grunt. "How bad?"

His combat-experienced eye glances at it. "A bleeder. She got you good. You'll need to be sewn up. Hold still a second."

Tearing a strip off the bottom of my t-shirt, he ties it expertly around my shoulder in a tight, makeshift bandage. The whole process takes ten or fifteen seconds, tops. Decker's a real-life Rambo, but I'm not complaining as I climb to my feet.

"Best I can do without QuikClot. Let's go," he says, running after where Dragoniis disappeared.

"Nassar, where the hell is she?" I ask over the radio, following suit.

"In a stairwell, going down."

"Take the escalator, get ahead of her," I tell Decker. "I'll take the stairs."

"You sure you're up for that?" he asks, looking at my shoulder.

"I'm fine. No more sword fighting."

While he takes off for the nearest escalator, I cut through the curtains to the stairwell.

"Don't stop at the main floor, Will," says Nassar. "She kept going down."

"Where the hell is she going?"

"Looks like the loading dock."

"Is there a motorcycle down there?"

Heart pounding, shoulder throbbing, and soaked in sweat, I fling open the door to the stairwell. Footsteps echo somewhere below me. I'm still in this. I can get the Unicorn back. One flight, two, three fly by. Making a turn onto the fourth and final flight, Nassar's excited voice returns to my ear.

"Yes! Found it. Red sport bike. Behind a white cube truck."

"Get on to the police frequency. Get them to block the top of the ramp. We can't let her out of here!"

"We don't have that frequency, Will. These are tactical only."

You're kidding me. Who bought these things?

"I can get to the uniforms," says Griffon. "I'm on the main floor."

"What about the Russian?" says Nassar.

"Cuffed to the stairwell. He'll be fine for a minute."

Blasting out of the stairwell into the hot loading dock, I stop on a small concrete landing, blinking in the dim orange-tinted light of a sodium arc lamp. Something flies at my head. Diving to the side, I'm careful not to hit my shoulder. Timber smashes on the doorway, showering me with splinters of wood.

When I come up, Dragoniis throws another piece of wooden pallet at me. Blocking with my good shoulder to deflect the pieces gives her enough time to leap off the landing. Drawing my Glock, I squeeze off two rounds after her as she runs away, deeper into the orange gloom. White puffs of dust from the concrete floor are a testament to what a lousy shot I am.

Dragging myself to my feet, I stagger down the stairs to find rows of trucks parked across the dock.

"Which one?" I ask Nassar.

There's only static in response. This far down there's just too much concrete between my little radio and a repeater.

A white cube truck, she said.

I spot one in the row, the opposite direction from where my shots chased Dragoniis off. She'll have to come back. Staggering around the front of the cube truck, I find the red bike that almost ran me over parked behind it, ready to go.

In this condition, I'll never survive another face-to-face battle with Dragoniis, so I get down on the ground, rolling underneath the truck to wait.

After what feels like a century or two, light steps approach from behind. Tentative at first, then quicker. From my hiding place, I swivel my head to see a pair of white leather boots. They stop in the middle of the dock, turning one way, then the other. A quiet moment stretches out. Holding my breath, the silence is broken only by the background whoosh of industrial air handlers. Eventually she runs for it, hopping on the bike and flicking the ignition.

With a grimace, I roll out from under the truck behind her. The engine coming to life masks the sound of me leaping to my feet. With a touch as light as I can muster, I reach for the case, sliding it off her belt while she revs the engine, shaking the entire bike underneath her.

Dragoniis twists the throttle hard, spinning the rear tire with an ear-splitting screech. Flinching, I cover my eyes and face from debris kicked up by her tire as she rockets toward the exit.

Taking only a second to catch my breath, I chase after her with the Unicorn in one hand and Glock in the other. Did I mention I'm fast? Well, not anymore. Snatching the Unicorn was the last of what I had in the tank. My throat is on fire. I gasp for breath, but I keep going. Each step up the spiral ramp is more difficult than the last.

Coming around a bend, I find a crowd of cosplaying kids, likely down here looking for a way to sneak into the Con. They're still coming back together after parting for Dragoniis. Maybe I'm closer than I thought. With whatever energy I can muster, I slip through the gap in teens.

Catching one last glimpse of her taillight as it turns onto the final ramp to the road above, I know it's no use. I'll never catch her. She's as good as gone. The world swims around me, dim at the edges.

From beyond the top of the ramp, a siren wails, followed by the crunch of plastic, tinkling of breaking glass, and tortured grinding of metal. Legs screaming, shoulder throbbing, and throat burning, I dash the remaining distance to the top of the ramp.

Dragoniis' bike lies on its side, the sleek red fairing now cracked and torn. Dragoniis is on the pavement next to it, rolling over onto all fours in front of the dark-colored sedan that just rammed into her.

"Don't fucking move!" Dana bellows, coming around the driver's door. She's still in black tactical gear, Smith and Wesson trained on Dragoniis.

The Chinese hacker glares at Dana and me, before collapsing back down on her stomach.

"Agent Parker," says Dana, as I sag to the ground. "You look like hell."

CHAPTER THIRTY-NINE

A black Escalade careens around the corner, roaring to a stop next to where I've collapsed on all fours to catch my breath. Though her gun never leaves Dragoniis, Dana looks with concern at the massive SUV until the door opens and Ace climbs out. With a gesture from the CEO, the burly security detail comes out next, to surround me protectively.

"Will, are you okay?" Ace pushes past the men, holding out a hand to help me to my feet. "You're bleeding."

Through their legs, I see Dana putting cuffs on a prone Dragoniis.

"Yeah, I'll be all right for now. Decker tied it up."

Decker. He'll be here any minute.

Blood has seeped through the bandage and trickled down to where I clutch the carbon fiber case holding the Fukushima Unicorn. Looking up at Ace, I manage a smile.

My usually stoic friend's face is creased with concern. The red bag, still slung over his shoulder, hangs heavy, the bottom bulging with the remainder of the million dollars. Strange to think he's carrying around that kind of cash, but surrounded by his security detail, there probably isn't anywhere safer for it.

My grimace turns into a grin.

"That's a sweet bag."

It takes Dana a minute to get Dragoniis up on her feet and bent over the hood of the police car, but once she does, she starts a thorough pat-down. Her hands find something and dig into a pocket.

"Will, what is all this stuff?" she calls, an edge of alarm in her voice. She shows me a bundle of wires coming out of Dragoniis' red and white leathers.

"It's not a bomb. She's got a full computer sewn into her costume," I answer. "Look for the largest, bulkiest block. That'll be the battery."

Dana quickly runs her experienced hands over the hacker from head to toe. For her part, Dragoniis isn't saying anything. She's smart. She knows that this opera is only in the opening act. And it won't be me or Dana participating in the next movement.

"Got it," says Dana, pointing to a wide, flat bulge in the small of Dragoniis' back. Opening a concealed zipper reveals the matte-black battery pack, wiring harness plugged into the end. "Now what do I do?"

"Unplug the wires and yank it out. No juice, no computer. No computer, no threat."

Dragoniis turns around to give me a silent glare, interrupted by a flinch when Dana pulls the pack out, accompanied by the sound of ripping.

"And of course, the swords," says Dana.

"Oh right, those." I cradle my wounded shoulder.

There's only enough time for Dragoniis to flash me a smirk before Dana pushes her into the back seat of the car, slamming the door.

"Where is she?" Decker bellows, exploding out of the door next to the loading ramp.

"Relax, Dana's got her," I say, pointing to the car.

He leans over to look through the window like a bride-to-be peering into a display case of wedding rings at a jewelry store. When he stands, it's nothing I've ever seen before. Decker's grin stretches from ear to ear, brilliant white teeth catching the morning sun.

"Oh yeah, that's what I'm talking about!" He hoots, offering Dana a fist bump. "Nice work, Detective."

"Hey, I ran her down."

"Really? Looks like she outran you, Parker."

"She was on a bike! And, you know, I'm hurt. There was a sword fight."

"A what?" asks Dana, her gaze settling on my shoulder.

"Which you lost," says Decker.

"I didn't have a real sword!"

"Where did you get any sword?" asks Dana.

"Well, you did get the Fukushima Unicorn, Parker," says Decker. "So, it's a good day all around. Speaking of which, hand it over."

"No."

Decker stands ramrod straight, as usual, but now his chest fills up and brow lowers into a hard stare that must have terrorized his troops back in the day.

"It wasn't a request, Parker," he says when I don't move.

Taking out my phone, I hit a speed dial number, setting it to speaker and placing it on the trunk of Dana's car.

Assistant Director Burke answers on the first ring.

"Parker?"

"I think it's about time you call off your hound," I tell him.

"What are you talking about?" he says cautiously.

"Director, he won't relinquish the case," says Decker. "You'd better hand it over now, Will."

He holds out his hand, expectantly. I look at it and turn away.

"Wait a second, why does he want the case?" asks Dana.

"Because he's the fourth bidder," I answer.

"The fourth . . . what?!" Her eyebrows launching skyward as she looks from me to Decker.

"How did you know that?" Decker demands, looming over me.

"He's smarter than you, Decker, I told you that from the start," says Burke. "His close rate is even higher than mine was."

"But we called you in," says Dana, turning to Decker. "How could you be the fourth bidder?"

"Ah, but he was already here. Before Caplan was killed."

"You're dreaming," says Decker. "Did Dragoniis hit you in the head, too?"

"I saw the car rental contract," I tell Dana, rolling my eyes. "He picked it up a day before Caplan was killed. He must have found Caplan on the Dark Web and was placing bids. He had no way of knowing if the Unicorn was real, or just another hustle. But he knew it would draw out Dragoniis.

"She was the mission all along, wasn't she?" I ask Decker.

"She was the principal objective," he admits, "but when Caplan turned up dead and the radiation result came in, it added a new dimension."

"You figured there was a chance there might actually be a genuine Unicorn here, so you called me in to confirm and find it for you."

"Correct. Hand it over," he says tilting his head and glaring at me. "Burke?"

"Parker, please give Decker the case."

"The Unicorn doesn't belong to him."

"It doesn't belong to you either."

He's right, it belongs to CastorNet.

The three of us are alone in the middle of a public street, the gathering crowd held at a distance by uniformed officers. Ace's Escalade has vanished, and him along with it.

Shrugging with my good shoulder, I heave the case up onto the trunk of the car. "Okay, have it, Decker."

"But, Will—" says Dana.

"It's all right," I interrupt, holding up a hand.

"Open it," he orders.

"Whatever you say." Placing my hand on the black panel, it flashes green, a soft click coming from the lock as it disengages. Sliding it over to Decker, I take a step back. Dana stays at my side, leaning around me to see.

Decker flips open the lid of the case.

"What the fuck is this?"

"What's happening?" Burke asks from the phone.

"It's empty," answers Dana. "Where is it?"

"On the way to California," I answer, letting out a sigh. "In the possession of the company it belongs to."

"What the fuck, Parker. How?" Decker blurts.

Dana puts a hand to her forehead. "Ace was here earlier with his security guys when Will first came out."

And now, he's on the way to the airport and a corporate jet with its engines already turning. The Unicorn's in the red bag over his shoulder for now, but I'm betting he'll move it to the backup case shortly. It *is* still radioactive.

"He won't have it for long," Decker says in a low, threatening voice. "Will, this was pointless. We'll have a warrant for it long before his plane lands. You're such a pain in the ass."

"Except that's not how it's going to go, is it, Director Burke?"

There's a long pause at the other end of the phone. Burke may be almost as uptight as Decker, but something else drives him. Decker follows orders, Burke follows the law.

"No, it's not," the director says finally, letting out a sigh.

"But, sir," Decker objects, squaring off with me, "we can force him to hand it over. It's evidence."

"That's questionable," says Dana, staying right by my side.

"That's up to a judge to determine," says Decker, "and I'm telling you now, he'll give it to us. Will's making this unnecessarily difficult."

"Let it go, Decker," says Burke.

"But, sir, he can't just flaunt the Bureau like this. The court will side with us."

"The court won't be siding with anyone," says Burke. "They're the legal owners. Getting it back means filing a motion. Which means going public."

"And?"

"You've been in the shadows too long, Decker," says Burke. "Think it through. If we had it, they'd file a motion to get their 'secret technology back from the government.' They'd sound like nothing more than conspiracy cranks and no one would pay attention. But we don't. They have it. And if we file a motion to seize it as evidence, it'll look like the government is out to spy on everyone and their mother. It'd be Snowden all over again."

"Dammit," says Decker slamming his hand on the roof of Dana's car. Through the window, I see Dragoniis jump.

"The Unicorn wasn't the mission, Dragoniis was, and you have him," says Burke.

"Her," I say.

"What?" asks Burke.

"Never mind."

"Listen, Decker," says Burke patiently, "this isn't a failure. The Unicorn didn't fall into the hands of an enemy."

"And don't forget we caught a killer," I add, "and rescued an innocent young woman."

"Yes, and that. All in all, good work for a weekend," says Burke with a tone that says he's winding it up. "Detective Lopez? Decker, Griffon, and Nassar will take custody of Dragoniis and bring him—"

Her.

"—back to Washington. Thanks for all your assistance. Great job," he finishes before hanging up.

"This isn't right," shouts Decker, shaking his head. "You can't just make up your own damn rules, Parker!"

Turning on his heel, he storms back off into the building.

"He's pretty hot under the collar," Dana says.

"Oh, he'll be all right. This isn't our first tango."

"Where's he going?"

"Don't know. Don't care."

"And what about you?"

"Well, I notice Burke didn't say anything about sending the jet back for me. So, I'll start with the hospital and figure it out from there."

"I also noticed he didn't say anything about when you have to be back at the field office," she says, tilting her head with a smile.

"I hear there's a Comic Con in town . . ."

CHAPTER FORTY

Dana didn't ask where I was going, and I didn't tell her. I don't think I knew until I bought the ticket.

Now, as I sit here sipping champagne in first class, I don't think where I'm going is as important as how. Tonight, as I chase the sunset west, I'm finally free to choose where I want to go.

After the hospital, Dana and I spent a brief but glorious time together. Celebrating our successes, we kept the world at bay until we couldn't avoid our futures. She has a mountain of paperwork to climb on the accidental killer, Russian gang members, and Hicks, the now disgraced Silicon Valley executive she has in custody. Meanwhile, the FBI field office in Los Angeles, and CastorNet's headquarters in San Jose, call me home to California. I'll see one of them soon.

At the airport, Dana wrapped me in a silent embrace. After a final kiss, she walked away without turning back. I know, because I watched until she disappeared out the door. There's a chance our paths will cross again, however unlikely. As I look out the window at the red sky, the possibility brings a smile to my face.

Ace has the Unicorn back in California where the brightest minds in Silicon Valley, save one, have already begun to reverse engineer it. Before long, they'll be able to replicate the portable quantum computer and the real work can begin, deciding what to do with the incredible power it offers. That visioning of the future, and the road map on how to get there, will take years. One thing is certain: it's going to change the world.

Saying something about the stress of "real-time work," Bradley's taken some time off, checking himself into a quiet meditation retreat in Big Sur. The fact that this fabulously exclusive resort is a favorite of the Hollywood set was barely mentioned.

A soft chime announces the dimming of the cabin lights, followed by a stir of activity in the pods around me as passengers settle in for the evening.

There hasn't been a peep from Decker, and I don't expect there to be. Storm Decker only moves forward, and with Dragoniis squirreled away in some secret location, he already has his next mission.

More surprising is the silence from Burke. There hasn't been any fallout from what I did with the Unicorn, nor has there been any direction on a future assignment. Though we've clashed over our vastly different approaches to an investigation, Burke's insight and uncanny ability to read people are things I've never doubted. Perhaps, then, the silence is his acknowledgment of the decision I have to make, and acceptance that he has no influence over it.

Eyelids drooping heavily, my head falls back onto the seat. In the darkened cabin, the siren song of sleep beckons and I have no reason to resist. It isn't the dim lights, or the white noise of the commercial jet. It isn't the champagne.

For the first time since my personal apocalypse, I have a conscience I can live with.